Melissa Oliver is from southwest London, where she writes sweeping historical romance. She won the Romantic Novelists' Association's Joan Hessayon Award for new writers for her debut in 2020, *The Rebel Heiress and the Knight*. For more information visit www.melissaoliverauthor.com, and follow Melissa on Instagram, @melissaoliverauthor, X, @melissaoauthor, and Facebook, @melissaoliverauthor.

Also by Melissa Oliver

Stranded with Her Forbidden Knight

Notorious Knights miniseries

The Rebel Heiress and the Knight
Her Banished Knight's Redemption
The Return of Her Lost Knight
The Knight's Convenient Alliance

Protectors of the Crown miniseries

A Defiant Maiden's Knight
A Stolen Knight's Kiss
Her Unforgettable Knight

Brothers and Rivals collection

The Knight's Substitute Bride

The Disreputable Marsden Brothers

The Lady's Bargain with the Rogue

Discover more at millsandboon.co.uk.

A SCOUNDREL FOR THE SUFFRAGIST

Melissa Oliver

MILLS & BOON

All rights reserved including the right of reproduction in whole or
in part in any form. This edition is published by arrangement with
Harlequin Enterprises ULC.

This is a work of fiction. Names, characters, places, locations
and incidents are purely fictional and bear no relationship
to any real life individuals, living or dead, or to any actual places,
business establishments, locations, events or incidents.
Any resemblance is entirely coincidental.

Without limiting the exclusive rights of any author, contributor or the
publisher of this publication, any unauthorised use of this publication
to train generative artificial intelligence (AI) technologies is expressly
prohibited. HarperCollins also exercise their rights under Article 4(3)
of the Digital Single Market Directive 2019/790 and expressly
reserve this publication from the text and data mining exception.

® and TM are trademarks owned and used by the trademark owner
and/or its licensee. Trademarks marked with ® are registered with the
United Kingdom Patent Office and/or the Office for Harmonisation in
the Internal Market and in other countries.

First published in Great Britain 2026
by Mills & Boon, an imprint of HarperCollins*Publishers* Ltd,
1 London Bridge Street, London, SE1 9GF

www.harpercollins.co.uk

HarperCollins*Publishers*, Macken House, 39/40 Mayor Street Upper,
Dublin 1, D01 C9W8, Ireland

A Scoundrel for the Suffragist © 2026 Maryam Oliver

ISBN: 978-0-263-41871-2

02/26

Printed and Bound in the UK using 100% Renewable Electricity
at CPI Group (UK) Ltd, Croydon, CR0 4YY

This is to all the amazing women in my life.

As well as all the women and girls
around the world who are striving to gain equality.
#womanlifefreedom

Chapter One

London—1884

The first time Cecily Duddlecott had met *him*, she could quite easily have throttled the aggravating man. The second time she'd met him, she imagined herself punching him on his all-too-perfect aquiline nose. The third time she'd met him, the exasperating bounder deserved to have his ears boxed. The fourth, fifth and sixth times were…frankly, no different than all the other times. Dominic Marsden was without doubt the most annoying and tiresome man she'd ever had the misfortune to encounter. Cecily, or Cecy as her friends called her, wasn't exactly bloodthirsty. She abhorred violence. But with Mr Marsden she was quite willing to make an exception.

'Well, Duddlecott, this is a predicament.' The man raised a sardonic brow and leant back in the chair, stretching his long legs and crossing them at the ankle languidly. 'I wager you got your days mixed up, eh?'

With that all-too-familiar manner and knowing twinkle in his green eyes, along with that lopsided grin, he was exceedingly confounding. His fine clothing befitted a gentleman, his manner quite the opposite, especially as he lounged in that casual way. Yes, he most definitely could do with having that supercilious smile wiped off that face.

As one of the owners of the Trium Impiorum or Three Wicked Devils, London's notorious yet exclusive gaming hell, as well being one of the three infamous Marsden Bastards, Dominic Marsden revelled in his role as a scoundrel. And he did it to perfection.

'It's *Miss Duddlecott* and, no, Mr Marsden, I have not got anything mixed up. You know perfectly well that your sister-in-law, and my dearest of friends, Eliza, has allowed me the use of her salon for my meeting with my ladies today.'

Why was the man always there wherever she happened to be recently anyway? It was quite disconcerting to find Mr Marsden these days wherever she was and at the oddest places. Only last week, she bumped into him at Hatchards bookshop, one of her favourite places in London, just ambling along in one of the many aisles apparently collecting some books for Eliza.

Another time, he just happened to be at the British Museum at the same time as Cecy. He was there, admittedly, with his youngest brother, who was, by all accounts, involved with a department of antiquity at the museum, but even so it had been an unexpected surprise to find him there.

Then there was the time when she had been on a promenade in Hyde Park, where yet again she spotted Mr Marsden in the distance as he walked beside a young woman she didn't recognise, laughing at something his companion had been saying. And then, to make matters worse, he caught Cecy staring at him and proceeded to acknowledge her by bowing in an elaborate manner, though not before he'd sent her a slow wink, along with that knowing smile, and all because he'd caught her staring.

It was likely to be her imagination, but she was befuddled and confused why the man seemed to be at the same places as she was. But then it was unfortunate that Cecy was so aware of him. This was what annoyed her the most—the fact that she was so affected by his presence. It totally disarmed her. And to make matters worse, she knew, just knew, that his smirks and that twinkle in his blasted eyes was somehow the scoundrel laughing at her. Behind her back. At some private little joke of his. Which frankly she couldn't care less about. Not one bit.

Cecy was, after all, used to ridiculous men thinking that someone like her—a learned woman who had pursued her dreams of academia and had them realised after attending lectures and meetings at Oxford University's Bodleian Library before finally being allowed to matriculate at Lady Margaret Hall four years ago—should be mocked and derided so.

Of course, all that euphoria and excitement of finally, finally doing the one thing that she had longed to do for so long had come crashing down around her. The sad truth was that it had all gone spectacularly wrong. A terrible scandal, that her brother Stephen had quashed and buried, forced Cecy back to London to live with him, as long as she put her *wild radical ways*, as he called it, behind her and adhered to a modest ideal of femininity as befitting her station. Which she had agreed to.

The truth was that Stephen had never approved of her academic pursuits and had warned her late parents about the dangers of educating of women beyond the schoolroom. And although she had always got on with her brother, especially when they were children, everything between them had changed when Cecy was admitted to Oxford.

Yet with her disgrace soon after, her brother liked to remind her that he could have predicted it all, as the education of women was not only unnecessary, but led to free and licentious behaviour. The kind of free and licentious behaviour that naturally brought about Cecy's disgrace, of course. Indeed, it was this apparent side of her character that he'd warned her about, deeming it unnatural, something he advised her to be conscious of.

In time Cecy was a model of propriety, giving Stephen no opportunity to reproach her further, especially in the efficient management of the household. Her sound business acumen, too, and the advice she gave him regarding investments and shares was something he listened to, absorbed, acted on, even if he was equally dismissive and shifty regarding his finances, deeming it unnecessary for Cecy to know more since their finances was his domain and not something she needed to worry her pretty head with.

The cheek of it!

Still, as a trade-off, Stephen had turned a blind eye when she'd arranged her meetings in her blue salon and had not resorted to selling off their father's first editions, rare tomes and manuscripts as he'd threatened to do many times. And so they rubbed along together for a number of years until recently. Everything changed when Stephen had married six months ago and Cecy realised that she could no longer have her secret meetings in the blue salon and was forced to have them elsewhere.

She changed the venue to the Marsden house, at the insistence of her closest friend, Eliza Marsden, née Trebarr-Bawden, who was married to Sebastian Marsden, brother of the bane of her existence, Dominic Marsden. Today's meeting was with the ladies of TWERM, or The Women's Enlightened Reform Movement, an organisation she'd formed with Eliza where they'd discussed the many reforms needed for the enlightenment of academia, science and the arts for women in society. Areas that notably prohibited or ignored women in many established organisations.

'Either way, Duddlecott, I think you're mistaken as I had already reserved the salon with my brother, purposely for meeting with the major-domo and others from the Trium Impiorum. They should be here soon, so you'd better run along.'

'I will be doing no such thing as the women from TWERM, Mr Marsden, will be here shortly.'

'You can use another room, Duddlecott. There are many within this house that can accommodate whatever it is you want to do.'

God, he was insufferable. But he *would not* get a rise out of her. 'May I remind you, Mr Marsden, that approximately fifteen women are expected here this afternoon. And, by the by, this meeting will be sombre, serious and important.'

'I'm sure it is.' A slow smile spread across his annoyingly handsome face. 'You're nothing but sombre and serious, Duddlecott.'

Cecy flushed, realising too late that this was precisely what a man like Dominic Marsden, who was by definition the opposite to anything resembling serious and always far more diverted by his own amusements, would believe her to be. Especially these days when propriety was as important to her as the very causes she championed. Still, it chafed that Dominic Marsden found her to be essentially boring.

He coughed as though he was clearing his throat. 'We could always share the salon. You stay in this half of the room and I'll stay over there in mine.'

She sighed deeply, glad to speaking about this predicament rather than any else that Dominic Marsden was implying.

'I suppose that is a reasonable suggestion.'

He shrugged. 'And I am nothing but reasonable, Cecy.'

'Please do refrain from using such informality when addressing me, Mr Marsden.' She tried to hide her irritation. 'In any case, I'm afraid that your suggestion will nevertheless be impractical for my ladies and me.'

Admittedly *this was* actually Dominic Marsden's home, where he resided with Eliza and Sebastian along with the youngest Marsden brother, Tristan, since their vast living quarters in the upper apartments at the Trium Impiorum gambling hell on Bury Street, St James's, were being refurbished.

Eliza was now with child and those nesting instincts of hers had not just extended to this elegant house here on Half Moon Street that her husband had obligingly bought for their expanding family and where she was busily refurbishing most of the rooms, but also at the club. Meaning that Mr Marsden also had a limited area in which to conduct his business affairs.

Being one of the owners of the Trium Impiorum along with his brothers meant that the man needed space in which to meet with his staff and discuss the daily running of the club, especially as his older brother, Sebastian, was preoccupied with their other ventures as well his wife's imminent confinement.

'Oh, and how is my reasonable suggestion so impractical?' he asked.

She lifted her head and looked at the man still lounging on one of the chairs. 'The problem I believe is that you and your fellow Trium Impiorum workers will be…you'll be…'

'We'll be what, Duddlecott…? Do put me out of suspense.' He raised a sardonic brow.

'You'll all be far too much of a distraction, Mr Marsden.'

Cecy had done her best not to get underfoot and go about her business as quietly as she could. And she would certainly have succeeded in that endeavour had it not been for Dominic Marsden. He loved to needle, prod and tease. For some reason known only to him, he'd singled her out just so that he could spar with her, probably finding it vastly amusing to do so, even when she did her best to stay out of his way. But the man just could not help himself.

Yet, if she was honest with herself, there were times

she found herself seeking him out. Not that she knew why. It was not as though she sought his company. But no one affected her in the way he did. Not that she could show the blasted man how much he vexed her as much as he did and certainly not how much he affected her.

Dominic grinned. 'You cannot know how this thrills me, Duddlecott. What are you implying? That your TWERM ladies are incapable of being in the same room as us pesky...men? Will they get the vapours and swoon at the excitement of being in the same room as our manly physiques?'

'Of course not. It's not that any of them have never been in the vicinity of strange men.'

'Good, because I can tell you right now that none of my men bite,' he said, crossing his huge arms across his chest. 'Not that I know any of them to have such a proclivity. But I can tell them to refrain from pouncing on your members, if they get the urge to, if that reassures you.'

'How very obliging of you,' she muttered through gritted teeth.

'Think nothing of it. I'm glad we have averted a possible problem here, Duddlecott. Sebastian and Eliza will be pleased that we have managed to resolve a disagreement ourselves without having to resort to asking for their assistance in managing our little squabbles. It would be rather childish to do so, do you not think?'

'Mr Marsden, I think your assertions are quite premature as we have yet to resolve this predicament.'

'Is that so?'

'Yes. It just wouldn't do for us to conduct our affairs in the same room.'

'Ah, but to conduct an affair one must be in the same room, sweetheart.'

Oh, but to wipe that wicked smile off his face. Instead, Cecy pinched the bridge of her nose and exhaled slowly. 'Mr Marsden, will you cease using such suggestive language? It is intolerable.'

'Apologies, Duddlecott, but a simple man like me can't help using such suggestive language when it's there for the taking.'

'Then consider refraining to take such liberties.'

'I shall keep it in mind.' He grinned at her. 'But I think I understand your predicament better, Duddlecott. It's not my men, but *me* who is a distraction. Tell the truth, it's not your ladies, but *you* who finds me distracting, eh? Well, in any case, I promise that I don't bite either, unless you're…well, no, those are the kind of delights I should perhaps also refrain from mentioning.'

'I should think so.' She huffed indignantly.

He chuckled softly. 'What do you know about such…delights, Duddlecott? I always knew under all that austere starch there was a passionate woman waiting to get out.'

'Mr Marsden!' she barked out his name, feeling herself blush yet again. 'You shall not use such vulgar language to describe my person. It's wicked and unbecoming.'

'Come now, Cecy.' He rose slowly from the chair and tilted his head as he studied her for a moment. 'You're giving yourself away here.'

She frowned in confusion. 'I beg your pardon, sir, but I cannot understand your meaning here.'

'Can you not?' He raised a brow.

'No.'

'The question is how on earth would you know about being wicked?' he murmured, leaning towards her, and for a moment Cecy wasn't certain she could breathe, let alone meet his eyes. But she did. She forced herself to lift her head and glare at the exasperating man, as an undercurrent of rage bubbled inside her at the audacity of Dominic Marsden believing he could say such words to her. Not that she could show any of her feelings; it simply wasn't the done thing. She tore her gaze from his and looked away.

But perhaps he'd seen something in her eyes as he softened his stance and held his hand up. 'In any case, I think you're right. I shall postpone the Trium Impiorum meeting for later today.'

'Thank you.' Cecy felt the tension in her body melt away.

'And attend your TWERM meeting instead.'

Just like that, it was back again. She snapped her head back up. 'Pardon me? What do you mean that you'll attend our meeting?'

'Just that, Duddlecott. I say, you're not going to get unduly excited with the vapours and swoon on me.'

'Not today, Mr Marsden.' She rolled her eyes and started to move away, putting out the pamphlets she'd brought with her for today's meeting, realising that was what she should have done from the outset and ignored the man.

'Well?'

'Well, what, Mr Marsden?' she said in a bored voice.

'Are you still going to ask me to leave?'

'If you'd be so obliging, I'd be most grateful.'

'Even though you'd know I'd like to attend one of your seriously somber, yet vastly important meetings, Duddlecott?'

'Mr Marsden, as you have already pointed out, there are many rooms in this house, so I cannot see why we need to be in the same company as one another.'

'The truth is that the subject of your meeting today fascinates me.'

'Does it indeed? And what about the subject of this meeting fascinates you?'

'All of it.'

'Interesting as I haven't told you the subject of our meeting.'

'I might be simple in your eyes, Duddlecott, but I

can read.' He lifted one of the pamphlets that she had placed on the table.

'Even so, I am afraid the meeting is for TWERM members so you cannot attend.' She prised the pamphlet from his hand and placed it back on the table.

'Can I not be an honorary member. Just for today?'

'No.' She shook her head. 'You may not. You do not have the necessities to join even as an honorary member.'

'And what are such necessities that I'm lacking, Duddlecott?'

'You need to be a woman, Mr Marsden.' She shrugged and turned around to get her papers and pamphlets in order. 'I am sorry, but even your brother has not been permitted to be part of our organisation.'

'That is rather discriminatory. Especially since Sebastian and indeed I have, through the Trium Impiorum, made generous donations to your organisation.'

'Which we are eternally grateful for.' She knew this to be true. Whatever she thought of Dominic Marsden and the Trium Impiorum, they had, as a gesture to Eliza, made huge donations to TWERM.

He trailed behind her, following everything she was doing and picking up another pamphlet from the table. 'I thought you were all about equality, Duddlecott.'

'I am. We are.' She grabbed the leaflet that he was holding and replaced it on the table.

'So you will bar me from attending this meeting even in my own home?'

Her shoulders sagged a little as she shook her head in resignation. 'No, I cannot do such a thing, since this, as you say, is your home and I… I am only a guest. However, I ask you, nay, request, that you kindly leave when the ladies arrive.'

'Oh, very well, but it is disappointing that you will not permit me to understand more about your organisation.'

What was this about? First, he insisted on conducting his business in the same room as her, then he acquiesced in ceding this space to her. And now, a sudden interest in the women's organisation that she had helped set up with Eliza Marsden. It did not make any sense. And the only way she could find out was if she allowed him to attend to see what he was about.

'Very well, Mr Marsden, by all means remain here, if you wish to. But I will be grateful if you could give me your assurances that you will remain quiet while we get on with our meeting. And that you will not in any way be a…'

'A distraction?'

'Yes.'

'I shall try, Cecy. Indeed, I shall do everything in my power not to be. But the issue is that I cannot help it…'

'Help what?'

He shook his head in an exaggerated manner. 'Being distracting with my manly physique. Do not worry yourself though. I shall sit in the corner at the back. You won't know I'm there.'

Cecy blinked before expelling a deep sigh. 'I cannot know why someone as busy as you purport to be would want to spend your time at such a meeting, but very well, Mr Marsden. I have had enough of this conversation. Do as you please.'

He grinned that irritating, lopsided smile again, his green eyes glittering with amusement. 'Oh, I invariably do, Duddlecott. I invariably do. And I thank you for your courtesy.'

'I suppose you're welcome, Mr Marsden.'

'I suppose I must be.'

She huffed, shaking her head, and moved away. Yes, Cecily found this to be just like all their previous encounters where she ended up feeling she'd been through the mill with Dominic Marsden, leaving her befuddled as always and once more imagining how she'd like nothing better than to kick the insufferable man on his legs. His absurdly manly legs.

Chapter Two

Dominic had nettled Cecily Duddlecott to the point that she'd finally relented, as he knew she'd do. It made him smile inwardly that, with just a few choice words, a nonsensical request, a single raised eyebrow and a smattering of hot and smouldering gazes, he'd reduced the woman to a fit of barely disguised anger and frustration.

Damn, but when she fixed him with that icy glare, that fire burning just behind her eyes and her fists clenched tightly, he wasn't sure whether she'd finally give in to that temper of hers that she tried and failed to hide and hit him over the head, as she no doubt wanted to do. Nevertheless, he'd worn the woman down and Cecily had eventually allowed him admittance into her meeting so that he could watch and observe the woman as he'd been instructed to do.

It wasn't exactly how Dominic would normally behave with anyone, least of all a prim and proper lady like Cecily Duddlecott, despite his rather overblown reputation with the fairer sex. He might be a charmer, a flirt and a bit of a tease, but Dominic was not much of a scoundrel. In truth, he actually liked and respected women too much to behave like a cad as so many of the patrons of the Trium Impiorum did. And women of all ages seemed to like him, too, many practically throwing themselves at him. But not this one. No, not her. Cecily Duddlecott loathed him. Admittedly, though, they had got off to a bad start.

The first time he'd set eyes on the woman was when he'd found her outside the Trium Impiorum's doors along with Eliza and all the women in their organisation protesting and causing trouble as a means to twist Sebastian's arm into helping Eliza. While his brother dealt with the woman who would later become his wife, Dominic was left with Cecily Duddlecott.

Initially, he was unexpectedly taken back by her beauty, grace and poise in that buttoned-up attire that made her seem unflappable but also unapproachable. And whether she liked it or not, Cecily Duddlecott was beautiful with her timeless features: all that jet-black hair and blue, almost violet eyes, heart-shaped face and that mouth… God, but that rose-pink mouth was probably better suited to the most seasoned courtesan instead of a pompous starchy harridan, who'd looked down her perfect little nose at him as though he was dirt beneath her feet.

In fact, the moment she'd opened her delectable

mouth that first day he encountered her, the woman shredded him to ribbons with that sharp tongue of hers, with a spectacular set down taking him off guard. By God, but the nerve of her when she'd made assumptions about him, just because he ran the Trium Impiorum with his brothers. As though they were the type of men who would take advantage of young defenceless women. As though they had two-penny doxies at their establishment.

Dominic could recall even now the anger he'd felt for her unjust presumptions about him and his brothers. But instead of correcting her, he did what he always did in situations like that and teased her, making light of her censure. And, well, they'd never seen eye to eye ever since.

Even so, if the bloody woman ever found out the real reason why he was paying her this much attention and seemingly following her about town, then she would probably want to throttle him after vowing never to speak to him again—not that she deigned to speak to him much anyway and not that he cared. But still.

'Are you with us there, Mr Marsden?' Cecily called out from the front of the room.

'Absolutely, Miss Duddlecott.' He smiled, catching her eyes over the heads of the women in her organisation, who were sat in front of him while he sat at the back, trying to be as inconspicuous as possible. She was giving her sermon-like speech at the far end of the salon, with rows and rows of chairs arranged with her ladies sat in raptures, hanging on her every word.

'I am most riveted by your, ah, interesting speech.'

'Is that so, sir? What precisely interested you about my riveting speech?'

'All of it,' he drawled, trying to recall bits and pieces of what she had said.

'Well…' she cleared her throat '… I'm glad to hear it. And yet it would be enlightening to know your thoughts on our proposals?'

'Your proposals?'

'Indeed. That is *why* we are meeting, sir.'

The cheek of Cecily Duddlecott, giving him a dressing down in front of these women, but then again, he had more or less invited himself along after initially conceding that he'd leave her to it. The truth was that Dominic did not have a meeting with Hendon, the major-domo, or any of his men at the Trium Impiorum scheduled in this room or indeed any of the rooms here. And if Dominic needed to have a meeting, he wouldn't need to have it here at Marsden House, when there were still plenty of rooms at the club despite his sister-in-law Eliza's penchant for decorating and refurbishing every bloody room. Of course, Cecily Duddlecott didn't know that. As far as she was concerned, he had decided on the spur of that very moment to follow her to this room, to this meeting where he was now listening to her proposal…

'They are very…sound,' he muttered. 'Especially education reforms for all children, especially girls from all societal classes.'

Dominic watched as Cecily blinked several times, as though she was wondering whether she had heard his words correctly. Well, of course she would, since it didn't quite sit with the scoundrel she believed him to be. But then, Cecily Duddlecott didn't really know him after all. She knew nothing of the work that he along with his brothers continued to do on behalf of his late mother. She knew nothing of how the Marsden brothers helped and funded schools for underprivileged children living in the slums after their club proved to be the financial success it eventually became.

'I see. And what are your thoughts, Mr Marsden?' She raised a brow. 'Would you also believe that this particular view to be…discriminatory?'

Touché, he begrudgingly thought, as she delivered his words back to him on a proverbial plate. 'No, I think ideas for educational reforms for every child, especially for girls, are very…commendable. As Plato said, "Women should have equal access to education and politics."'

'True, yet his student Aristotle believed that women were fit only to be the subject of male rule.'

'Ah, but I defer to the master's words, rather than the student's.'

'Even when the student is considered to be one of the greatest minds of all time?'

'Even then. To be human is to err. We are not infallible, Miss Duddlecott, and we all have our many flaws and imperfections, so even the greatest of minds have been known to be wrong about many of their findings. All of which means that we constantly need to rigorously challenge accepted ideas that are passed off as empirical facts.'

'I'm glad you think so, Mr Marsden. But going back to the advancement of women, what we believe along with our sister suffragists is that while there have been many prestigious girls' schools that have been opened in the last fifty or so years, one of which I was lucky enough to attend, they are still very much the preserve of the middling and upper orders of society. What we believe is that school should not be limited only to those who can pay for the privilege.'

It astounded him how much Cecily's words were similar to what his mother would have endorsed when she was alive. Even during those years of hardship after they'd lost everything. It was both familiar and uncomfortable at the same time. 'I heartily agree.'

'You do?'

'Absolutely,' he said quietly, forgetting about the other women present in the room. For a brief moment it felt as though Dominic and Cecily were alone, devoid of the banter and quarrelsome manner that marked their usual interactions. 'As someone who has...who has known privilege, lived and breathed it only to have it snatched away, I know the value of a first-class education. Which is the point, is it not? For that first-class education to be available to all regardless of class or background...or even sex.'

Some of the women gasped at his casual reference to a word that was certainly not acceptable in polite society—even Dominic knew that. Yet Cecily Duddlecott did not look away. Her blue-violet eyes were fixed on his as though she was seeing him for the first time, her intelligence, warmth and something else he could not put his finger on shining through.

She eventually blinked as though she'd realised what he'd said, which made him smile inwardly, noticing Cecily flush that delectable pink shade that infused her skin, spreading from her forehead, to the tips of her ears and down to her neck and the top of her buttoned-up dress. He wondered absently whether it spread beneath that austere dress, if he gave chase to it, undressing her to find out. And just as quickly he admonished himself for such lewd thoughts about a woman who'd likely skewer him than allow such liberties.

He had to remind himself that he'd been assigned to keep an eye on Cecily when she visited Eliza at Marsden House and elsewhere in town, as well as her feckless brother at the Trium Impiorum, which was frankly not what he'd choose to do when he was a busy man with all his normal duties as part-owner of the club.

Yet he could hardly deny that a strange kind of spark existed between them that somehow managed to get his fingers metaphorically burned every time he sparred with the woman. He wondered whether Cecily was even aware of it or not. Even so, there was a side to him that wondered whether the more he pushed and probed her, the more that tamped-down passion she had hidden inside would rise to the surface.

'May I ask a question?' one of the women from the front asked loudly. 'Is there a reason why a man is here with us today, Miss Duddlecott?'

'I believe I have already explained about Mr Marsden's presence here, Mrs Drewer. And I hope it is agreeable to you and everyone else here?'

'Yes, you have explained, although I am still puzzled by this, to be perfectly honest with you.' The older woman then turned around in her chair and addressed him directly. 'And I hope you don't take this the wrong way, sir, but you must understand that it does make us women feel a bit uncomfortable having a masculine presence here.'

The other women murmured among themselves, while Cecily darted her head and looked at them with concern before catching his eyes and raising a brow accusingly, as if to say *see what you've caused, Mr Marsden.*

This was perhaps his cue to walk out discreetly, to leave the women to their business, knowing full well that was what all these women, especially Cecily, would want him to do.

Instead, Dominic stood slowly and ambled to the front to stand beside Cecily. He turned and faced the women sat in rows with their arms crossed, scowling at him.

'Ladies, ladies. Please forgive my presence here. I had certainly meant no harm by being here. In fact, I wished to learn more, since I had heard so many wonderful things about your organisation that I wanted to see for myself. And as I said earlier, I have certainly not been disappointed thus far. Your impassioned stance to change the iniquitous difference in society between the sexes is, as I said, very commendable. Especially in relation to education for girls and women. I believe it might even be what I would call a noble cause, despite the many challenges you face and will continue to face surrounding these issues.'

'Let me understand you, Mr Marsden, but are you implying that you agree with what we stand for?' Cecily asked from beside him, clearly still sceptical.

'I do, yes.'

'Then you are a rare man.'

'I'd like to think so.'

The murmurs of the women in the salon, evidently surprised by his words and the possibility of his being an ally to their cause, gave way to the women softening towards him and becoming a little more welcoming than just a moment ago.

'There are many such inequalities in society. Whether it's workers' rights, voting rights and other social injustices,' Cecily said beside him. 'Why the interest in our cause particularly?'

'One can champion more than one cause, Miss Duddlecott.'

'True, but I've never known you to be interested in social inequities of any kind.'

'No, but you do not know me.' He shrugged, pinning her eyes with his own for a moment…a moment that seemed to suddenly and quite unexpectedly make him a little wistful because of what he saw in the depths of those blue-violet eyes. He didn't have the language for what it was and he had more than likely imagined it. But what he saw somehow made him forget where he was and whose eyes he was transfixed by. They told of a long-ago emotion. Something he did not quite understand and frankly did not know whether he wished to.

Just as quickly, her eyes masked over, making him think that it was just his fanciful imagination. There was nothing in her eyes that resembled the longing that he believed he'd seen. Not her. Not Cecily Duddlecott. God, he really needed to get back to his club. Why had he stayed? Here in this room, he'd insisted on remaining to learn what exactly? Nothing. There was nothing for him to learn here. This went beyond what he'd been asked to do.

Someone coughed, clearing their throat and bringing him back...to a room full of suffragists and Cecily Duddlecott staring at him now in muted shock. Dominic blinked, looking away before speaking again. 'However, the inequalities that women have always faced are something that is strangely personal to me as well.'

'It is?' He had never heard Cecily speak so softly to him, as though they were quite alone. And for a moment he wished he could drag her away and ask her about what he thought he'd seen in her eyes. He wanted to know what it was that made her look at him like that. But, of course, he didn't.

'Yes. I, along with my brothers, have seen many forms of injustices and feel, like many of you good women here, to be outside the parameters of those who are reluctant to share this great nation's wealth, prosperity and equality. It is like looking on the other side of the glass pane and never being admitted inside. Yet shouldn't we be admitted within or is it only the preserve of a privileged few? Indeed, my brothers and I were born into that very privilege before it was snatched away and we were declared to be unworthy, undeserving and flawed in some way. And all because of circumstances beyond our control.'

The irony was not lost on Dominic that he, along

with his brothers, was referred to as one of the disreputable Marsden brothers when trust, honour and loyalty were the very tangible things that bound them together. He would do anything for them. Anything. Including protecting both his older brother, Sebastian, and his younger brother, Tristan. Indeed, there was nothing disreputable about any of them.

'So, yes,' Dominic continued, 'I understand far too well the need to have the same acceptance, choices and rights as the men who run this country of ours. For all of us.'

'Hear, hear,' said Mrs Drewer.

'Absolutely, sir,' said a woman behind her.

The small smile that curled around Cecily Duddlecott's lips was possibly the first true one that she'd directed at him and he almost gasped at how much it transformed her face.

It didn't sit well with him that he had been forced into all this subterfuge, but for the love of Trium Impiorum and his brothers it was something he had to do. To find out more about any possible links Cecily Duddlecott and her brother, the politician Stephen Duddlecott, had with the newspaper tycoon Samuel Millington, who had recently branched out into many other businesses, his fingers in many pies.

With the unlikely duo, the politician and the tycoon, frequenting the club, Dominic—the one brother who worked the floor of the club and was perhaps the most hands-on out of the three—had been the one who was approached by Sir Algernon Pendle from the Intelligence Office. He'd been the one pressured to observe the men in his club and find out more about their business dealings, and where, if anywhere, Cecily Duddlecott fitted in.

Not that he knew what it was that he was supposed to uncover. Dominic was a damned club owner, not an intelligence officer. But he had been made to comprehend that if he did not do his patriotic duty and comply, then they would see to it that the Home Office would come down hard on the Trium Impiorum and any of their own future business ventures. And he was then sworn to confidentiality.

Not that he could discuss any of this with his older brother, Sebastian—especially with the imminent arrival of a baby and his concerns over his Eliza's health. Dominic had not wanted to add to his brother's worries. And although it did not sit well with him to keep this from Sebastian, Dominic wanted to resolve it by himself so that everything could then go back to normal. And he would no longer have to follow the captivating, yet aggravating, Miss Cecily Duddlecott.

'Could I ask how you have become so…?' she asked. 'So…?'

'So valiant a supporter of workers' and women's rights. You have, after all, acknowledged yourself to be outside the parameters of those who have all the privileges.'

He wondered whether he should answer her and also how he'd even got to this rather private area of his life. This, he had certainly not accounted for.

'My mother, Miss Duddlecott,' he said quietly. 'She was not treated as well as she…as she should have been. What happened to her has come to inform many of my opinions. And her life afterwards became much harder than it should have.'

His mother, who had been the Countess of Harbury, was once considered an impeccable lady far beyond reproach. That was before she was publicly disgraced and dishonoured after their father's death, when it was discovered that his father had been married in secret years before his marriage to his mother and thus been a bigamist posthumously. His mother's whole life changed overnight and all three of her sons were then declared bastards, losing all their inheritance and standing in the world.

Before long they were left poor until the wrangles of the estate and his father's will, which had not been entailed to the Harbury title, had been finally decided upon after years of bitter dispute with his uncle, to whom the Harbury estate and title had passed. By then it was too late. His mother had died and from a broken heart since she had never been the same afterwards.

Dominic still missed her, his sweet and gentle

mother whom he'd always try to cheer up with his silly quips and funny stories. Nothing had worked, not really, and it wasn't long before Dominic and his brothers were left to fend for themselves after her untimely death. God, it had been a miserable time, one he did not want to dwell on. Pushing the memories away, he turned to the woman beside him.

'Yes, I believe as in…we all do that it must have been particularly difficult for your mother.'

'It was, Cecy.' They both almost jolted at the use of her given name, which he hadn't intended to use in front of others, especially since it spoke of an intimacy that didn't actually exist between them. His gaze caught on a large green glass vase filled with flowers on a small table in the far corner of the room that had once belonged his mother.

'The truth is once you lose your standing, your place in the world, you realise that you never really had it in the first place. It was never there and you were always powerless, you were always vulnerable, but had no idea of the truth. So, you see, I firmly believe that the inequity in our society must and should be addressed, whether that's workers' or women's rights, which then instigate reforms in all areas of society and the law, including, of course, education. Change must be brought about for the betterment of all.'

Perhaps Dominic had overdone it. He certainly hadn't meant to make a speech such as this, but it was done now and all the women in the salon, including Cecily Duddlecott, were staring at him in amazement before standing and clapping.

'It seems you've won them over,' Cecily whispered from the side of her mouth.

'It seems I have,' he murmured softly back. 'Which naturally makes me wonder.'

'Oh?' She snapped her head around, her eyebrows furrowed in the middle. 'It makes you wonder what, Mr Marsden?'

A smile curled around his lips, slow and unbidden. 'Whether I've won *you* over as well?'

Chapter Three

It had been a week since the TWERM meeting at Marsden House where Dominic… Mr Marsden had surprised her so much that she'd been left speechless. He had been so unlike what she had always believed him to be that it made her wonder whether she knew him at all.

He'd gone from sitting at the back of the room, teasing her with his usual wry sardonic manner, to revealing far more about himself. Perhaps even more than he had intended to after explaining that he actually believed in the emancipation of women and the need for education for all. It would explain why he'd suddenly and abruptly left soon after, making his excuses about being needed at the Trium Impiorum.

And yet…and yet, there had been a moment when he had talked so earnestly about his past and especially about his mother that Cecily could not deny being drawn towards him when he spoke. It felt as though a veil had been pulled back for her to glimpse the real man beneath the affable yet annoying scoundrel. As though perhaps this was the real Dominic Marsden and not the one he presented to the world.

But just when she looked more deeply, trying to ascertain all the questions piling in her head about him, the mask was suddenly fixed back so quickly, it was as though she had imagined it all. This was what she had been pondering on this last week as she went about her business, which was much more closely observed than ever before at home.

Since her brother's marriage to the meek and malleable Lady Victoria Duddlecott, Stephen had been questioning Cecy's every movement far more than before, especially with his mother-in-law, Lady Honoria Saxby, who had moved in with her daughter and her new son-in-law so that she could give them the benefit of her counsel. And that counsel had also extended to Cecy.

Everything was scrutinised, from her conduct and behaviour, to what she occupied her time with, as though she were a child and not a woman of almost thirty years who had come into her majority many years ago. It was becoming intolerable how the old baggage wanted to insert herself into Cecy's life through Stephen, who shared his mother-by-marriage's views.

It was as though Honoria's opinions confirmed and corroborated everything he had always believed about

Cecily—especially the scandal nearly five years ago when she'd attended Oxford. This he must have shared with the older woman, for how else would she have known?

Now Cecy was underfoot in her own home and not because of her sister-by-marriage, Victoria, but Victoria's mother. The old baggage had not only taken over the reins of running the household from Cecy, but would constantly undermine her at any opportunity.

She found fault with everything Cecy did and managed to convince her brother that the meetings for her TWERM organisation needed to be stopped as they were not for the acceptable charitable work as he believed them to be, but Cecy's secret meetings were actually something far more pernicious, unfeminine and unnatural since they were for the advancement of women.

The disapproving woman advised Stephen that her young daughter Victoria, even as a married woman, should not under any circumstances be exposed to such radical beliefs in her own home. Stephen was naturally persuaded and forbade Cecy to hold any such meetings in his home ever again. What had made matters worse was that their arguments had extended far beyond her organisation to Cecy's character, which was constantly put to question.

Once again she felt judged and found wanting, just as she did after her scandal. Although perhaps in that, there was some justification. Still, Cecy couldn't help feeling hurt by her own brother's behaviour towards her. Stephen had seemingly cut the ties of familial loyalty and attached them more to his wife and her family, knowing they would serve him far better for his political ambitions than any obligations he felt for her. And he'd also made up his mind that the only way that she could overcome all the avarice and confusion of her disordered mind, making her so unlike other females, was if she agreed to marry;

'Only in the blessed marriage state will you find your true calling, dear Sister,' he'd say. *'You shall find your real purpose as a wife and mother, Cecily. I am convinced this is the only way for you to find lasting happiness and purpose. You are now approaching your thirtieth year and as a mature woman can only hope to find an older gentleman who will not mind that you're no longer in the first bloom of youth or beauty.*

'He will also need to overlook your other, ah...past proclivities, which I always warned you would one day hold you back rather than open doors for you. No man would be in want of a wife who is openly and vocally more intelligent than he is. But you, my dear Cecily, are a fortunate woman. As luck would have it, there is an older gentleman of great means who has spoken to me of his interest in you... One who would be a great asset to both of us.'

All this had forced Cecy to rethink her future as it

was becoming clear that she could no longer continue as she was. She could no longer continue to reside at her childhood home. She'd have to soldier on stoically until she found a solution through this mess that had become her life.

'Are you going out, Cecily?' Stephen was standing in the back of the marble-floored hallway with his hands behind his back, looking down at her with a frown etched on his forehead, clearly displeased that she hadn't told him of her every movement.

'Yes, I'm just going to Hatchards to pick up a few books I ordered.' She picked up her gloves and slid them on as she turned to face her brother. 'If it meets with your approval, of course.'

She had said the last without being able to contain the sarcasm from her voice. After all, Stephen was only a year older than her, but being born a male saw himself superior in every way to Cecy.

'Of course not, Sister, and you needn't take that tone with me. But if you'd be so obliging I would have you postpone your outing today.'

'Oh, and why would you want me to do that, Brother dearest?' She sighed. 'I've just fixed my brooch on my cape that Clayton kindly found on the Kent table. And I have several other appointments after my visit to Hatchards. Can whatever it is not wait?' Cecy knew she was babbling, which wasn't like her, but she didn't quite trust the way her brother was looking at her, so much more reserved—even for him.

'No, Cecily. And if we may have this conversation in my study room, rather than out here in the hall, where we might not be overheard by the servants.'

'Very well.' She walked past her brother and back into the large square hall, marching into Stephen's study room that hadn't changed much since it once belonged to her father. 'What is it that you wish to speak to me about, Stephen?'

The study room still had that familiar scent of old papyrus, piles of old tomes and even a trace of pipe smell from when her father was alive, with wall-to-wall mahogany wainscotting and two wing-backed chairs either side of the crackling fireplace, cupboard space with a wooden filing system that Cecy used in the main for bookkeeping and a large mahogany desk with elaborately carved legs in front of the square window.

It was the one room at least that Lady Honoria Saxby hadn't dared to find fault in and want to remodel for her poor daughter who wasn't used to living in such reduced circumstances. The cheek of it. All of their parents' knick-knacks were to be boxed up and put into storage soon—all their memorabilia from their travels in the Far East, through to Russia, Mesopotamia and Persia. Cecily could remember even now talking to her father in this very room about her parents' next adventures that would take them to Egypt and into the Holy Land.

However, they never got that far. It was in Paris a month later that they had both contracted typhoid fever and perished soon after. She could remember as if it were yesterday when she received that tragic news at her lodgings in Oxford. It had been one of the worst days of her life.

'Will you sit, Cecily?' Stephen motioned to her father's old mahogany chair as he made his way around the huge desk and sat on the other side, watching her for a moment, his fingers steepled.

'Very well, but I must say this all seems quite ominous, Stephen. What are you about?' she said as she perched on the elaborately carved chair.

'How like you, Cecy, to want me to get to the heart of the matter. You were always like this even as a child—so impatient with everyone and everything.' He said this so softly that it made her instantly go on her guard. Especially as he called her *Cecy*, a shortened version of her name that only those closest to her called her—well, that was except for Dominic Marsden.

'Indeed, I find that there is much to do and very little time to do it.'

'Quite. Well, Sister, it seems that you have been making quite an impression.'

'I have?' She lifted her head, frowning, wondering what on earth Stephen was jabbering about. And for one moment thinking whether he was referring to Dominic Marsden. 'Who are you referring to?'

'Why, Samuel Millington, of course. He has told me how much he enjoys your forthright conversations and robust opinions. I never believed you would draw the attractions of a man such as Millington, but it seems that fortune has looked very favourably on you, my dear.'

Millington? Samuel Millington? Cecy could never have imagined that their conversations were in any way forthright or that the man valued any of her opinions, especially since their only interactions consisted of two short walks to Hyde Park and an evening soirée here at her home.

'Well, the long and short of it is that he has asked me if he could formally court you, old girl.' Stephen stood up. 'Allow me to say, Cecy, that I am very pleased for you.'

She blinked several times and looked up at her brother, who was smiling warmly at her. 'You are?'

'How can I not be when you have caught the attention of one of the most prominent men in the country. A man whose wealth and stature are most estimable. And, of course, a man whose vast connections would be most welcome allied to my own. Who could and would help me realise my goal as a politician and could help me rise within the Tory party and secure a top-ranking government role.

'And after my good fortune in my own marriage, this is beyond what I had ever expected for you. Especially after what happened in Oxford and your scandal. However, it might be best if we did not speak of that at this time.'

She nodded slowly, trying to take all of this in. 'That is very good of you.'

'Now, Cecy, why the sullen face?' Stephen came around to her and grabbed her hands, tugging her to stand. 'Didn't you hear that I bring you good news?'

'Yes, it is most welcome news, but you must allow me to think this all through before I make a decision about whether or not I would accept Mr Millington to court me.'

Her brother let go of her hands and took a step back. 'What do you mean, *if*? I have already given the man my permission, Cecily.'

'Without consulting with me first. Perhaps you were too hasty, Stephen.'

Her brother dragged his fingers through his dark hair irritably. 'Why must you always make everything so difficult?'

'Stephen.' She reached out and stilled her brother. 'I have not said I would not accept Mr Millington's attentions. Nor have I said that I would do anything to make things in any way difficult for you. Can you not allow me some time for this surprising news to sink in? You do not need to resort to anger to get your own way.'

He took in a deep breath and nodded, rubbing his forehead for a moment. 'You are right. I apologise. But you don't understand how important this is for me, Cecy.'

For him? Stephen was pushing this because an alliance between Samuel Millington and her was that important to him? She couldn't help think that this was all rather odd. Why should a proposed courtship with Mr Millington be so important to Stephen aside from the usual familial concerns? She didn't, however, say anything. Not yet.

'Well, if there's nothing further you wish to discuss with me, I believe I might leave for Hatchards now.' She stood up, as her brother held up his hand.

'Actually, Cecily, if you wouldn't mind waiting for a moment.'

'Really, Stephen, I have to go. What else do you wish to discuss?'

'About Samuel Millington…'

'Yes, yes, I said that I would give the matter some thought.' She put her gloves back on and bent low to get her mother's old portmanteau.

'What it is, Cecily, is that Samuel Millington is taking you out so you can spend more time with him.' She looked up and saw he'd drawn the dark-green velvet-brocade curtains aside to glimpse through the window that looked out on to the road. 'He's here now.'

Cecily hated this. She hated being managed and manipulated in this highly irregular manner. As though she couldn't be trusted to make an informed decision about her own future and needed more or less to be coerced into a courtship and ultimately, marriage. All of which she needed time to give proper consideration. None of this endeared her to Mr Millington's suit at all. What on earth was Stephen thinking?

'This does seem neatly arranged, Stephen. Perhaps you might have allowed me the courtesy of some time alone to consider everything you have said thus far.'

'Which is why I arranged for you to have this outing with Samuel himself. He can explain himself far better than I, all those difficult queries you might have regarding his suit and about your future together.'

She clenched her fists at her sides. 'I have not yet given my answer to any of this, Stephen.'

'I understand, Sister. And as Lady Honoria said, it would be wise for me to make some of these decisions for you, otherwise you might get cold feet and all that. I predict that the more time you spend with Samuel Millington, the more you'll come to appreciate the seriousness of his suit.'

A knock at the wooden door prevented Cecy from giving Stephen the set down he deserved.

'Enter,' Stephen called out. The next moment, Clayton, their officious butler, announced Samuel Millington, who stepped into the study and greeted them both in his usual cool and self-important manner. And before long, Cecy found herself in Samuel Millington's rather plush open-topped carriage along with her maid, Mary, as he navigated the busy streets of London.

'You are rather quiet this morning, Miss Duddlecott,' he said.

'I suppose I am. I have rather a lot on my mind, Mr Millington.'

She glanced across at the man sitting beside her with the ribbons grasped firmly in his gloved hands as he stared out in front of him. He was a handsome man for someone who was in his fiftieth year. Tall, with a mop of dark hair threaded through with grey, especially down his sideburns, warm brown eyes with fine lines in the corners, set within a chiselled face along with a rather imposing moustache, the man could never be mistaken for anything other than the epitome of virile masculinity.

Yet he did not set her world ablaze, not that she needed any of that nonsense, of course. In truth, Stephen was right—she should feel exceptionally honoured to have been singled out by him. She would have to give his suit her full consideration, not that she'd ever believed herself on the cusp of a courtship with the man. Those considerations had long been discarded, the notion of marriage something she had not thought of in years. Perhaps this was the reason her brother had been speaking so freely about the subject to her. In any case, this had been an interesting day so far, along with an equally surprising proposition.

'Am I too presumptuous to guess that your musings might be in some way to do with the meeting you had with your brother before my arrival, Cecily? May I call you Cecily?'

'Perhaps—that, too, is one of the many things I have to consider, Mr Millington. And, yes, the conversation I had with my brother before your arrival is one that occupies my mind. Perhaps it might have been best if I had come here alone with Mary, for I fear I might not be good company at present.'

'Nonsense. Your company is always welcome—in fact, I'd say it is something that I enjoy very much, even when your mind is occupied elsewhere.'

She swallowed uncomfortably. 'You are too kind, sir.'

'Not at all. And you will tell me when you're ready to give me leave to use your name freely.' He smiled at her. 'And I hope…yes, I hope it will not be too long.'

Cecily stared out ahead as the road passed by, her mind racing. This was all happening far too quickly. What on earth was she doing here alone with a man she barely knew, all because he wanted to court her for some reason?

'May I ask you a question, Mr Millington?'

'Of course, and please call me Samuel.'

'Before we dispense with such formalities, sir, I'd

like to ask why after such a short acquaintance you have formed…you have formed such a strong attachment. As in…well, why me, Mr Millington?'

'We are both of an age and I had no desire to pursue a much younger woman with no sense or intelligence. Both of which you possess. I like your plain-speaking, no-nonsense attitude. I find that it amuses me somewhat. And your brother tells me that you have been running his household accounts as well as giving him financial advice for many years prior to his own excellent marriage. So you see, I find the whole package very attractive to a man like myself.'

Well, now. Cecily could not ever recount being described in such a manner, especially as an 'attractive package'. Nor her age, so blatantly stated and used as a back-handed compliment. She had to say, if nothing else Samuel Millington was proficient in plain speaking himself.

'Thank you,' she murmured lamely, not knowing what else to say.

'I hope it answers your question?'

She smiled. 'Not exactly, sir. We still hardly know one another.'

'Which is why there is the need for this outing. For us to get to know one another today and, if you'll allow it, for the next few weeks or so.' He pulled the reins outside the famous London bookshop and turned to face her. 'I would hope to hear your answer by then?'

It seemed the man was also rather efficient in his dealings as well—even when acquiring a wife. 'I can make no promises, sir. However, I will do my best to engage with our outings and provide you with an answer soon enough.'

His whole body seemed to tense, his jaws clenched for a moment or two before he expelled a long breath and smiled at her. 'There it is, the plain speaking I was talking about.'

Yet Cecy wasn't convinced Samuel Millington actually liked what he purported to at all. Her plain speaking seemed to grate and annoy a man used to getting his own way. Either he didn't know himself well enough or the man was insincere. Both of which were as surprising as they were worrying.

It seemed that the next few weeks were going to be exceedingly long as she tried to ascertain whether to accept Samuel Millington's suit, knowing that it was flattering to be singled out by the man. But did she really need a marriage such as this? Cecily was no fool and knew that being attached to a powerful, wealthy man like him who had the kind of political connections she could only dream of would potentially open doors to her organisation in a way nothing else could. She could effect change far more by being married to a man like Samuel Millington then she could ever hope to do as a spinster.

However, none of that would be possible if the man

was against the advancement of women's equality, especially the education of girls. Still, Cecy had to find out before she made her decision. She had to give his suit her serious consideration, even if the man seemed to possess an insincerity in his regard for her. Even so, marriage could be mutually beneficial to the both of them—not that she could quite see what he hoped to gain from an alliance with her when he could frankly marry any woman.

No, the question of why he'd chosen her had not been adequately answered. Not to Cecy. And she was not foolish enough to fall for all his honeyed words and effusive flattery without considering this whole courting and marriage business from every angle.

He helped her down from the carriage as she took his arm and made their way inside Hatchards on Piccadilly, one of her favourite places in London. With the little bell ringing overhead as they entered the large wooden door, Cecy walked along to the large counter and smiled at the manager, Mr Pickles, who beamed at her.

'Miss Duddlecott, a pleasure to see you. I have the books you requested wrapped up and ready for collection. Although you might be interested in the new delivery we've had earlier this morning?'

'Good day to you, too, Mr Pickles, and thank you. Yes, in that case, I should very much like to browse through your new collection.' She turned to face Mr Millington. 'That is if you wouldn't mind?'

The man's smile didn't quite reach his eyes. However, he inclined his head in deference as he spoke. 'Of course not. I shall wait here and have a read through my newspapers in that comfortable-looking armchair. Take as long as you need, my dear.'

There was something proprietorial about Samuel Millington's tone and manner that made Cecy feel a little uncomfortable. Still, it was flattering that a self-assured and self-made man like Samuel Millington, with his wealth, position and influence, was attracted to her. It was probably because she hadn't known the attentions of such a gentleman—not in very long time anyway. This was most likely the reasons for her reticence about him. After all, it had only been a few hours since she'd learned the nature of his interest in her.

'Thank you. Which aisle have you arranged the new delivery in, or are they scattered all over, Mr Pickles?'

'Since the books are predominantly…ah, well…' Mr Pickles coughed and glanced at Samuel Millington before proceeding to speak. 'Scientific and mathematical, they're all grouped together in the usual spot, Miss Duddlecott. The furthest aisle and right down the back.'

'Thank you,' Cecy muttered as she rushed to the back of the shop, hardly able to disguise her excitement at the prospect of new books in the areas of study that formed the basis of her interest and intellectual curiosity.

From a very young age Cecy had excelled at every area of her studies, from literature, Latin, history, classics, Greek, French and Italian, but the area that she excelled at the most was science and in particular mathematics, much to the chagrin of her brother, who was extremely embarrassed and resentful not to be brighter and cleverer than his high-achieving sister. Even so, it was in the field of mathematics that Cecy had attracted a sponsorship to gain entrance to Oxford all those years ago, with such high hopes and eager excitement for her future, only to have them all dashed later on.

Still, she kept abreast of things with all the new developments and discoveries in the scientific journals and books that she got her hands on. She wondered whether the new volume of *The Compendium of Mathematics* had been published yet. Cecy had collected all ten volumes and had been waiting patiently for this one.

She hurried down the aisle until she reached the back of the shop and looked across the new editions along the row upon row of books. Aha, she'd found it. Cecy reached across to pulled out a copy, only to find a smiling face of a man who not only irritated her but made her pulse race on the other side of the bookcase, peering through the gap she'd created by removing the book.

'Hello, Cecy. Fancy seeing you here.'

Naturally it would be the one man who plagued her like the devil himself.

Mr Dominic Marsden. And he was grinning like the cat who'd got the cream.

Yes, of all the men she'd thought to encounter at Hatchards and at the back of the blasted shop, he was the last one she'd have expected to find here.

Chapter Four

Dominic had paid the manager, Mr Pickles, a pretty penny to ensure Cecily Duddlecott would come to the back of the bookshop on her own. Though he hadn't taken any chances in case Millington had decided to accompany her, too, hence Dominic hiding in the adjacent aisle, not wanting to draw attention to himself. Thankfully she had come alone.

'Good afternoon, Mr Marsden. Yes, *fancy*...it seems that I encounter you in the most unlikely of places.'

'Unlikely, Miss Duddlecott. Why ever so? No, don't answer that.' He walked around the bookcases and down the aisle to where the woman was impatiently tapping her feet. 'But I'll let you into a secret. This isn't my first time here in Hatchards.'

She flung her arms in the air. 'I do know that, since you were here again the last time I was here.'

'How could I forget?' He winked. 'You must stop following me all over the place, Cecy.'

She visibly bristled. 'I am certainly not following

you—in fact, I would say that it is you who are… Oh, you are jesting with me.'

'I am.' He grinned. 'You are so easy to provoke, Cecy.'

'I must be.' She sighed. 'Especially by you. What are you doing here anyway?'

'The same thing as you, I should imagine. Collecting a few books I ordered and browsing through the new collections.'

She frowned. 'It still doesn't explain why we happen upon on each other at the same time, on the same day. Once again.'

'We can put it down to a happy coincidence that we keep bumping into one another.'

'Oh. Indeed.' She rolled her eyes. 'Very happy.'

He leant closer, her warm floral scent teasing his nose. 'But I am glad to have bumped into you again. Here in the back of the shop. It's almost as if we're conducting a secret rendezvous, here behind all these bookshelves where no one can see or hear us, Cecy.'

'Don't be ridiculous, *Dominic*.'

'I do like the sound of my name uttered in that almost contemptuous tone. It makes me realise how close you and I have become recently.'

The woman flushed that pretty pink fusion so becoming against all that dark hair pinned into an eye-wateringly tight chignon beneath her jaunty little hat. He realised her reaction warmed the blood pumping through his veins. The idea that he affected this proud no-nonsense woman in some measure was strangely gratifying.

'You realise nothing of the sort, as it is certainly not true.'

'You wound me.' He shrugged and crossed his arms over his chest. 'For shame. And here I was thinking that after all our recent encounters we might have come to some sort of understanding.'

The moment he said the teasing words he regretted them. It reminded him once again of how he'd erred the last time he'd seen Cecily by revealing far more about himself than he should have. He'd felt far too exposed in that meeting of hers at Marsden House where he found himself talking about his late mother of all people, which was not something he often did. If ever. Which was why he'd felt so shaken up by that whole episode that he'd stupidly kept away from Cecily Duddlecott.

At least Dominic had had the foresight to arrange receiving updates by one of his own men who'd trailed Millington and had reported back that the man had been in Cecily's company several times in the past week or so. It was the reason why he then followed Millington and discovered that the blasted man had ordered an engagement ring from Bentley and Skinner.

It was also why Dominic could kick himself for his stupidity for keeping away. He needed to somehow warn Cecy about a man he was observing without actually warning her of anything exactly. Not yet. Not when there was still nothing conclusive that had been discovered about Millington or his association with her brother, Stephen Duddlecott. But the men from the London Intelligence Office, especially Sir Algernon Pendle, his main contact and head of the office, who'd employed or rather forced him to find out information, confirmed that they were close to gathering all the information they needed for Millington's traitorous activities.

It seemed that Millington was knee deep in bribes and blackmail as a means to have prominent politicians in his pocket. If he somehow secured Cecily's brother into the government itself, then anything might happen. Not that it was certain whether Stephen Duddlecott was actually involved in all of Millington's plans or whether he was yet another pawn in the large and intricate web that the newspaper tycoon was constantly spinning. All of which meant that Cecily did not deserve to be unknowingly dragged into any of it, even if she was a difficult and belligerent female.

Even if this was not part of what he'd been assigned to do, Dominic felt obliged to protect her. God only knew why. Perhaps because she was his sister-in-law, Eliza's, dearest friend. He felt obliged to protect the blasted woman. Without her knowing any of it while playing his part. Now how to do it…

'Mr Marsden? May I remind you that you and I have no such understanding.'

Dominic felt he was standing on safer ground when the woman was insulting him as it meant that they were both reverting back to their usual roles within their odd dynamic. Which was far more preferable than acknowledging this strange pull of what might be described as attraction, every time they met.

Still, it chafed that Cecily believed his interests did not include the love of books. But then she only formed her opinions based on what he'd presented her, which wasn't too far from the affable scoundrel she believed him to be. For a brief moment he wanted her to know him as he really was. But, no, there was no point in that. And that was not the reason he was here in any case.

'Do we not?' He smiled slowly, looking at her from top to bottom. 'But I wonder whether I have this all wrong. Perhaps you hoped to find me here again, Cecy.'

'What the devil do you mean?'

'I mean that you look particularly lovely in all your finery, Cecy…' he gazed at her, taking his fill '…and why I conclude that it must be for my benefit alone that you have come to a mere bookshop looking so… enticing.'

Cecily Duddlecott did look rather lovely dressed in a deep-green promenade dress with a navy-striped wool, trimmed in black velvet and a waterfall pleating effect over those cumbersome bustles. She wore this with a matching short jacket and that jaunty little hat fixed to the side of her head, her appearance seemingly a lot softer than her usual starchy buttoned-up look.

'You are insufferable, Mr Marsden. And, no, I did not come to Hatchards to meet you.'

Dominic stilled her as she turned to go as he knew she would, his hand wrapped around her wrist. And even with all the layers of clothing, he could feel her pulse racing; he could still feel the heat emanating from where he touched her. He resisted exploring more of that heat, yet he couldn't quite allow himself to remove his hand as he really should. 'Are you quite certain?'

'Yes, Mr Marsden, and my attire is absolutely none of your concern.' She exhaled before lifting her head. 'Now you will desist from holding on to my person.'

Dominic allowed his hand to drop to his side as he clenched and unclenched it, wondering why he'd felt so compelled to touch the woman in the first place. What the hell was the matter with him?

'By the by, Cecy, I was complimenting how lovely you look, or is that also frowned upon?'

'Of course not. But I think it was a little more than that, don't you think? Your observation of my appearance was to suggest that it was for your benefit, which is highly inappropriate. When in fact it is…'

'When in fact it is…?' He raised a brow. 'Good lord, do not say it was for another's?'

'I did not say that.'

'But you were going to.'

'I am so glad that you're on hand to tell me what I am about to do.'

He laughed softly. 'If only, darling.'

'I have never in my whole life encountered such an ill-mannered, rude, discourteous, unrefined man as you, Dominic Marsden.'

He pretended to brush off a little lint from his frock coat. 'Don't forget insufferable.'

'That, too.' She continued to glare at him before expelling a breath and shaking her head. 'Why do you happen to be everywhere I seem to be? Why?'

This was precisely what Dominic did not want the woman to be thinking about. His turning up at the same places where she happened to be was evidently beginning to gain her notice, which was unavoidable, even if it was true.

'Keep up, Cecy, we have already established all of that.'

'Ah, yes, it's by *a happy coincidence* that you're always there wherever I am. Was that it?'

'Indeed.' He smiled. 'You're a lucky woman.'

She rolled her eyes and turned back to grab another volume of whatever it was she was…wait, was Cecily Duddlecott reading *The Compendium of Mathemat-*

ics? Evidently. The woman was full of surprises, even if she loathed him. Perhaps it was better that she did.

'So?'

'So…what, Mr Marsden?'

'So who is this paragon, who has you all in this state of excitement?'

'I am not in any state of excitement.' Her nostrils flared. 'And you wouldn't know him, anyway.'

He smiled inwardly, wondering whether she knew that she'd given herself away there. 'I know everyone who is everyone, sweetheart. Most of London's gentlemen visit the Trium Impiorum. It's the place to be seen and the place where one can indulge in many vices. Not that I should be speaking to you about such things.'

'Why, because I'm such an innocent miss that I wouldn't know what on earth you could mean when you speak of indulging in your particular brand of vices?'

'What do you know of men's vices?'

'More than you think, Mr Marsden.' She exhaled a shaky breath as she clutched her books tightly against her chest.

He frowned. 'What on earth does that mean?'

'Nothing,' she said and he couldn't help notice that all colour had drained from her face.

'Cecily?'

'I said it means nothing.' She lifted her head. 'And

I doubt a man as busy as Mr Millington would have time to come to your club.'

Dominic wanted to question the woman about the haunted look in her eyes that he'd witnessed, but doubted that she would even consider confiding in him. Why would she when all he'd ever done was tease and annoy her mercilessly? And he wasn't quite done yet.

'Samuel Millington? *The* Samuel Millington, with gold watches and diamond pins and the huge wads of money he likes to throw around. That is the man you've set your cap on?' He whistled. 'Well, well, well, you are a high flyer underneath all that starch that you've put aside for the day, Cecy. And quite the contrary, he visits the club often. Along with your dear brother.'

He watched as a myriad of emotions flickered across her face. 'Stephen visits your club? Stephen? Surely he no longer does since his marriage?'

It was interesting that she was more disappointed and surprised by her brother's visits then a man who hoped to win her hand, if that was indeed what he was doing with the purchase of that blasted ring.

'Sorry to disappoint you, darling, but he was there just last night.'

She shook her head in apparent disbelief. 'That can't be. I'm sure you're mistaken.'

'I am afraid I'm not.'

'But my brother... He is such a stickler for... I cannot believe it. He has always believed that such places as the Trium Impiorum to be a vastitude of sin, vice and licentious behaviour.'

Dominic didn't want to tell Cecily that her brother, Stephen, was in fact quite a regular at the club and had been attending for many, many years.

'Sadly, most people who judge others along the lines of morality and proper behaviour tend to be hypocrites themselves.'

'It seems so.' She turned to leave again. 'Well, good day to you, Mr Marsden. I wish I could say it was a pleasure to meet you again.'

'Wait one moment, if you will.'

'How can it be possible for you to have more to say to me?'

'And yet I do.' He leant across to block the aisle so that she would be forced to listen to him. 'I would urge you caution. Take care, Cecily. I tell you in good faith that Samuel Millington isn't quite as he seems. Remember that I know the men of the *ton* in ways that you cannot and I tell you that he is not the man for you.'

She snapped her head up. 'Oh, so now you know what is best for me, do you?'

'In this I do. And while I appreciate that a woman of your standing, who has gained his attentions, must seem flattered, but know this—the man is not what you believe him to be. He is not quite what he presents himself to the world.'

'Is that so? Well, he must be quite like *you* in that respect.'

What the devil...?

'What on earth do you mean?'

'Surely you know?' She raised a brow. 'One minute you are expressing your feelings about a number of issues as well as being sympathetic to the causes that matter to me, the next you're back to...*this*.'

'Back to this? What can you mean?'

'The usual. You naturally find it excessively amusing that I have a potential suitor and are doing all you can to be a nuisance.'

'Is that what you think?' He scowled at her in disbelief. God's blood, but did the woman believe that he'd stoop so low? For amusement? Evidently.

'Why not? When you're back to being...'

'Insufferable?'

'Precisely,' she muttered. 'So, which one are you, the sensitive, intelligent man or the scoundrel?'

'Perhaps I'm a bit of both.' He smiled before giving himself an inward shake. Why the hell was he talking about this nonsense? 'But that's neither here nor there. We're discussing Samuel Millington. I ask you to take heed. The man is in want of something and it may not be what you want it to be.'

'Perhaps he is in want of a wife, Mr Marsden?'

'I rather doubt it.'

'Naturally, because why would a gentleman like Mr Millington desire such a thing from a woman like me? Is that it?'

He saw hurt and indignation flash in her eyes before being extinguished and replaced by the same implacable look of disdain she always had whenever she glanced in his direction. Dominic might have ordinarily accepted her loathing, but he couldn't have her believe this was his opinion of her. He was not that insensitive, nor that much of a martyr.

He stepped closer and cupped her face and tilted it upwards, his thumb grazing her soft skin. 'Of course not. I would never have you believe that about yourself. Don't you know that you're so much more than that?'

Cecily locked eyes with him and for a moment they just stared at one another, neither of them saying much, but wordlessly assessing, exploring, uncovering. Her eyes were so bright, so vivid, so damn beautiful with every shade of blue and mauve and even strands of silver, as she held herself still, not allowing him to see more than she was prepared to give. So together, so in control. But hanging there by only a thread.

He could see that his touch was affecting her just as much as it was affecting him. The fact that she hadn't moved, the fact that the little shallow breaths against his hand were a little ragged. The fact that her pupils were swallowing up all that blue in her eyes. The fact that she'd moved closer to him and the fact that her eyes had dropped to his lips.

Desire, hot and potent, hit his blood so suddenly that it made him want to tear his hand away from her and take a step back. But he didn't. He continued to touch her, wanting more.

Wanting...wanting...wanting.

The word kept running through his mind.

What the hell?

'Miss Duddlecott? Cecily?' Millington's voice boomed from further along the bookshop, getting closer and closer.

She flicked her gaze up at him and wordlessly pleaded with him. He pulled her close and bent his head, his nose brushing against her neck as he whispered in her ear, 'Remember what I said about Millington, Cecily. Take care.'

He then released her and moved with lightning speed back to the adjacent aisle where he'd initially been hiding. Dominic watched her through the narrow gap above the stacked books on the bookshelf, allowing him to see the aisle where Cecily moved quickly away.

'I am here, Mr Millington.' She spoke louder than she probably would have, warning Dominic that he should remain hidden. It would naturally be unseemly for Cecily to be discovered with him, but there was a part of him that wanted the man to know just so he would leave her alone. For some reason he couldn't quite put his finger on, Dominic felt uneasy about Samuel Millington being anywhere near Cecily.

'So you are, my dear.' The man practically purred as he smiled down at her. 'I thought you might have lost your way in the shop.'

'No, of course not,' she said with amusement. Had he heard correctly? Had Cecily Duddlecott just chuckled inanely like pea-brained miss? Why was she acting so differently in front of Millington? 'I believe I must have been immersed in my reading that I forgot about the time. I hope you can forgive my unpardonable behaviour, sir.'

'With pleasure, my dear.' The man held out his arm out to Cecily, which she took, tucking her gloved hand into the crook of his arm. 'And if you're finished here then I'd be delighted to take you for luncheon. I took the liberty of acquiring a table at Verrey's. The food is excellent there, if you wish to accompany me.'

'I'd be delighted, Mr Millington, but perhaps another time.'

'Come now, the table awaits us.'

'I'm afraid I have a prior engagement this afternoon, sir.'

'Which you can surely postpone?'

'Not at this late notice, Mr Millington. I am sorry to disappoint you.'

Dominic could hear the man sigh deeply. 'Very well.

I'll let you off this time. But allow me to postpone it and make it a dinner reservation, instead. How about tomorrow night?'

'I should like that very much, thank you.' Dominic could see Cecily glance over her shoulder before giving the man a smile.

'It's all part of my plan to win you over, my dear.' The obsequious rat returned her smile, which Dominic was itching to wipe off.

'I am honoured.'

'Good, good.' Millington patted her hand. 'Shall we?'

'Yes, thank you. I must first settle my account for the books.'

'No need. I have already done that.'

Even from this distance and watching her over the top of the stacked books, Dominic could just about make out Cecily's spine straighten in that familiar way when she was displeased.

'You should not have gone to the trouble for me, Mr Millington.'

'No trouble at all, my dear.'

'Thank you, but there was really no need. I must recompense you, sir.'

'There was every need and you shall do no such thing.'

Dominic backed against the far wall as Millington's eyes darted over Cecily's head, perhaps trying to ascertain whether or not there was someone else there along the aisle. He didn't want to jeopardise what he'd been assigned to do, with Millington possibly starting to suspect Dominic of watching his movements and being anything other than the affable, friendly co-owner of Trium Impiorum. But in that moment, Dominic didn't seem to care about any of it as much as he did about Millington's possessiveness, while escorting the woman out of the shop. He couldn't help the feeling of dread and concern in the man's interest with 'Miss too good for her boots' Cecily Duddlecott.

Chapter Five

Cecily's mind was still reeling after that odd encounter with Dominic Marsden at the back of Hatchards bookshop yesterday. She couldn't stop thinking about everything that had transpired between them even now as she sat opposite Samuel Millington the following evening on apparently the best table at Verrey's, London's most exclusive French restaurant, sampling from their exclusive à la carte menu.

She had been reliably informed of this by Mr Millington, who proceeded to show his apparent good taste, which also equated to his very expensive taste, by the arrival of the finest champagne before they made their order, something which she would ordinarily have minded. Not this evening, however.

All she could ponder on was Dominic Marsden's words to her the previous day. His warnings about Mr Millington just before he vanished behind the bookcases. And then there was the matter of how he'd touched her and caressed her face when she'd believed that his warning must have been some kind of jest at her expense. But then he'd earnestly told her that it was not so.

'Of course not. I would never have you believe that about yourself. Don't you know that you're so much more than that...'

Cecily had wanted to ask what he'd meant, but had been left motionless by the touch of his bare, callused hands against her skin. God, she could still feel the press of his fingers into her nape and how the pad of his thumb gently grazed along her jawline, her cheeks and her lips, even now after a day.

The man had then repeated his warning about Mr Millington, with all his usual humour stripped from his handsome face as he asked her again to remember what he'd said about Millington. Cecily could not understand any of it. Least of all the fact that he had almost kissed her. God only knew how much she would have welcomed it.

Yet... Dominic Marsden? She must be going mad.

'Cecily, you are not attending again, my dear. Are you unwell?' Mr Millington said as he wiped his mouth with his crisp white napkin, clearly displeased that her mind was elsewhere. And how was it that he felt that he could drop formalities altogether and call her by her given name, especially after what she'd said only a day ago.

It was this expectation that she would agree to his

suit that was particularly galling. Even so, Cecily was being discourteous when he'd sought to impress her by bringing her to this marvellous place, which she wasn't appreciating as much as she should.

A haven of opulence and modernity, the dining area of Verrey's was simply stunning, with half-oak wall panelling, and huge Venetian mirrored glass imported from Italy above it, and a massive chandelier above, and large potted plants creating the ambiance of some of those Parisian salons that her parents had described in their letters.

'I apologise, Mr Millington. I think I'm left quite speechless by the grandness of this place.'

'Then I'm glad it meets to your approval,' he said, tossing back the champagne from a crystal flute.

Honestly, she didn't know anyone who drank champagne as though it was water. A part of her felt giddy, considering how so much had changed in only a day. How she was here at this expensive establishment with a man who clearly wanted to court her. Who wanted to marry her. It was all so unexpected. Yet all Cecily could think about was another man altogether. 'I cannot think how this establishment might not meet with anyone's approval.'

He leant forward and covered her hand with his. 'But you are not just anyone, Cecily. I do hope you know that.'

'Thank you.'

It was strange that Samuel Millington's touch, this time on her hand, made Cecily feel none of that burning heat of Dominic Marsden's. One touch from that scoundrel and she'd wanted to throw herself at him. God, but even now she could remember how she couldn't take her eyes away from his mouth. She had found herself leaning in closer and closer until she was just a hair's breadth away from his lips.

What had happened to her? She didn't even like the man, did she? And he was certainly all the things that she'd described yesterday in Hatchards, when he'd made her so angry after he'd admitted to wanting to get a rise out of her. Yet she couldn't deny that she had also wanted to kiss him. Perhaps it was just some kind of passing madness. Perhaps it was getting caught up in the heat of the moment. Or perhaps it had more to do with the fact that, lately, she seemed to be pushed and pulled and jostled into place to do what others expected from her.

First, from her seemingly hypocritical brother, Stephen, and then Mr Millington, who was pushing too fast. The man was behaving as though it was done already—that this proposed courtship had been accepted and agreed by her. And then there were Dominic's words coming back to her again about having to take care with Mr Millington. What had he meant? And when had she started thinking of Dominic Marsden by his given name?

'Are you not hungry, my dear?' Samuel Millington asked, a brow raised. 'Perhaps I shouldn't order the duck à l'orange as it might be too rich and order the lemon sole instead. Yes, that might do.'

'It all sounds delicious.' She smiled dutifully. 'But I must admit, Mr Millington, that I do usually enjoy ordering my own meals. I am not used to another person being so…solicitous of my needs.'

'Do not worry yourself. You shall get used to it soon enough, my dear.' He returned her smile.

'Will I? I have not given you my answer yet, Mr Millington,' Cecily said softly. 'Surely you know, since I have been honest with you, that I need time to consider your suit.'

His smile slipped from his face, the angles of his face suddenly harsh and unforgiving. 'I admit that I'm not a patient man. And I am not used to failure in any aspect of my life. Something which I'm not about to start now. You should know, my dear Cecily, that I usually get what I want in the end, one way or another.'

His words made her feel uneasy. What did he mean 'one way or another'? Did the man mean to force her down the aisle? How terribly Gothic of him.

'While I am deeply honoured to be the object of your, er…want, Mr Millington, I cannot help think that your words sound too…dare I say it presumptuous?'

'Apologies, my dear. But I do mean to win your favour and, as I said, I'm used to getting what I want.'

His smile was somewhat vulgar for a man who believed himself an arbiter of good taste and gentlemanly behaviour. 'I just can't help being a little passionate about the object of my…want, as you put it.'

'I am flattered, sir.'

'Good.'

They resumed drinking champagne in silence. She lifted her eyes just then as a small group of diners wove their way through the restaurant and passed their table.

'Eliza? Mr Marsden?' Cecily said, surprised to see her friend, along with her husband and her two brothers-in-law. Her eyes took in Sebastian Marsden, then Tristan Marsden, before settling on Dominic Marsden looking so handsome and dashing in his evening attire that she almost gasped. 'What a…*happy coincidence.*'

Dominic Marsden gave her a ghost of a smile before bending over her hand, his green eyes glittering. 'Good evening to you and, yes, it is, is it not, Miss Duddlecott?'

She dragged her gaze to Eliza, trying to ignore the rampant beating of her heart. 'I must admit that I didn't think to see you out and about, Eliza.'

'Yes, perhaps this whole outing is a little concerning for a woman in my wife's condition,' Sebastian Marsden muttered under his breath. Clearly, he'd come out this evening against his better judgement. 'Not that I can deny Eliza anything.'

'I'm well, Sebastian, please don't make a fuss. I know it's not the proper thing, but I hardly subscribe to doing what is proper. As you well know,' she said, smiling up at her husband who smiled back, before addressing Cecily. 'This is my last few days and nights in London before we're away to Cornwall for the last months of my confinement. And we…' She glanced at Dominic Marsden before glancing back at her. 'As in I was desperate to leave the house, where I have been cooped up for far too long.'

Cecily smiled at her friend and slid her hand into her gloved hand, giving it a squeeze. 'Then you must join us. That is, if it is agreeable to you, Mr Millington?'

The man sat stony faced throughout this whole exchange, not even rising to stand in the presence of another lady, which reflected very badly on him. He did stand eventually and exhaled before inclining his head at Cecily.

'Of course. It would be our pleasure, Marsden, Mrs Marsden I shall see to it.'

'As long as we're not intruding?'

'Not at all.'

'Thank you, Mr Millington. We're much obliged to you.'

He bowed before clicking his fingers and gaining the attention of a handful of waiters, who quickly and efficiently came to do Mr Millington's bidding. And in no time, they all found themselves sat around a much larger dining table, with all their table settings artfully arranged around it.

'It's very good of you to accommodate us, Millington,' Sebastian Marsden said, raising his flute and nodding at the man sat beside Cecily.

'Not at all, Marsden.' Mr Millington covered her hand once again with his own. 'If Cecily wishes for Mrs Marsden's company along with your own and both your brothers, then I'm delighted for you all to join us.'

'Thank you,' Mr Marsden said.

'Although I am curious how you are able to be away from the Trium Impiorum. And in the evening. Even curiouser that you're not dining at the club, where the food is quite excellent.'

'True,' Dominic murmured from across the table before his brother could reply. 'However, we were all the more curious about this place, having heard so much about it.'

'And Eliza wished to be somewhere outside the four walls of Marsden House and the Trium Impiorum,' Sebastian said gruffly. 'Now, shall we order?'

'I must say that I am excited to be sampling the menu at this fine establishment after hearing so much about it,' Dominic said to no one in particular after another efficient waiter poured wine for the new guests around the table. 'It makes one realise what we might need to do to improve the standards at the club.'

'The dining experience at Trium Impiorum is already excellent, Dominic,' his older brother retorted, clearly taking offence at the implication.

'Yes, but it never hurts to evaluate the competition—not that Verrey's is a club, but its dining experience is certainly similar,' Dominic said after speaking to the waiter about the à la carte menu.

'I'd say that's good business practice, Marsden. I approve.' Mr Millington flashed a brief, hard smile. 'The food is excellent here, so plenty to compare with.'

'Do you have any recommendations?'

'Of course. Allow me to choose the best dishes that this establishment has to offer,' Mr Millington said to the surprise of the Marsdens. Apparently, it wasn't just the wine or the hors d'oeuvres that he liked to order. Perhaps this was what he enjoyed doing. And perhaps she'd been quick to judge Mr Millington. 'I would recommend the following dishes which are all first rate.' Samuel Millington then reeled off all the dishes for the four-course meal. 'Starting with oeufs à la Kavigote, bisque d'écrevisses, consommé Okra. And then rougets à la Muscovite. Selle de mouton de Galles, haricots panachés to follow, tomates au gratin with pommes soufflées, timbale Lucullus and fonds d'artichauts, crème pistache and grouse. As well as a few side dishes of salad Rachel. To finish with biscuit glacé à la Verrey, soufflé de laitances and dessert.'

'Thank you, Mr Millington. That all sounds delicious.'

'My pleasure, Mrs Marsden.'

'Indeed, Millington, I'm not certain what we would have done without your excellent, ah…taste in such matters.'

'Not at all.' It seemed Mr Millington hadn't quite picked up on Dominic Marsden's sardonic tone, something which his older brother had, giving him a reproachful glare. Oblivious to all this, Mr Millington continued to speak. 'However, as I said before, we can all agree that the chef at Trium Impiorum is a real asset to your club. The food is excellent.'

'Thank you, Millington.'

'Yet not all of us can quite agree on that, so I will have to take your word for it, sir.' Cecily found herself saying these words and wished she'd kept her mouth shut, as all eyes around the table turned to her.

Dominic Marsden was watching her intently from the other side of the table. 'What could you possibly mean, Miss Duddlecott?'

He knew well enough as this conversation was not a new one. Cecily had often debated it with the man about the fact the Trium Impiorum was exclusively a male domain. 'I do not wish to be impolite, but I am the only person around this table who has not had the privilege of knowing how excellent the food at the Trium Impiorum is.'

'You may sample the chef's table with Eliza any time in our living quarters on the upper floors once my wife has completed the refurbishments, Miss Duddlecott.'

'I thank you, Mr Marsden, however…'

'However?'

Eliza smiled at her husband. 'That is not what Cecy meant, Sebastian.'

'I apologise, Miss Duddlecott, but I fail to comprehend.' The older Mr Marsden's brows furrowed in confusion. 'What is your meaning, then?'

But once again Eliza spoke on her behalf. 'Cecy and I believe that the Trium Impiorum should not just be the exclusive reserve of gentlemen. That women should also enjoy the gaming rooms as well.'

'You do?'

'Yes, Sebastian, I do. It would be wonderful that perhaps once a week or once a month the Trium Impiorum could host an evening that would include us. It's high time the club included us ladies.'

'And not be discriminated against?'

'Yes, exactly, Dominic.'

Mr Millington began to laugh. 'You cannot be serious, Mrs Marsden?'

'And why not?' Cecily asked the man sat beside her. 'Why is such a notion so laughable?'

'Because it is, my dear. No respectable woman would ever consider such a notion.'

The man must have realised how clumsy his words were considering he was sitting with two such women. It would seem excessively rude and disrespectful, especially since the table descended into silence, with a thrum of tension that he quickly averted. 'Apologies, Mrs Marsden, Cecily, I did not mean to cause offence. What I meant was that I cannot see why a respectable woman would want to patronise a gentleman's club such as Trium Impiorum in the first place.'

'Would you not think that it would be something to ask us women, Mr Millington, instead of making that assumption?' Cecily took a sip of her wine. 'After all, there was once the common belief that it was not desirable for respectable women to dine in such establishments as this and yet here we are. Attitudes to such matters are changing and evolving all the time.'

Mr Millington laughed. 'My dear Cecily, a gaming table, however, is a very different case altogether.'

'I cannot see why. The demands for changes are happening right now. From workers' rights to women's rights, the inequities within every aspect of society are being constantly scrutinised and challenged. An exclusive gaming club is no different here.'

'And yet it is so unseemly.'

'Is it?' Cecily said softly. 'I wouldn't know, sir.'

'No, you wouldn't, my dear, which is how it should be. And that's why you should defer such decisions to people who know better. Perhaps there are some institutions that are and should remain the preserve of men. Otherwise, where will we be?'

Cecily was momentarily speechless. It was attitudes such as this that both she and Eliza encountered time and time again. At least her friend was now married to a man who accepted that part of who she was and didn't want to change her.

'You forget, Mr Millington, that as an Oxford woman, I am used to such views. Most people still believe it unnatural that a woman should be allowed to study at university.'

'Ah, I had not known that.' Mr Millington drew his finger along the stem of his glass before addressing her. 'And while I think it commendable, it is hardly necessary, my dear.'

'Being intellectually curious and having a thirst for knowledge may be quite a necessary for some, Mr Millington,' she said, trying to keep her voice steady. 'It was for me.'

'Well said.' Dominic nodded. 'Couldn't have put it better myself.'

'I agree, Miss Duddlecott,' Tristan Marsden, the youngest brother, added. 'I wish Cambridge, my alma mater, would follow Oxford's suit and admit women. But they're far too stuck in their ways.'

'How very disappointing.' Cecily gave the young man a tentative smile.

'Ah, but change and progress doesn't all come at once.'

'No, indeed.' Mr Millington nodded taking a sip of wine. 'And in the case of the Trium Impiorum, for me, I hope it remains as it has always done. A club exclusively for men.'

Eliza smiled that polite impersonal smile that usually meant she was hiding her disapproval. 'You make it sound as though the Trium Impiorum is a hub of sin, vice and debauchery, Mr Millington. It is far from that. And no one is saying that the club should admit women every night—well, not right away, but perhaps one night a week or once a month.'

'I'm afraid you shall find many of the gentlemen of the *ton* who are members of the club rescinding their membership, if there was a gaggle of their womenfolk at the same gaming table as them. It just wouldn't do.'

Cecily bristled with indignation at Samuel Millington's ridiculously old-fashioned views, which she found to be contradictory for a self-made man like him. She had hoped that he was progressive enough to see Cecily as she really was, as well as the many causes she was passionate about.

But perhaps his views were only in relation to the Trium Impiorum. Or if they were, she had the power within her to change his views. After all, many gentlemen had views such as this, including her own brother.

She glanced across at Dominic Marsden, whose eyes had been fixed on her throughout this whole exchange.

'And you, Mr Marsden? What are your thoughts regarding this?' she asked, turning her attention to him.

Dominic shrugged. 'I believe both you and Eliza may have a valid point.'

'You do?' Sebastian asked.

'Why not? I believe the ladies may have hit on something here. It seems ludicrous that we haven't thought of it before, Sebastian.'

'Do you not think that it might alienate some of our members?'

'It certainly will,' Samuel Millington said with a huff, even though Sebastian Marsden had not actually addressed him.

'But why? I see no problem with admitting women once a week, for instance, and I like to think of the Trium Impiorum as a club that isn't stuck in its ways and can adapt to change, rather than resting on its laurels.' Dominic paused and glanced at Mr Millington. 'And if some of our older, more conservative patrons are so outraged by the idea of women being admitted to the club once a week, then they can always patronise another club on those particular evenings or they can leave altogether if they're so incensed by such a thing.'

'It's a huge risk.' Sebastian sighed. 'What if every one of our members leave?'

'Will they?' Eliza turned to her husband, who was

rubbing his jaw. 'Because you admit women to the club occasionally?'

'Possibly. It might seem radical and progressive for many of our members who are resistant to change. And they're hardly going allow their womenfolk to enter the club anyway.'

'True, but as Cecy explained, that has always been the case when society constantly restricts the movement of women, binding them to acceptable modes of behaviour.'

'Exactly.' Cecy nodded. 'And if we do not challenge these beliefs, then nothing ever changes.'

'Yes, but what of the women in society themselves, who would never dream of entering a gaming hell, believing that the kind of woman who would partake in what a club has to offer as someone they would not want to associate with. It would be a pointless exercise, would it not?' Sebastian raised a brow.

'I can tell you that would be exactly the case. No right-minded man would want their women to enter a gaming hell, even one such as the Trium Impiorum. It would be too unseemly,' Samuel Millington said with a challenge in his voice.

'Would it now?' Dominic asked slowly as he sipped his wine. Cecy threw him a grateful smile for the way he stood up to Millington, in a way she could not.

'Naturally it would,' Millington said through gritted teeth.

But this was precisely the attitude that had always followed everything that Cecy ever did in her life and yet it was Samuel Millington who felt annoyed by the opinions around the table? Well, then she would add her voice as well. And if it ruined his estimable opinion of her, then so be it.

'I am one such woman who has faced negative aspersions, Mr Millington, and only because of my interest in what society at large perceives to be the domain of men. And in the case of the Trium Impiorum, there may be many women who would look down at others who enter its hallowed walls, but a change of attitude needs to start from somewhere, otherwise where would we be?'

Dominic raised his champagne glass at her. 'Indeed, Miss Duddlecott, change can sometimes be a force for good, even if it is difficult at first.'

Cecily nodded. 'It might be deemed enlightened, forward thinking and, dare I say it, modern.'

'Yes,' Dominic murmured with a faint smile on his lips.

For a long moment she simply stared at the man on the other side of the table, transfixed by the inscrutable flash of emotion in his eyes. Time stretched for a moment and drowned out the low hum of the restaurant noise, and even their companions faded into the background.

Then she blinked and heard someone clearing their

throat, bringing Cecily back to the room and back to their table. Good God, what on earth was she doing, mooning over Dominic Marsden in full view of his family? And in front of Mr Millington as well. She tore her eyes away, trying to recover her misstep, but still managed to catch the blasted man smiling at her.

Thankfully the waiters arrived just then with the first course that Mr Millington had taken upon himself to order.

'Well, this looks marvellous,' Sebastian said, looking at the platters that had been artfully placed in front of them. 'Bon appétit.'

The table descended into a silence before Eliza returned the conversation back to the subject of their discussion.

'But you know I cannot see all your patrons leaving if you admitted women. And you can always explore the possibility of this venture for one night and gauge its success?'

Sebastian smiled and lifted his wife's gloved hand to his lips. 'I thank you for your wise counsel as always, my love. In any business one must keep abreast of developments and introducing new and exciting ideas. Some might be rejected while others? Others might well prove to be a success.'

'Exactly.'

Cecily felt a sharp pang in her chest, as she realised that this here, this intimacy, connection and mutual respect between her friend and Mr Marsden, was what she'd want if she were to marry. It was this that she'd longed for: to be accepted as she really was. Eliza and Sebastian were extremely lucky to have found all of that in each other. As well as finding love…

Which naturally made her think of the man sat beside her, who for a reason unknown to Cecily wanted to make her his wife. Samuel Millington was disappointingly set in his ways; yet could he be persuaded to think differently? After all, as a leader of industry he must be similar to the Marsden brothers in knowing that change could be a good, even a necessary thing at times. But the question was whether he would ever consider changing his opinions for her and accept Cecily and her radical beliefs.

When she lifted her head, however, there was a different man who met her eyes. Dominic Marsden was once again watching her as though seeing right inside her soul. His eyes felt as though they were burning a hole into her skin and the intensity made her heart pound in her chest. She only hoped no one saw, especially not Samuel Millington. But then after tonight, Cecily was even more curious than before to understand what Dominic Marsden had meant when he'd warned her off the man, as she was hopeless with cryptic messages.

Chapter Six

For the next couple of days Marsden House had been a hive of activity which was a good thing as Dominic was trying avoid his sister-in-law, who was determined to question him ever since the evening at Verrey's restaurant. So far, he'd managed to dodge her since he was naturally quicker and always one step ahead of a heavily pregnant woman. However, he had not been so lucky today.

'Ah, there you are, Dominic,' Eliza said as she walked into the library and closed the door behind her after finally cornering him. 'I have been meaning to talk to you since the other night.'

'Have you, indeed?' He looked up from the behind the desk that he'd been working at and put down his quill.

'You know very well I have, since you have been doing your best to avoid me, dear Brother.'

'I? Avoid you, dear Sister?' He rose as she came closer. 'Nothing of the sort. Sit, here on the armchair,

Eliza. Take the weight off your feet. I'll ask Cairns to come and fuss over you with a nice tray of tea and hot buttered crumpets.'

'Not so fast, Dominic. I don't need to sit and while I very much appreciate a nice cup of tea, I think I can do without one for a moment. Besides, I'm not too addled in the head that I need help to ask Cairns for anything.'

'Very well. Out with it, then. What is it that you want to talk to me so urgently about?'

'I wanted to ask whether you knew Cecy would be there with Mr Millington the other night?'

'No.' *Naturally he did.* 'It was a happy coincidence.'

God above, but he needed to stop repeating that ridiculous phrase.

'Was it, though? I cannot help thinking that you orchestrated the whole thing. Persuading me to ask Sebastian so that we would all go to Verrey's together, only to bump into Cecy and Mr Millington once we got there. I cannot put my finger on it, but you're up to something, Dominic, and it somehow involves Cecy.'

'What a fanciful notion. Are you sure your mind isn't addled after all, Eliza?'

'Very funny, Dominic.' She sighed deeply. 'I just wish I knew what you're up to.'

The last thing he needed was Eliza and, for that matter, Sebastian poking their heads into his clandestine assignments and the real reason he was keeping a close watch on Stephen Duddlecott, Samuel Millington and, by association, Cecy as well. 'I assure you that I'm not up to anything.'

'Either way it's a shame that I'm going to Cornwall later this afternoon, as I might eventually have got the truth out of you.'

He rose to leave, having had enough of this conversation. 'Was there anything else, Eliza?'

'Just one last thing.' She held up her hand. 'You seemed quite different with Cecy the other night.'

'Did I?' He did not like her perceptiveness, which at times felt far too invasive. His brother had always said this about Eliza: that she was far too clever by half. 'I can't say I know what you mean, dear Sister.'

'Can you not?'

'No.'

'It's odd, Dominic, but lately...' Eliza peered up at him from behind those round gold-rimmed spectacles of hers and studied him for a moment before shaking her head.

'Lately I...?'

'Lately, you seem...to be taken with her.'

'Good God!' He shook his head. 'Taken? With Cecily Duddlecott? Are you mad?'

She shrugged. 'I know what I saw, Dominic. At the dinner you couldn't quite keep your eyes off her.'

It had been true, not that he could explain it himself, let alone to his far too inquisitive sister-in-law. Cecily Duddlecott stirred his blood in a way that was disconcerting at best and downright disturbing at worse. But Dominic could hardly deny how lovely she had looked that evening.

The low light of the candles and gaslight of the chandelier had cast a soft glow over her exposed skin, making him want to touch her again, to see if her skin was really as soft as the first time he'd touched her in Hatchards. Her dark sable hair had been artfully coiled into a high chignon with silver, onyx and lapis lazuli hair combs holding up the arrangement, allowing a few curls to frame her heart-shaped face.

Her evening dress was simply stunning in midnight-blue velvet, draped and following the curves of her lush body as it flowed and puddled down to the floor, with a simple bustle at the back. She looked the epitome of grace and elegance even if her off-the-shoulder neckline showed too much of her décolletage. It was by no means indecent, not by the evening dresses worn by fashionable women lately.

But Dominic could not explain how much it bothered him that Millington's eyes constantly dropped to her bare shoulders and her plunging neckline. It was ridiculous as Dominic had really no claim on the woman and yet he hated the other man's pursuit of her in his usual brash and aggressive manner. That was surely the only reason. He was merely acting in concern for his sister-in-law's good friend.

'Well, you were wrong, Eliza. I find Miss Duddlecott amusing, that is all.'

'Fine. You don't have to confide in me, but I hope that your amusement doesn't extend to anything that might…?'

'That might…what exactly?'

'Hurt her,' Eliza almost whispered the words, but he'd heard them all the same.

He was outraged. 'How can you think that of me? That I would ever hurt anyone, let alone a woman, simply for amusement's sake?' He shook his head in disgust as he started to walk away. 'If there's nothing else, Eliza, I shall see you at dinner.'

'No, wait.' She stood and waddled after him. 'Please, Dominic, wait. I apologise. I didn't mean to cause offence. I can be so direct and thoughtless, especially in my current condition, but I do apologise. I was unpardonably rude and you're rightly annoyed with me.'

He sighed. 'It's hard for anyone to stay annoyed with you for long, Eliza.'

She smoothed her hands over her large round bump and inhaled. 'You know I would never suggest such a thing. I know you'd never intentionally hurt anyone, least of all Cecy.'

'I know that.'

'Friends?' She raised a brow.

'Friends.' He caught her hand in his.

'Good.' She smiled, squeezing his hand in return.

'All I ask is to tread carefully with Cecy. She may have a strong, stiff exterior, but it's a way to protect herself after what happened at Oxford and the scandal that followed.'

'What do you mean?' He frowned. 'What happened at Oxford?'

'Oh dear, that is another bad habit of mine, lately. I keep babbling things I really shouldn't.'

'Eliza?'

'All I will say is that she has been hurt before. The rest you will have to find out yourself, as it really is not my place to disclose any more than I have.' She rubbed her forehead. 'I shouldn't really have said anything in the first place.'

What the hell did Eliza mean? What scandal had occurred in Oxford that would make such a proud woman such as Cecily Duddlecott need to protect herself? None of this made any sense. And none of it was exactly Dominic's business, yet he could not help being intrigued by everything that Eliza had said. Not that he would acknowledge any of it to his nosy sister-in-law.

'I doubt Miss Duddlecott would confide in me about anything like that, Eliza. But I will say that perhaps you should be more concerned about Samuel Millington, if you want to prevent her from getting hurt.'

'Yes, about him—it's obvious that you share my view that the man is a complete coxcomb?'

'Among other things.'

'Nevertheless, Mr Millington is inordinately wealthy, is of huge influence and he has set his sights firmly on Cecy.'

'It seems so.' He couldn't quite keep the bitterness from his voice.

'The truth is that I will not be able to be here for Cecy since I'm travelling later and retreating into my confinement. So I will ask you, since you seem to have taken an interest in Cecy, whether you will look out for her while I'm away, Dominic?'

'A minute ago, you were warning me about hurting her for my amusement. Now you want me to look out for her? Which is it, dear Sister?'

'I put it badly as I know you would not hurt her. I did explain, Dominic, do keep up.'

Dominic rubbed his forehead. 'It's quite difficult to at times, Eliza. I do wonder occasionally how my brother gets on.'

'Very well, if you must know.' She rolled her eyes. 'Anyway, as I was saying about Cecily.'

'What about her?'

'It's just that my intuition tells me that Mr Millington's interest in Cecy is a little worrying.'

He raised a brow. 'How so?'

Dominic was intrigued to get a woman's insight about Millington, especially Eliza's as it might offer a different perspective to the one he already had.

'I don't know, Dominic, and, in truth, I could be

wrong about him. Not that my intuition has ever let me down before. But Mr Millington seems possessive. He seems resistant to the changing world around him, especially in terms of women's emancipation, which as you know is important to Cecy. I don't like the idea of him changing Cecy or making her unhappy. I can't put my finger on it, but the man is shifty. And he seems to keep all his cards to himself, without giving much away.'

'He is a newspaper man, Eliza. He's always shifty. But fear not, those cards aren't always kept so close to his chest. Not the way he plays at the Trium Impiorum. In fact, it's at those times when he is engrossed in his game that he's far more open.'

She sighed deeply. 'I could have this all wrong and Mr Millington might be just the man to deserve Cecily—however, I cannot be certain at the moment. This is the reason that I would ask you to keep an eye out for her. Be there for her if she needs your assistance, especially as I won't be here in London.'

'What of her own family?' Again Dominic knew the answer to this question, but would have it verified from someone as astute and intelligent as Eliza who was also close to the lady.

'Her brother won't be any good, as he is the one pushing for this alliance with Samuel Millington.' She leant forward. 'Say that you'd do it for me?'

Dominic was already doing it, with or without Eliza's request, yet this now gave him the perfect excuse for traipsing after Cecily. It would be as if he was doing his sister-in-law's bidding all the while.

He smiled. 'For you, Eliza, I'll keep a look out for Cecily Duddlecott. Don't worry about a thing.'

'Thank you.'

It was then that Cecily walked into the library and without the butler announcing her. The woman was at Marsden House so often that there was really no need for it. However, it did make a slightly awkward atmosphere since she had walked into the library at the very moment he'd been discussing her with Eliza. Dominic hoped that Cecy hadn't heard any of the exchange, but he could not tell, her face was so impassive as she held herself in her usual rigidly composed manner.

Her hair was scraped back and pinned tightly beneath her small hat, without a strand out of place, the softness of the other night a thing of the past. Even so, it was bad enough that she was already suspicious of running into him all over town, Dominic did not want the woman to think any more about their 'happy coincidences'.

'Good morning, Eliza. Good morning, Mr Marsden.'

'Cecily! We were just talking about you.' True enough, Eliza was blabbing before she thought it through.

'You were? How fortuitous then that I am now here,'

she said as she walked to her friend and exchanged a kiss on the cheek before turning to him without meeting his eyes. 'Good morning, Mr Marsden.'

He inclined his head. 'Miss Duddlecott.'

'Ah, perhaps I should also start by saying good morning, Cecily,' said Eliza. 'How lovely to see you.'

'And you, Eliza. You say you were speaking about me? May I ask in what regard you were discussing me?'

'Certainly,' Dominic said before Eliza spoke and gave them away again. 'I was just saying how much I enjoyed everything about the evening at Verrey's the other night.'

It was perhaps not the most refined manner in which to address the other night, but it was the only thing he could think of at that moment.

'I dare say you did, Mr Marsden. Especially after yet another happy coincidence where you happened upon Mr Millington and myself. And on the same night.'

Thank God, Eliza kept her mouth shut and didn't let on that he'd more or less said the same asinine thing to her a few moments ago.

'Just so.' He smiled pointedly before changing the subject. 'Allow me to get some refreshments for you, ladies. That is if I can find Cairns. Where has the man got to?'

'On an errand that I've sent him,' Eliza said. 'Don't

worry about us, Dominic, I'll get one of the footmen to ask Cook to send up the tea things.'

Cecily turned her attention to her friend. 'Are you packed and ready to leave?'

'Almost, but I can finish later. Come, sit a while.' Eliza linked arms with her friend, a comfortable intimacy passing between them, and together they navigated the elegant, though somewhat cluttered, room. Sunlight streamed through the expansive square window, illuminating the rich textures of the various furnishings as they reached a pair of generously proportioned leather armchairs, nestled invitingly near the window, each adorned with a collection of plush cushions and soft, woven throws.

'I am going to miss you, Eliza, but I do understand the reasons why you'd want to birth the baby in Cornwall.'

'Thank you, and, while I admit to being a little nervous about the whole thing, I am pleased that my husband and both my brothers-in-law have finally come round to the idea that the baby's birth will be in the beautiful county of Cornwall.'

'None of us had much of a choice,' Dominic muttered.

Eliza chuckled. 'No, indeed.'

His sister-in-law came from an old noble family of Cornwall and had only regained her ancestral family seat, Trebarr Castle, after she'd married Sebastian, who'd owned the deeds. Now that the castle was habitable again with all refurbishment and modern plumbing completed, it was ready for Eliza, Sebastian and their team of physicians, along with local midwives, to welcome the first of a new generation of Marsdens, even if it was nerve-racking for both of them.

His brother in particular was highly apprehensive with concern for his wife and unborn child, but had put on a positive face for Eliza's sake. All this was even more reason why Dominic hadn't wanted to involve his brother with everything that was going on, what with the Intelligence Office and Sir Algernon Pendle's demand of him.

'But before I leave, Cecily, I wanted to talk to you about the march at Parliament Square tomorrow afternoon.'

March? What march?

'We can postpone joining the march with all the other women's groups until you are ready to come back with us, Eliza. I'm sure that there will be more such rallies at some point in the future.'

'I think not. The organisation does not exist merely because of you and me, Cecy. It's bigger than both of us and must continue to move forward. And this march is an opportunity for TWERM to be part of something of great import. You must still go, even if I can't.'

'While I agree with you, I'm not quite certain I can lead our ladies on my own.'

'Of course you can.'

'Indeed, from what I have observed, Miss Duddlecott, you have all the necessary leadership qualities and your ladies seem to respect and admire you.'

'Thank you, sir.' The woman flushed as her eyes flicked in his direction without meeting his gaze.

'So you'll go?' Eliza said.

Cecy nodded slowly. 'Very well, I'd be very happy to lead the way and join all the other women's organisations.' Her eyes fairly sparkled with excitement.

'As well you should, but what of the safety of you and your ladies?' he said, raising a brow.

'What do you mean? The whole of Parliament Square will be filled with women from various organisations.'

'Yes, but so often these marches can suddenly turn and become quite dangerous. It is something that must be taken under consideration.'

'Quite right,' Eliza said, turning towards him. 'Which is why you should also attend the march with Cecy and the ladies of our organisation.'

Cecily shook her head. 'Oh, really, there's no need to impose on Mr Marsden's time. We shall do well on our own.'

'But what if there's trouble, as Dominic says? It would be useful to have him with you. I know if I were attending, Sebastian would insist on being there with me.'

'That's because he is your husband, Eliza.'

'Pish posh, what does that matter?' Her gaze turned to him. 'And, Dominic, do remember what we spoke about before? Otherwise, I can always ask Tristan.'

God, but sometimes Eliza was a like a dog with a bone. In this case, however, she was perfectly right. Still, he had the odd suspicion that he was ever so gently being manipulated by his dear sister-in-law.

'No need.' Dominic smiled at Cecy. 'I'm at your service, Miss Duddlecott, and happy to attend this march of yours.'

'I'm much obliged to you, sir.'

It was then that Cecily met his eyes, having looked everywhere but at him since she'd walked through the library door. And once again, just as the last few times he'd locked eyes with the woman, he found himself transfixed by those fathomless blue-violet eyes, sparked with emotion. Something he'd wager she'd desperately tried to hide, especially that vulnerability hidden in the depths speaking to him in a way he could not understand.

Cecily did not seem to be quite herself this morning. She was quiet, reserved, watchful and even a little coy. Where was that infamous sharp tongue of hers? It unnerved him and made him hot under the collar. This reaction to being close to Cecily was downright disturbing. And once again in front of Eliza. Yet he couldn't help wanting to know more about Cecily. Especially what had happened to her to cause a scandal in Oxford.

'It's nothing, Miss Duddlecott. In fact, it would be my pleasure.'

Damn, but did he need to use that word... It was disconcerting that he was so aware of everything about her. The way she was breathing, the rise and fall of her chest, the way her pink tongue quickly moistened her lips before she swallowed, the way she twisted the fabric of her day dress with her elegant fingers, the way her skin was suffused in that pink blush that seemed to spread the longer she watched him. The whole room felt as though it pulsated with some kind of electric undercurrent and, if he didn't leave soon, he would no doubt combust.

His mind tried to comprehend why he was having this visceral reaction to her, which only a month ago would have made him come out in hives. Was it because he hadn't had the pleasure of a woman's body for a long while? Was he overtired from the work he was doing for the Intelligence Office as well as running a club? And with Sebastian's departure to Cornwall, he would be doing it more or less on his own. Was that it? Or was he glutton for punishment or simply just a fool?

He'd always said that he would never get entangled with a woman again after the last disastrous time many years ago. And he would damn well stick to that. But there was something about Cecily that called to him. That made him want to take her into his arms. Not that it was of any consequence. He could never give her that one part of himself that he'd locked away.

Eliza spoke of hurt, yet no one knew of his hurts. Not even his brothers.

Dominic tore his eyes away. He needed to leave and he needed to leave at that moment.

'If there's nothing else, I shall leave you ladies. Eliza, Miss Duddlecott.' He inclined his head before heading out, glad to be away from Eliza's knowing smile and Cecily's curious eyes, which had once again fixed on to him.

'Good day, Mr Marsden,' Cecily said.

'Dominic?' Eliza called out, once again stopping him in his tracks. 'As I said earlier, you seem very much taken…'

Chapter Seven

Parliament Square was a hive of activity the following day, with many women's and workers' groups and organisations united and gathered together before they were due to commence their rally through the streets of London. It had been spearheaded by The National Society for Women's Suffrage and even eminent speakers and activists such as Millicent Fawcett and Emily Davies were in attendance. Cecy admired both women greatly for tirelessly working the universal suffrage of women and was excited to meet them.

The march was born out of the recent Reform Bill which was proposing to give the vote to many new classes of men, such as working men and agricultural labourers, yet failed to include women. And with the amended Married Women's Property Act, which had passed into law only two years ago, affecting the properties of women that passed to their husbands the moment they entered a marriage state, it was the time now to capitalise on such momentous changes and push for the emancipation of women.

It might be a hard and arduous road ahead, but if they gained the vote for women, they would pave the way for laws to protect women and allow social and economic, and, importantly for ladies of her organisation, educational emancipation for girls and women. This was why it was important. This was why Cecy was here, even though her brother would hit the roof if he found out about her involvement here at Parliament Square, let alone her role within TWERM. Cecy knew that Eliza had been right about TWERM being bigger than the both of them, even if she risked her brother's wrath.

She looked down the long line of women readying themselves to commence the march. All members of the groups and organisations present had been informed and advised that they were all to take a lot of care of their appearance. So, there was a sea of women dressed in soft pastel-coloured clothing, emphasising their femininity, including Cecy, who was dressed in a powder-blue and dove-grey ensemble. Far too often their apparel was used as a way to dismiss and ridicule their organisations as being unnatural. So to counter this they dressed with deliberate care to accentuate their femininity. Their hats, too, were trimmed with bows, flowers and ribbons, as though they were attending a social function, rather than a march. But the banners of all their various groups certainly gave them away.

Cecy was waiting and talking to many of the women in the organisation before they were ready to go on the march. But she patently did not meet the eyes of the man who had come to accompany her, at Eliza's request. She kept herself busy by making sure that everyone knew the formation of the march and the route that they would take, and told herself she didn't have time to talk to Dominic Marsden. And yet there was much to say.

For one, Cecy needed to thank him for coming today. She knew that this was last place he wanted to be, but had agreed anyway to somehow keep Cecy safe to mollify Eliza. That told her so much about who he was as a man, as someone clearly reliable, trustworthy and honourable—traits that she would never have attached to Dominic Marsden. Not even a week ago. Then there was the night at Verrey's when he'd effectively backed her up in the argument about whether women should be admitted to his club occasionally. Again, she had not expected that.

To her shame, Cecy was beginning to realise that she did not actually know the man as well as she thought she did, since she'd been so wrong about him. She had done what many in society had done over the years and made too many presumptions about him. Wrong ones, at that.

Quite aside from all that, there was the very inconvenient attraction that was getting in the way of a possible friendship, which in truth Cecy would welcome far more than anything else. She could certainly do with more friends to rely on, now that Eliza was going to be away from London. And in all honesty, it had never dawned on her until recently that Dominic could possibly become that to her.

If only she could stop this ridiculous pull of attraction, which was terribly embarrassing, especially as she wasn't particularly good at hiding her feelings whenever she was in his presence. She seemed to forget who she was or registered the people around her when she was around Dominic. Cecy had made that faux pas at Verrey's restaurant when she had arrived with one man, but couldn't stop ogling another.

What made it worse was that Samuel Millington had taken note of it, but had tactfully expressed his displeasure of the whole evening, rather than take her to task about Cecy mooning over Dominic Marsden. She had to stop behaving so inappropriately, especially as she had promised to consider Mr Millington's suit. And as for Dominic Marsden, she must treat him as Eliza's brother-in-law, whom she no longer loathed, but whose friendship she'd welcome and enjoy. It would be far safer that way.

'Thank you once again for coming today.' Cecy smiled across at Dominic, who was dressed impeccably in a dark-grey suit and black frock coat, looking impossibly handsome and rather imposing with his dark hair swept back under a top hat. 'I know that you must have had better things to do with your time than come here today with our ramshackle group of women.'

It was something Dominic had once called their organisation when she had assisted Eliza with organising a demonstration outside the Trium Impiorum over a year ago. It had also been the first time she'd set eyes on Dominic Marsden. Yet so much had changed since then. For one thing, she enjoyed his company now and wanted very much to get to know him. But as a friend, of course.

'I won't lie and say that I don't have a thousand things to do, Cecy, but I'm happy to accompany you.' He bent lower and whispered in her ear, 'Even if it's filled as far as the eye can see with your ramshackle group of women.'

She chuckled. 'Not mine, but collectively part of all of us.'

'So I see. Besides, I wanted to see what the fuss was about.'

They began to move now, slowly, walking down into Parliament Street, which would lead to Whitehall where they would soon pass the Prime Minister's residence in Downing Street.

'And what do you think of all the fuss and bother that we women are belligerently causing?'

'I will say that it's impressive.'

'You would?' This surprised her. Dominic Marsden might be a bit of a non-conformist and different to men such as her brother and Samuel Millington, but he was still a man. The fact that he was unfazed by being seen with her on this march made her realise that he was not only intelligent, but enlightened. Both rather unexpected. It made her feel as though she could say anything to him.

'Yes, I would. It's well turned out and seems well organised.' His eyes flicked to the long line of women on the rally, which was interspersed with a handful of men who, like him, were there to add their support.

Cecily leant her head closer conspiratorially as they ambled along. 'I'll let you into a secret, Mr Marsden.'

'Mr Marsden?' He raised a brow. 'You know you do slip up now and again and call me my given name, Cecy. Do you not think that you and I are beyond such formalities by now?'

True, she had done that many times now. 'Very well. Dominic it is.'

'Good. Now what is this secret of yours?'

'Oh, that I've done this before.'

'I don't follow.' His brows furrowed in the middle 'What exactly is it that you have done before?'

'I've helped put a rally like this together with all the

other groups that are present here. But as I said yesterday, I never thought of myself as much of a natural leader. That was always Eliza's strength.'

'And as I said yesterday, you also have the capabilities to lead. Just like my brother Sebastian and I have different strengths, we still both lead in our way. Likewise, your organisation has the benefit of not one, but two formidable women at its helm. Don't underestimate yourself.'

'Thank you. I always thought my natural strengths were organising, advising, administering.'

'And very efficiently too, I'd wager.'

'Well, I did run my brother's house for years and…' She paused for a moment before continuing. 'That is before he didn't need me any more.'

'That must be difficult?'

'Yet it is inevitable. Stephen was always destined for matrimony.'

'And you are not?'

'No. I never thought so.'

The truth was that until recently, until Samuel Millington's surprise interest in her, Cecy had never considered matrimony for herself. Not since the scandal that had cost her far more than just being barred from studying at Oxford. Not since her reputation had nearly been irrevocably damaged. And once she had come into her majority there had not been much point to it, until Stephen's recent marriage, when she was no longer made to feel welcome in her own home. Besides, with everything that had happened in the past she needed to be careful whom she gave her heart to. If anyone at all.

Cecy was still not certain whether matrimony was the path for her. And she was still mulling over whether Samuel Millington would be the ideal husband for her. He had made his views very clear on something as banal as women gaining entrance into a gaming hell, so what on earth would he think of her involvement in TWERM or being part of this rally? It didn't bear thinking about.

The more she thought about it, the more Cecy was convinced that they would not suit. But she would give him one more chance. She would see whether she was able to change his mind about the causes that were important to her. And if he was still not going to accept her as she was and wanted to prohibit her from being part of her organisation, then she could not accept his offer. It was that simple.

She could accept many things, even a loveless marriage, as long as there was mutual respect and companionship, but she could not accept a man who would restrict her thoughts, her beliefs and her movement. It might be a difficult path to live life as a spinster, but she would not compromise any of that simply for the comfort of having a wealthy and influential husband.

'Then what are you destined for, I wonder?' Dominic said from beside her as they took in the sights and the rows and rows of white stucco-fronted government buildings at Whitehall.

'This. This is my calling. It's a hard, challenging, sometimes unforgiving and fruitless endeavour, but I believe, as do the women here who are from all walks of life, that it is our obligation to demand our rights for now and for future generations of women and girls. To push for the enfranchisement for women, even if change is slow to come. It is worth the fight. To keep going. To remain strong, to remain resilient. Even if we fail.'

'I have to say that, despite everything, I cannot help but admire that, Cecy. There is something very commendable about what you're trying to achieve. That your beliefs and convictions are so strong that you are willing to fight for them.'

'Thank you.' His admiration made her heart skip a beat. 'Am I right to assume that you speak from experience?'

Cecily wasn't certain he would reply as he remained silent for a while, his gaze darting from one place to the next. Eventually it returned back to her.

'Yes, I speak from experience,' he said in a low quiet voice. 'I know all about fighting for something. For my brothers and me, it was also a case of needing to survive, more than anything else.'

Cecy, like many, knew how Dominic and his brothers came to be known as the Marsden Bastards, when it was discovered that their father had in fact been a bigamist. It must have been a terrible time when all three young boys had lost their privileged upbringing as sons of the Earl of Harbury in the aftermath, having to then adjust to a life they knew nothing about.

No, she was not surprised to learn that Dominic, along with his brothers, had learnt to survive, especially after their mother's death when nothing must have been the same again. God, but to think that they were left entirely on their own and had to clothe and feed themselves, putting a roof over their heads before eventually starting the Trium Impiorum from the ground up.

'I can imagine how difficult it must have been during those years when you were on your own.'

'I wasn't on my own.' Dominic shrugged as they strolled side by side. 'I had my brothers. It might not seem very much, but the bonds that tied us together gave us, as odd as it is to say, an indominable strength after the heartache of losing our father, our home and then our mother.'

'You must be very close.'

'We are.' He nodded. 'It's also comforting to know that we could always rely on one another, no matter how bad things got. And knowing that we always have each other's back, even when we disagree or argue about anything.'

'That's equally commendable, Dominic, to look out for one another in the manner that you've done and still do. It seems those ties of brotherhood served you well, since you then worked together and achieved everything with the Trium Impiorum, making it the success it was always destined to become.'

'Thank you. But it wasn't easy.'

'In what way?'

'Well, for one, we had to start again, which at times felt like an impossible feat to accomplish. We were constantly trying to make ends meet, not knowing how to adjust to the hovel we were living in. But we had to learn fast. Firstly, by living together in one small room in the roughest part of London. And we did it. We put up and shut up. Then after our mother's death, the money we scraped together began to dwindle, so Sebastian and I had to get any work just to put food on the table, while looking out for Tristan, who was too young and sickly to work. There were, of course, many children younger than Tris who worked, but we needed to protect him until he became bigger and stronger.'

'That was a brotherly thing to do.'

'It was a necessary thing to do.'

'And what kind of work would the sons of the Earl of Harbury do? What were you fit for?'

'Nothing. We were fit for nothing. At the time of our father's death Sebastian and I had both been up at Eton. But once we knew we had to find money, something that would have been considered vulgar in our previous lives, we got any work we could find. From working as a dockhand, lifting and carrying cargo, to working in a factory, a butcher and even an assistant in a haberdashery shop. Sebastian and I even managed to get jobs as clerks at a family law practice, since we spoke well, had a good level of education and were well turned out in our Sunday best.'

'As I said, very commendable. And to think you went from that to building the Trium Impiorum.'

He nodded. 'We initially put down the capital from the unentailed inheritance that was finally released to us after years of bitter entanglement with our uncle.'

'And it was your uncle who became the Earl of Harbury after your father's death?'

'You're well informed. He was also the man who tossed me, my brothers and my mother out of our home once my father was declared a bigamist,' Dominic said bitterly. 'In any case, it would have taken us far longer to build the Trium Impiorum, as you say, had we not gained the capital to pump into the business.'

'Either way, you must be proud of your achievements with the club?'

'Yes… I am.' Dominic blinked and turned towards her, his lips curling into a smile. 'Never say that you actually approve of our gaming hell, Cecy?'

'I can hardly approve or disapprove of a place I have yet to visit.'

'Which is one of the reasons you wish to come and see for yourself?'

She sighed deeply before responding. 'There are many places that women are banned from visiting in this country, let alone London itself, Dominic. And many, many things that women are prohibited from doing—all endorsed and upheld rigidly by society and for no real reason other than to keep women shackled to the home and hearth.'

'Not all women think of their role in society in such an extreme manner.'

'Perhaps not, but maybe that's because some women are fortunate to have the head of their family to do their duty by them and actually care, respect and protect them as they're expected to do. But not all women and girls are that lucky. Especially those born in the slums who had very few choices.'

Dominic Marsden didn't say anything for a moment as they walked side by side, his manner a little pensive. 'No, you are right,' he said eventually. 'Which was why my mother believed in the advancement of education for all, especially for young disadvantaged girls.'

'She did?' Cecy murmured, taken aback by this revelation.

'Yes. As the Countess of Harbury, my mother endorsed many charitable causes, but nothing was as close to her heart as educating those who had little access to it. Which was why she started the Harbury

Education fund, a charity that helped many children from various local parish schools in country towns and villages to those in big cities.' He stopped and took a deep breath. 'However, after our family's…change of circumstance my mother went into decline and one of the many things that helped her was the few hours she dedicated to reading stories to young children in that part of London we lived in.'

'She sounds like an incredible woman.'

'She was.' He gave her a small smile. 'And after her death I vowed that if the Trium Impiorum became successful, I'd continue our mother's work and support local schools by setting up the Alice Marsden Education Fund.'

Cecy was astounded. 'I had no idea. Eliza never told me.'

He shrugged, looking away. 'Perhaps because my dear sister-in-law didn't know. Few people do.'

'But why? It's a remarkable thing to do, Dominic, and you should be rightly proud of doing such a thing.'

'That was not the reason I did it. I did it because I wanted to honour her memory in a meaningful way.'

'Which you are doing.' Why would he hide this side of himself? It made no sense other then make Cecy realise that Dominic Marsden was a more complicated man than she'd given him credit for. And a far kinder one, too. 'I am certain your mother would be proud of you.'

He looked at her and nodded his thanks, perhaps a little uncomfortable that he'd revealed so much about himself. 'So, yes, I do support your endeavours, Cecy. To change society's attitude so that all these long-held views simply crumble away is good in theory, but difficult to achieve.'

'Most good things are. Besides, one day they will have to.' She sighed. 'Many statutes of law that govern women's rights are outdated by quite a few hundred years. I would have hoped that we might start to improve the conditions for all the people of this great country of ours and not just a select few who were lucky enough to be born male and come from the right sort of families who have all of the advantages granted to them.'

'I agree with you there. Even though it will take a long time to change such attitudes that have been embedded within society for so long.'

'But believe it not we have already made a start with the Married Women's Property Act. It will have huge consequences for many women, although only a few will once again benefit from the bill at this time. But one step at a time. This is why we need to continue our pressure on the government and make certain that we women are not excluded as we were in the Reform Bill. But you're right, it will take time. Perhaps even well into the new century, but I hope to see change within my lifetime.' She turned towards him and smiled sheepishly. 'However, for now admittance to Trium Impiorum will have to suffice.'

A bark of laughter escaped his lips, surprising Cecy. She wasn't always certain when she had said something funny. 'Is that what you want, Cecily Duddlecott? To carouse, wager and gamble?'

'I also want to see what the fuss is about, Dominic Marsden. Just as you did when you accompanied me on this march. And if you and your brothers decide to admit women to the club, I'd be honoured to visit the Trium Impiorum.'

'Honoured, eh? It would be quite tempting to invite women just to see what your impressions of the club would be.'

'Is that all?' She glanced up at him. 'You don't think I can play?'

'Would you like to play, Cecily?'

Dominic's voice was soft and low, his words so enticing that for a moment she wasn't sure whether they were still talking about gaming at the Trium Impiorum or something else altogether. Something far riskier and more potent. She snapped her head around before changing the subject.

'Oh, by the by, I wanted to also add my thanks for having *my* back, as it were, the other night at Verrey's. I'm not used to anyone taking my side in any argument. Well, other than Eliza and not since my parents were alive.'

'Not even your brother?'

'No,' she muttered quietly. 'My brother and I have very differing views on many things. We do not often see eye to eye.'

'Is that why he is not here with you today?'

Cecy shook her head at the absurdity of such a notion. 'Stephen attend a rally such as this? Absolutely not. He doesn't even know that I'm here, let alone approve of any of my activities.'

'Then where does he believe you are at this moment?'

'At one of the charitable organisations that he approves of and which I sometimes attend. I find it serves its purpose as a foil for such occasions such as this.'

'Very neatly done, Cecy.' He smiled. 'Let's hope you don't get caught out, not that you should mind what your brother thinks.'

'If it were only that simple. Besides, Stephen is far too busy to take note of my movements at present.' And since her brother was keen for Cecy to accept Samuel Millington's suit, he had been far more amenable recently than he had in a long time. 'In any case, my maid will cover for me. I have been topping up her wages for years to buy her loyalty, a fait accompli by now.'

'It seems you have thought of everything. I hope this march is worth all your effort.'

She sighed. 'It has to be. These are the small sacrifices I have to make. As I said before, we need to push to bring about change in all areas of society. And my particular interest is in allowing women and girls to pursue their academic interests into higher education just as men do.'

'Is that why all this is important to you?' He paused walking for a moment and turned to face her in surprise. 'The education for girls and women?'

'Yes. Very much like your late mother, it is of great importance to me.'

'Is that so?' He cupped her face with his gloved hand. For a long moment she just stared transfixed by those soft green eyes of his before looking away, making him drop his hand to his side.

Cecy nodded. 'Not all girls and women were as lucky as I was, with parents who were supportive and encouraging, allowing me to use my portion to fund and obtain sponsorship to attend Lady Margaret Hall at Oxford. Take Eliza, your own sister-in-law, who was and still is one of the cleverest, most intellectually curious people I have ever known. Since Eliza was a young girl, she'd always dreamed of matriculating at Oxford, but was denied this by her overbearing father who forced her to marry a terrible man just for his title. Her life made miserable until…well, until she met and married your brother.'

Dominic held out his arm which she took, as they

resumed walking side by side in a sea of people. 'Yet *you* did attend Oxford.'

'Yes, I did.'

'But never completed your studies?'

Cecy felt the blood drain from her face as she abruptly stopped walking again and snapped her head up. 'No. I did not.'

'May I ask why?'

'I cannot imagine why you'd want to know.'

'No reason other than natural curiosity. After all, for someone who states how important education is, I cannot understand why you would not complete your studies after working so hard to gain a place at Oxford in the first place.'

Surely Dominic had heard something about what happened at the time, even if her brother, Stephen, had tried to bury the story, paying large sums of money for it to be forgotten. 'Tell me, Dominic, why the sudden interest in my past now?'

He shrugged. 'I suppose after I disclosed so much about my past, I thought you might do the same. But no matter. You don't have to, of course. Your past is your affair.'

God, what a terrible turn of phrase. 'True. You did confide in me about your past, which I am most grateful for. So I shall try to do the same. Although I admit, I find it quite difficult to talk about it.'

'Then you don't have to.'

'It's fine.' She lifted her head and met his eyes. 'But tell me whether you have heard anything of it.'

'I know that there was some kind of scandal.' He said this so quietly that she wondered whether she imagined it.

'Yes…yes. There was a…a scandal.' She nodded and worried her bottom lip between her teeth, wondering whether to say more.

'I've been told that I'm a good listener, Cecy,' he murmured, as though he could read her mind. 'You can trust me.'

'I can?' She glanced up at him at the same time that a ray of sunlight caught her eyes, making her raise her gloved hand to shade her eyes.

'Yes,' he said quietly as they resumed walking, taking in their surroundings, neither of them saying anything for a long moment.

'The truth was that I was thrilled to be admitted to Lady Margaret Hall, just a year after the first women were allowed.'

'Impressive. What did you study?'

'Mathematical sciences.'

Dominic whistled under his breath. 'Mathematics? Good God, woman you don't do things by half, do you?'

'I don't know what you mean?'

'Yes, you do.' He shook his head, smiling. 'You know as well as I that of all the areas you could study you opted for the one area that is and has always been a male domain.'

'I'm hardly England's first female scientist, Dominic, let alone mathematician. From Ada Lovelace, Mary Somerville, to my friend, Sophie Bryant, there have been quite a few of us interested in this field throughout the ages.'

'And yet it's still an anomaly.'

'Even so, I can hardly help that this is the also an area that I excelled at.'

'You misunderstand me. Although it's not a surprise when you've always had to defend so much of your actions.'

She sighed. 'Yes. How did you know?'

'A lucky guess. But let me reiterate that I think it splendid that your clever brain was put to good use. In truth, it doesn't surprise me that you're a mathematician.'

'Is that a compliment?' she asked, not quite trusting herself to believe it. Cecy was always cautious when she was being praised, since she had always been mocked for her interests in the past, making her rather defensive as Dominic astutely observed.

'Undoubtedly. I'm more than impressed.' He chuckled. 'And surely you must have wanted to matriculate at Oxford with all of its dreaming spires and so on?'

'Why, yes, I had dreamt of those spires as I said since I was a little girl. It had been the most exciting thing to finally be there.' She paused for a moment before continuing. 'But sadly dreams have a nasty habit of turning into nightmares. And this one was a veritable disaster.'

'Why?' He frowned. 'What happened?'

She stopped walking for a moment, allowing some of the marchers to overtake them. 'I… I fell in love.'

Chapter Eight

It would be an understatement to say that was the last thing that Dominic had expected Cecy to say. He felt his jaw drop as he stared down at the small woman looking up him expectantly. He gave himself a mental shake.

'Apologies, I believe I misheard you.'

'I believe you understood me perfectly.'

'You fell in love? *You?*'

Cecy huffed and began to walk ahead, leaving him behind. Ah, he seemed to have insulted her, inadvertently. Dominic followed her, his legs eating up the distance between them as he wove his way back through the crowds and towards the most surprising and confounding woman he'd ever met. 'Wait, Cecy, don't storm off.'

She spun around, her gloved hands fisted at her sides. 'I know it must come as a shock to you that I could possibly have the capacity for such an emotion, but it was, nevertheless, true.'

'That's not what I meant.'

'Then what?'

'It's just that I cannot quite take in that *this* was the scandal?' He made a face. 'Falling in love?'

'You don't need to say it as though it's a dirty word,' she hissed under her breath. 'And, no, Dominic, my scandal was not, as you so charmingly put it, because I fell in love, but because I fell in love with the wrong person.'

Dominic was flummoxed to discover that Cecily Duddlecott had once been so idealistic as to have fallen in love—an emotion he always avoided. It made him realise that there was so much more to this woman then he'd initially believed. And aside from that, he didn't quite know how to feel about the fact that she'd once given her heart to another, but it bothered him for some reason. It bothered him a lot. And for the life of him, he could not understand why.

'So, who would be the wrong person to fall in love with that would cause such a scandal?'

She exhaled. 'What you must understand about the first cohorts of female students who entered the university, Dominic, is that there was a lot expected of us. We had to be exemplary in everything we did. Not just in how we applied ourselves to our studies, but in our conduct, our comportment and how we lived day to day. We were highly supervised and could not go anywhere, even our lectures, without a chaperon. Far more than I had ever experienced. As well as this, we were prohibited from entering many areas of the university, especially communal areas, in case we somehow managed to excite the predominantly male student body. So you see, our behaviour had to be beyond reproach. And yet, even with all those precautions in place, I still managed to find myself in a situation of my own making.'

'What happened?'

'My chaperon was careless, lazy and didn't care a jot about her charges, as long as she was well fed and well paid. And my professor, a man whom I had worked on many new theorems with, was enigmatic enough for me to believe that I was in love with him. All because he'd said so much nonsense about my brilliant mind, interesting ideas and that I could outmatch any of his other students. It certainly gave me comfort to know another kindred mind—one who accepted and encouraged me. He also seemed to care and made me feel valued, something that I had missed after losing both my parents. And I truly believed he wanted to marry me since he intimated as much many times during our brief…time together. The naivety of the young, I suppose.'

'But your professor never intended to marry you despite what he intimated?'

'He could hardly marry me when he was already married, now could he?'

He shut closed his eyes briefly and cursed under his breath. 'Hell, Cecy.'

'I was foolish because I believed every word he uttered. And it appeared that my brilliant mind was actually rather foolish after all. I failed to comprehend that the man was already married.'

'That was hardly your fault,' he said, gently threading his fingers with hers.

'That's not how the university saw it. To them I was the embodiment of a Jezebel preying on a poor unsuspecting academic who just couldn't resist my seductive advances.'

Dominic was not a violent man, nor had he ever felt the need to seek retribution for anything that had ever happened in the past. He was even on friendly terms now with his cousin, Henry, the current Earl of Harbury, after the death of the man who brought about the change in circumstances for Dominic and his brothers' lives, causing so much misery.

But this, now, was the first time he'd ever felt a visceral need to go and rage against someone—a damn no-named professor who took advantage of a young girl whose head was filled with those dreaming spires and the university itself for crushing those dreams. He wanted to take up arms for this outspoken yet brilliant woman, so she should never have to suffer such shameful cowardice and injustice again.

'And this was the extent of your scandal, Cecy?'

'Was it not enough?'

'Oh, aye, but the shame of it belonged to another, not you,' he said through gritted teeth.

'Thank you, Dominic. Sadly, most people would not agree with you. Women are often the ones who are blamed in such situations as this. Even my brother did not believe me when I informed him that I had been deceived and knew nothing about the existence of the professor's wife.'

'Your brother is nothing but a coward, a bounder and a fool with little sense in that over-inflated head of his.'

'You don't mince your words.'

'No, Cecy, I don't.' Without thinking Dominic lifted her fingers and pressed his lips to them. 'He should've taken better care of you. He should have protected you.'

'Thank you.' She shrugged. 'But in many ways Stephen did.'

'Even so, if he blamed you and didn't believe your explanation, then he didn't do as well as he should have by you.'

'Perhaps not.' They resumed walking again side by side for a long moment before Cecy spoke again. 'In any case, it gave Stephen the excuse to set the conditions in helping me out of "my disgrace", as he called it, and hushing up any gossip that made its way back to London, although of course some did leak back here and for a while I was shunned in some quarters. Gradually, however, things changed.'

'How so? Never say you charmed your way back into society because the *ton* is not known to be so forgiving.'

'No, they're not. I agreed to Stephen's demands and changed my…my…' She stopped again and looked away. 'Perhaps I have said too much.'

He nodded encouragingly at her. 'You can say as little or as much as you like. But know that I will never betray your confidence. As I said before, you can trust me.'

'Very well.' She lifted her chin in that determined way of hers and met his gaze. 'I changed myself, Dominic. I changed everything about myself—well, outwardly at least. I ironed all the parts that made me seem wanton, as my brother would say, and became the model of respectability. I became his hostess and companion when he needed me and ensured that nothing would ever stain my reputation again.

'But there was one point I would never change and that was my continued involvement in the organisations that I am passionate about, working tirelessly for equality, and universal suffrage. Such as this march here today. If I can do one thing, it would be this. To atone and make amends for my past mistakes where I squandered the privilege of furthering my studies at Oxford. Perhaps in some way it would continue my parents' legacy and all that they instilled in me. That education is our right and not just for a select few.'

Dominic knew first-hand how cruel society could be. His mother had experienced its devastation once it had come to light that she'd married a bigamist. Something she never quite recovered from.

Even so, in that moment Dominic wanted to wrap his arms around this fearless and spirited woman and just hold her until he could somehow assuage the hurt of her past, but he didn't. Instead, he squeezed Cecy's fingers gently and gave her a weak smile. He could hardly believe that this beautiful, intelligent, vital woman had been made to feel so wanton and unworthy that she felt the need to change herself.

No wonder she dressed as she did in the buttoned-up manner with that tightly coiled hair. It all made more sense now. Cecily made more sense now, as he had always thought she was a mass of contradictions with her fierce manner while being a stickler for propriety.

Although of late Cecy no longer dressed in that manner, it explained how she 'ironed the parts that made her seem so wanton'. Damn Stephen Duddlecott for making his sister believe all that nonsense. Damn society for making women have to fit a certain mould. And damn the bastard who took away Cecy's dreams by seducing her and leaving her out for the wolves.

'It should never have come to that,' he said. 'You should never have had to change yourself. There was nothing to atone for and nothing to make amends for. Nothing.'

The smile Cecy gave him was the warmest and truest one he'd ever seen directed at him and he felt it deep in his chest. 'I thank you for your confidence, but I was not entirely blameless. In any case, it is usual for women to pay the consequences of getting entangled in such terrible…affaires of the heart.'

'True, but that is not always the case.'

Her brows shot up as she studied him for a moment. 'You seem to be talking from experience.'

As usual, Cecy was far too perceptive. It was remarkable that from only a handful of words she could tell that he'd also had a similar experience to her, where he had once been just as idealistic resulting in the same hurt and the same humiliation. Although not the same disgrace.

'I am, but I'll leave that sad story for another time,' he said, making light of it.

'Another time? Are we going to be in the habit of confiding our deepest, darkest secrets to one another?' She chuckled.

'I'm willing if you are.' He shrugged as they continued to walk under Admiralty Arch before emerging on to the Mall.

'I'm not sure if I have anything more to share.'

'I'm certain you do, Cecy. For instance, why Millington? Why would you consider his suit?'

'For the simple reason that he asked.' She held up her hand, sensing that he was about to speak. Which frankly he was. 'And before you say anything more, I'd like to add that I'm not worried about remaining a spinster, Dominic. Far from it. But when my brother apprised me of Samuel Millington's suit, I knew that only a fool would turn down a man of his influence.'

'Despite his views at Verrey's the other night?'

'Well, that's the part where I consider everything about him, which includes an evening where his views were, I admit, quite different from my own.'

'Come now, they were far more than that, they were the antithesis of your views and opinions.'

'Perhaps. But I will give him my full consideration and not be swayed by sentimentality as I might have been once.'

'Even after what I told to you about him?'

'Yes, about that, Dominic. What do you have against Mr Millington?'

'I didn't realise I had anything against the man other than that he doesn't deserve you.'

'That's kind of you to say, but what did you mean about not trusting him?'

'Precisely that, Cecily.'

'I see. So, you want me to trust *you* then and not him?' She narrowed her eyes. 'Is that it?'

'What if I said, yes…'

'I would say that I do not understand. Unless you can tell me the reasons of your prejudice against him.'

How could she not see that even if Millington was not guilty of what was suspected of him, he would still crush her spirit just like another man did all those years ago.

'I'm not prejudiced against him. I just don't like the basta…blighter. And there are many reasons not to trust him, by the way.'

'Such as?'

Before Dominic could explain himself without revealing that Samuel Millington was under suspicion of colluding in bribery and corruption, there was suddenly a huge commotion up ahead, with the sound of horses whinnying and raised voices in the distance. Many people had now stopped walking around them and were looking around as though they were assessing what was happening ahead.

'What do you think it is?' Cecy muttered from beside him, as she went on her tiptoes to look around the heads of people ahead of her.

'I don't know, but I'm going to find out.'

'I'm coming with you.'

'No, you're not.' He wrapped his hand around her elbow, guiding her back to on to the pavement. 'You stay here with your ladies.'

'But…'

'Please, Cecily, do as I ask. Allow me to ascertain

whether the safety of you and your ladies has been compromised.'

'And if it has?'

'You will know what we have to do.' He gave her a pointed look before addressing their group who had huddled together, looking decidedly concerned as well. 'Ladies, before we know what is going on, I ask you to stay back against the buildings on this side of the pavement. It would be better actually if you go down that mews there, away from the thrum of people, until we know what is happening. I will get a few of my men to escort you all.'

This naturally caused the women to start to talk and debate among themselves at this sudden change of plans, while Dominic ordered a few of his men whom he'd brought to assist the women. He asked one of the smaller scouts hired at the Trium Impiorum to weave his way quickly through the crowds and find out what the problem was.

'I'm certain it must be some trifling matter that will be smoothed over soon and we continue on the march,' Cecy said from beside him, still standing on her tiptoes.

'I hope so, too, but we can't take any chances. I'll go and find out what is going on.'

Dominic ventured into the middle of the road, which was densely populated with people standing and waiting to find out whether they could continue on this blasted march. He saw the club's young scout, Jimmy, make his way back, zig-zagging around the stationary people to reach him.

'What's going on, Jimmy?'

'A couple o' coves arguin' and splutterin' with the bobbies on 'orseback, guv. It's lookin' ugly an' I fink it's meanin' to.'

'Why? Who's causing the disturbance?'

'If you askin' me, guv, it looks like a set-up. Dunno why. Some well-heeled coves might not like these bluestockin' skirts to be paradin' an' at 'ere today. Lot o' grumblin' an' at the front. My guessin' is it ain't real.'

'Real or not, things could easily get out of hand, especially with so people who have come along today.'

That's when they heard it. A piercing scream and then another followed by a palpable panic that suddenly seemed to spread throughout. The people who had stood waiting until they could resume marching suddenly turned back around and start to run in every direction, turning the whole area into bloody pandemonium. Placards were thrown on the ground as people tried to get away from the area.

On the side, a handful of the mounted constables on horseback from the newly formed Metropolitan Police, who had been keeping the march moving while ensuring there was no trouble, suddenly found themselves surrounded as people tried to leave the area. One of the horses, which was far more skittish than the others, reared up and threw off the rider, and galloped into the crowd, causing even more mayhem with the sound of screaming echoing through the air.

From the corner of his eye, he caught Cecily also viewing the scene with confusion and horror. He tried to make his way back to her, but Dominic was jostled around in every direction and had to watch in growing panic as Cecy made her way into the middle of the street to help those who had fallen over.

'Cecily!' he roared, but his voice was drowned out by the din. Quickly, Dominic wove his way around the throngs of people, trying to get to her. He turned to see a handful of the Metropolitan constables on horseback riding in Cecily's direction. 'Get out of the way, Cecily! Move!'

Dominic launched himself and managed to reach her as she fell to the ground. He grabbed her by the waist and yanked her across and out of the way just in time, shielding her with his much larger body, otherwise Cecily, who'd had her back to the constables, would have been trampled on. Hell and damnation, what a bloody mess this whole day was turning out to be.

'Cecily, talk to me. Are you hurt?' he said, cradling her in his arms and feeling her tremble. 'Lord above, woman, what were you doing in the middle of that chaos?'

She pulled away, her body shaking violently as she

opened and closed her mouth several times, unable to utter a word.

'Are you hurt, Cecily?' he said, breathing heavily.

But the woman seemed to still be in shock as she gasped for air. Dominic gently guided Cecy away from the commotion and down one of the narrow mews that was thankfully empty and far away from the scene. He held her closely, running his hand up and down her spine, trying to soothe her until he could feel all the tremors of her body subside.

'Are you hurt?' he asked again.

'No,' Cecy said eventually, still panting. 'No, I'm fine.'

'Are you sure?'

'Yes.' She tried to smile, but failed. 'I'm in one piece.'

'Good, I'm glad to hear it.' He exhaled the air he hadn't realised he'd been holding in. 'But tell me—what the hell do you think you were doing back there?'

'I saw a child,' she said before taking another gulp of air. 'She had fallen and if I didn't get to her she would have got trampled by the crowds. By the time I lifted her up, her mother had come and claimed her from me, thank God. But I hadn't seen them coming. I hadn't seen the horses. I hadn't seen how close it had been.' She flicked her gaze up to him. 'I don't know what would have happened if you hadn't come and got me when you did.'

'No.' He rubbed his forehead and shook his head. 'It's not worth contemplating. At least you're safe.'

'And the ladies of TWERM?'

'All accounted for.' He pulled her tightly and held her for a long moment before loosening his hold just to look at her. 'You scared me half to death back there, Cecily Duddlecott.'

'I didn't mean to.'

'God above, don't ever do that to me again.'

'I was thinking of the child, Dominic.'

'But who is there to think of you, woman?' He shook his head. 'Who is there to look after you, protect you…?' Dominic cupped her face, his fingers shaking as he stared at her in frustration. Did she not comprehend how bloody dangerous it had been, how close she had been to getting hurt? But as he looked into her eyes, he could see that same longing he'd witnessed before. 'Damn it,' he whispered before he bent his head and touched his lips to hers.

For a moment Cecy did not move, seemingly too surprised that he was kissing her. But just as he thought to end their admittedly chaste kiss, Cecily Duddlecott kissed him back. Tentative, and uncertain at first, the buttoned-up woman who once loathed him wrapped her arms around his neck and slid her lips across his, soft, open-mouthed, sensual, languid. He coaxed her mouth to part so that he could taste her and, wonder of wonders, Cecily Duddlecott deepened the kiss.

A bolt of lust shot straight to his groin as she pressed herself to his body, making him deepen the kiss, nipping her bottom lip and slanting his lips over hers, devouring her mouth. His hands roamed over the curve of her body beneath all that clothing as Dominic slowly walked her backwards so that she was now pressed against the wall and continued to explore her mouth.

It had been a long time since he'd wondered what it would be like to hold this woman, to have her soft curves pressed against him, what it would feel like to glide his hands over her body and cover her lips with his, learning the shape of her mouth and what she might taste of. Now he knew. Damn, but it made his blood rush through his veins. And as for her mouth, she tasted of coffee, dark, rich and bitter, with the sweetness of honey which perfectly summed Cecily up.

He pulled his mouth away and trailed hot kisses along her jawline, the column of her neck before her naked skin disappeared beneath the collar of her cape. He then made his way back up, nipping and sucking her earlobe, making her groan.

'Christ, Cecy,' he murmured in her ear and turned her head around by hooking his fingers beneath her chin so that he could kiss her mouth again.

Bloody hell. What was he doing? He was ravishing Cecily Duddlecott down a dingy deserted alley, only a handful of yards away from Pall Mall. He suddenly released her and found himself staggering back a few steps, his breathing ragged. What the hell had possessed him? The woman had only just told him of one scandal and here he was leading her merrily into another. And all it would take would be one of those women from TWERM or any of the others from this disastrous march catching a glimpse of them together and that would then be the end of that. What then?

'Don't you dare.' Cecy's chest rose and fell as she clung on to the wall behind her. 'Don't you dare think to apologise, Dominic Marsden, because I won't accept it.'

'I wasn't going to.'

She glared at him, smoothing down her skirts. 'Good, because I kissed you back and don't you forget it.'

As though that was likely to ever happen. Dominic finally, finally knew what it meant to hold her, to kiss her, to taste her. And he wanted more.

He smiled slowly despite himself. 'Again, I wasn't going to. And, yes, you did kiss me back. Rather thoroughly, Miss Duddlecott. Tell me, where did you learn to kiss like that?'

'A lady never tells.'

'Guv?' a young voice called from behind his shoulder. Dominic turned on his heel to find Jimmy at the entrance of the mews. 'Guv, dose old skirts are waitin' for yer. 'Tis quiet back there now, empty up nice and clean, like. Ans I gets this to pass to yer abouts yer meetin' 'bout the newspaper cove, Millin'ton.' The boy held up a small sealed parchment that most likely held the details of the time and place that Dominic was to meet Sir Algernon Pendle, who assigned him with the surveillance work on both Stephen Duddlecott and Samuel Millington. And the man who had arranged a meeting later that day.

'Very well, Jimmy, you run along now.'

'But he said it was important.' The boy shuffled nervously from one foot to the other.

'Very well, hand over the missive and get going,' he said as the boy gave him the parchment before running back the way he came.

Dominic slipped the damn missive in the inside pocket of his frock coat while he watched Cecy's soft eyes change to a cold wariness as she tried to decipher what the young boy had said. Damn, but he was going to have words with the young scamp revealing too much information in company. For now, however, he had to think fast.

'Come,' he said, giving her a bland smile. 'I'll take you back home.'

'Yes, thank you,' she said stiffly, her whole demeanour very different now. 'But firstly, allow me to check that everyone is unharmed.'

He held out his hand. 'Very well.'

'And one other thing.' She lifted her head. 'May I ask why your young lad there mentioned Mr Millington?'

Chapter Nine

Cecily did not get any answers from Dominic Marsden that afternoon. In fact, he hardly said a word as he escorted her back home. It might have been because they'd had that intimate conversation about their pasts while on the march before disaster struck, or the tumultuous events that led to being rescued by the man, or that incredible kiss where she still felt the warmth of his body pressed against hers many hours later.

Yet, Cecy knew that it was not because of those reasons alone. She knew that it had something to do with whatever was written on the parchment the young lad had given to Dominic about some meeting or other. And none of it would have been her concern, had it not been for the fact that the young boy mentioned Samuel Millington's name. It had made her wonder why his name had been bandied about by Dominic's young worker. And it had made her suddenly so aware of the man who she had writhed against and kissed so fiercely in that secluded alley. It made her question everything about Dominic and what they had been discussing moments before the chaos had ensued.

For one thing, why had he constantly warned her against Samuel Millington, which he had still not explained? Which was why, as soon as Cecy had been escorted home, she turned back around and followed Dominic as he left for a secluded part of Hyde Park on foot, thankfully.

She needed to see if she could discover more and find out whether it was mere coincidence that Dominic Marsden's young lad had mentioned the man whose suit she was supposedly considering. Dear Lord, but the whole thing was so mysterious. And she'd been determined to get to the bottom of it. Which she did… up to a point.

After following Dominic without him realising, Cecy had managed to hide behind an old oak tree as he spoke to a tall, bald man in his middling years and she listened to some of their conversation. She had learnt some of it, although she hadn't been able to hear everything that the two had discussed.

In fact, there was quite a lot that still puzzled her the following day after a night of tossing and turning, unable to sleep. But one thing was for certain—Dominic and this older man, whom she'd never seen before, had not only discussed Samuel Millington, but also her brother as well.

'Cecily?' Stephen had been taking her to task all afternoon after returning early from his work in Westminster. Somehow, he had been informed of her involvement in the march the day before and was chastising her as he often did with one of his boring preaching sermons, as though he was her father and not her brother. 'Cecily? Are you listening to me?'

'Of course, Stephen. What on earth do you think that I am doing, otherwise?'

'With you, anything is possible.' He threw up his arms in frustration. 'I cannot fathom how you can justify such an outrageous decision to attend a march with all those odd, unnatural females.'

'With that wonderfully concise description, perhaps you would label me as an odd, unnatural female, too?'

'This is no time for one of your jests, Cecily,' he said in a clipped tone as he pinched the bridge of his nose. 'What you did yesterday was egregiously wrong of you after everything that happened before.'

'Good God, Stephen, must we always bring all up all that hullaballoo from all those years ago?' Cecy chuckled mirthlessly. 'It seems that I am forever to be judged for the misdemeanours of the past.'

'When you participate in a march filled to the rafters with radicals and agitators such as Millicent Fawcett and Emily Davies, then, yes, you need very much to be reminded of your lack of judgement.'

'Well, thankfully I have you to remind me. However, I still do not understand why you would believe that my participation in the march yesterday was so egregiously wrong, as you put it.'

'Can you not?' He shook his head. 'My discussion with Lady Honoria was quite illuminating and revealed the extent of your deception to me, pretending to be at a charity event while conspiring against me by going to that damn march.'

'Conspiring? Will you listen to yourself?' she said, trying to temper her growing anger. 'And when did you start conferring with your mother-by-marriage about my movements?'

'When she kindly offered to keep an eye on you for me, since I cannot readily trust you to behave in an appropriate manner, Cecily. And do not talk about the lady of this house in that manner.'

Cecy's brows shot up at his surprising outburst. It was never actually said out loud that the mother-in-law rather than the wife was the lady of the house, yet it was surprising to hear it. 'I had believed that Victoria held that title and not the lady's mother.'

'If you must know, my wife is happy to allow her mother to guide her in such matters as running a politician's household. And when Victoria has learnt sufficiently from her excellent mother, Lady Honoria will naturally step back. Anyway, I digress. None of this has any bearing on my wife or her mother, although your conduct is a source of embarrassment to them both.'

'It was a march, Stephen. Just a march.'

'Oh, for goodness sake, Cecily, how can you be so naive?' he spat out the words. 'I'm a bloody backbencher with ambitions of getting into the government, but your behaviour and conduct is hardly going to be helpful in that. Can you not see how badly this reflects on me?' He shook his head as he exhaled. 'And getting servants to lie, leading them into the same deception and dishonesty as yourself. What kind of example are you? Have I not explained that your behaviour needs to be beyond reproach?'

Cecy felt her face become more and more heated, her anger and frustration mounting, but she did not give into it. She allowed her nails to dig into her hand and welcomed the pain as she continued to listen to Stephen's ridiculous nonsense. Still, this was outside of enough. 'Let it be on your conscience that I've had to let Mary go and without a reference.'

This Cecy had not known. Oh, devil take him. 'You can't do that, Stephen. Mary is *my* servant.'

'Strange, but I believe I pay her wages.' In theory, but Cecy more than supplemented it. 'So that decision is not yours to make. Besides, it's already done. I have Lady Honoria to thank for the speed and efficiency of overseeing this problem.'

'Which can be simply rectified, Stephen. Matters do not need to get to this drastic state.'

'Ah, I'm afraid you're too late, Sister. As of an hour ago Mary McAndrews was ushered out of this home.'

She stared at her brother in disbelief. 'How dare you do this behind my back.'

'You wish to discuss going behind one's back? Because it's not a good feeling, Cecily. And if I can't have loyal and trustworthy servants reporting to me, then there's no point in keeping them on.'

'You had no right, Stephen. No right at all. Mary is my loyal maid who has been with me since I was fifteen. And yet you dismissed her as easily as that?'

'Yes, as easily as that,' he said, snapping his fingers together, showing her just how quickly. 'I hope that Millington doesn't hear about this hullaballoo as you call it once he returns to town. It doesn't bear thinking what he will say and he was certainly not in charity with you after the night at Verrey's, let me tell you, Cecily. Be thankful he is not presently in London.'

God, but she'd had enough of Stephen and his machinations as well as Samuel Millington for that matter, whose views she cared little for at present. Always being told to behave in a particular manner, always found lacking. Always reminded of her past, always found wanting. Always the same thing from her own brother. Enough. She'd had enough of Stephen and would find a way to leave her family home once and for all. Plans. Yes, she needed to start making them. That's what was needed to be finally free of all of this.

Cecily rose from the wooden chair and strolled around the blue lounge, her mother's favourite room with its soft palette of blues, golds and lilacs in the sofa, armchairs, bolsters, cushions and other furnishings as well as a large Aubusson carpet in the centre. It was a room Cecy used to enjoy spending time in, sometimes with Eliza, debating and discussing about many things that mattered to them, as well as hosting many of TWERM's meetings here without her brother's consent, of course, because had he known, he'd never have allowed it. She ambled towards the fireplace, the flames roaring and spitting, and dragged her fingers across the smooth marble mantelpiece above it, absently picking up some of her mother's small figurines before placing them back again. She then took a few steps back and tilted her head at the portrait of her parents above it, studying it for a moment.

'I've always loved this painting of Mama and Papa. They sat for it in this very room because the light through the French doors was so vibrant, casting a golden luminosity around the whole room. Which I suppose was how they wished to be captured by the artist: bold, striking, true to form without hiding their flaws or blemishes. But above all they wanted the brightness of this room to capture their enlightened spirit.' She turned to face Stephen watching her, his whole manner stiff and unyielding. 'Which is why I have continued to honour everything they instilled in me, in both of us. And yet you have gone against everything they stood for, Stephen. I have often wondered why.'

He smirked, shaking his head. 'God rest their souls, but our parents were idealists, with all their unattainable futile beliefs and principles, none of which amounted to anything.' God, but each word he uttered was like another knife cutting into her chest. 'Whereas I am a realist, Cecily. I know exactly what the world is and who it belongs to. Who yields the real power. So you see, none of your marches for social changes will change that. Not now, not ever.'

She watched her brother as he spoke and realised then that she had stayed all this time under this roof not just because of her scandal, trying to regain her reputation, but also because she believed that by being the sister he wanted her to be, she could somehow influence him not just as an MP, but as a sister. For the sake of those familial ties and for the sake of what their parents had stood for. But it was all futile, as he'd said himself. Stephen would never change.

'I care very little for your reasons, Stephen, but your explanation is nothing that I did not expect, which is a shame for your sake as it is for Mama and Papa.'

'How dare you!'

Cecy continued as though she had not heard his outcry. 'And neither, for that matter, do I care a ha'penny whether Mr Millington may or may not approve of me.'

Her brother stood abruptly and stared at her. 'But you should, otherwise he may no longer have you. And that cannot be borne.'

'If Mr Millington's regard towards me has cooled because of this, then we simply do not suit. I am more than resigned to that as it's something I have been reflecting on, of late.'

'No, Cecy! Please refrain from thinking that,' he pleaded, yet somehow it didn't quite ring true. 'Millington is more than enamoured with you and will not be so easily put off.'

Her brother started to pace back and forth about the room, muttering to himself.

'And yet you said quite the opposite, just a moment ago.' She frowned. 'Either way, Stephen, I have not agreed to his suit as you well know.'

'Yes, yes, yes, of course,' he said dismissively, not actually listening to what she had said. 'Millington, however, wants you and I think it would be the best for all of us, if you do accept him, Cecy. You will, won't you? At least do not reject it out of hand?'

'I... I had not said I had.' Her frown deepened.

'It's of great importance that you do, my dear.'

Her brother's sudden change in demeanour was beyond strange, but at that moment, Cecy had just about had enough of her brother's erratic behaviour. It was odd even for Stephen to swing from admonishing her for participating in a march one moment to this snivelling man before her the next. What on earth was going on? For a moment she stared at him, not knowing what to think about him. It dawned on her that his need for her to accept Millington could be used to her advantage. For now, she could rectify his mistake, while she tried to understand what Stephen was about.

But there was one person who might be able to shed some light on what was going on...

'Very well. I shall continue to consider his suit. But on one condition: you must reinstate Mary in her job.'

A man who had repeatedly warned her against Samuel Millington.

'Absolutely not. I shall not hear of it.'

'Then I'm afraid that I can no longer agree to your terms.' She started to walk towards the door.

Stephen moved before her, blocking the entrance. 'Wait. No need to be hasty.'

'The choice is yours, Brother. What will it be?' She folded her arms and raised a brow.

'But what will I tell Lady Honoria?'

'You'll think of something, I'm certain.'

Stephen nodded in resignation. 'Very well, but I want an answer by the end of this week.'

A man who had been turning up at the oddest of places all over London...

'As long as Mary is back and living under this roof by the time I get back. I might then be amenable to listening to your views regarding Samuel Millington.' She skirted around Stephen and opened the door.

'Back?' He followed her out of the room and into the large hallway. 'Back from where? Haven't we established that you are not to leave this house without my say so?'

A man whom she had followed and discovered furtively discussing both Millington and her brother with a stranger...

'I shall take a footman.' She walked to the entrance and glanced in the looking glass, adjusting her hat and smiling at Clayton, who helped her into her grey overcoat. 'Since we have also established that I am not a child.'

Indeed, she needed to meet with Dominic Marsden and she needed to do it this instant. But after buttoning up her overcoat and grabbing her matching reticule and umbrella, she found herself on the pavement outside wondering how she was going to get herself inside the Trium Impiorum. Stephen would have a fit if it ever got back to him that she'd visited the notorious club alone.

So, after asking Peter, the footman, to obtain a hansom cab to take them to Marsden House on Half Moon Street, she formulated a plan.

* * *

Once they had arrived, the Marsden butler, Cairns, was naturally surprised to see Cecy, especially since Eliza had left London for her confinement in Cornwall, but being the consummate professional he was, he didn't give anything away in front of one of her brother's footmen. And like all the servants in the Marsdens' employ, he was very discreet and loyal to all the Marsdens, especially a close friend of his mistress's even if she had just arrived unannounced.

Thankfully he played along with her when she asked to see Eliza and was ushered into the small lounge while her brother's footman was told to wait downstairs in the servants' quarters until his mistress was finished, which she informed him would be of a long duration. Cecy only hoped that the young man would not question why there was such a skeleton group of servants tending the Marsdens' house and not guess that it was because the master and mistress of the house were away with only two of the brothers currently in residence.

Once she was alone with Cairns, she asked him to arrange another conveyance to take her to the Trium Impiorum with her brother's servant being none the wiser. Again, the man showed little regard to her outrageous request from a single woman on her own. He did, however, insist that a Marsden footman accompany her.

So, after a short time in a Marsden cabriolet, they arrived. Cecily pulled the netting of her hat down to cover her face and stepped outside the Trium Impiorum on the corner of Bury Street in St. James's, an area notorious with gentlemen's clubs. But instead of entering the imposing four-storey red-bricked building at the front, she did so from the back entrance that tradespeople and workers used and where deliveries were made.

She clambered up the narrow stairs with the Marsden footman in tow and waited as the major-domo, Mr Hendon, whom Eliza had often spoken about, approached her and asked her to follow him through the narrow corridor that took her to the servants' stairwell and on to the third floor, then down another long passage until she approached one of the many wooden doors. Cecy knocked and, after waiting for that familiar low voice to respond, she was ushered inside an office. There, on the other side of large oak desk, was Dominic Marsden, evidently not in the least surprised to see her.

'Hello, Cecy.' He stood and inclined his head a little. 'I've been expecting you.'

She raised a sardonic brow. 'So I see. Apologies for my tardiness, but there were a few matters I needed to tend to before embarking here. The first being to deposit my brother's footman somewhere away from the club. I decided on Marsden House, which is where I ensconced him with the excellent Cairns.'

'Quite industrious of you.'

'Quite. It was only a trifling matter.'

'Just as it was yesterday when you followed me to Hyde Park?' Dominic motioned towards the chair in front of the desk. 'Please, take a seat.'

Cecy sat down and watched Dominic amble towards the cabinet by the side of the room. 'Ah, so you knew I was there, did you? Shame you didn't introduce me to your friend.'

'Yes, it was remiss of me.' He fetched two cut-glass tumblers from the side of the cabinet and reached for a crystal decanter. 'Care for some brandy?'

'At this time?'

'I fear this is going to be one of those discourses that will require some libation.'

'The way that you put it. Very well, then, just a drop.' She caught her lower lip between her teeth. She'd never actually drunk brandy, other than a mouthful or two, but took the glass that Dominic held out to her. At least it gave her hands something to hold on to.

'So...'

'So?'

'To your health.' She took a sip, feeling the amber liquor slide down her throat chased down by a rather pleasant warmth in the pit of her belly.

'And yours.' Dominic smiled and also took a long swig before watching her for a moment over the rim of the glass. 'Why are you here, Cecy?'

'I wanted to ask about the meeting with your friend in the park yesterday.'

'And what exactly did you want to ask?'

'Why it was that you were discussing Mr Millington and my brother with your friend?' she said, taking another sip.

'Heard that, did you?'

'Indeed.' She nodded.

Dominic sighed and shook his head. 'You shouldn't have followed me there yesterday, Cecily Duddlecott.'

She grimaced, annoyed by his pithy response. 'I've been reminded of late of the many things I should and shouldn't do and I must say that I find it all quite tedious.'

'And you should not have come to the Trium Impiorum either. What of your reputation?'

'Apparently it's hanging by a thread.'

'Your outing is hardly going to help.'

'And yet I remain unmoved by that possibility.' She took another long sip. 'Addictive, isn't it? The warmth hitting just the right places.'

'There are many things in this building that are very addictive.'

'Which I know little of.' Her brows furrowed in the middle. 'Weren't you going to show me around this place?'

'No.'

'I'd love to see the various rooms of this hallowed place.'

'And still the answer remains the same.'

'Spoilsport.' She lifted her head and watched him for a long moment. 'So, are you going to answer the question? I can stay here all day until you decide to explain it to me.'

'And if I do, will you promise to leave? You might not care much about your reputation, but I find that I do.'

'How very gallant of you, Dominic.'

'All part of the service.'

'Yes, about that.' She frowned, tapping her fingers against the wooden armrests of the chair. 'I cannot ascertain whether your pursuit of me and all the various times you and I happened to bump into one another was that happy coincidence you spoke of or something else altogether.'

Dominic dropped his head, unable to meet her eyes, wordlessly telling her everything that she needed to know. Her heart sank. How very disappointing. Just when she'd let her guard down and started to trust the man—at his request, no less—he had to let her down with deception. God, would she ever learn about trusting handsome men who showed an interest in her? Did it mean everything between them had also been a lie? Their friendship? That all-consuming kiss, which perhaps she should push to the back of her mind.

'I see,' she said coldly. 'Why don't you start from the beginning and tell me everything…?'

Chapter Ten

Dominic watched Cecily, sensing that she was retreating more and more behind a wall of hurt, anger and confusion. He couldn't allow her to think the worst of him, even though he probably deserved her scorn. Well, some of it at least. And after everything that had happened, she deserved to know all of it, despite Sir Algernon Pendle warning against sharing any covert information with anyone.

He'd had enough of that old fart ordering him about. If he wanted Dominic's help, then the man needed to understand that he would do this his way or he could find someone else to do his bidding. As he'd told him yesterday, he was not actually someone whose livelihood depended on this covert work, even if the Home Office were to cause trouble for the Trium Impiorum. Still, he did not want to worry either of his brothers.

In fact, Dominic wanted all of this to go away and for him to go back to just running the club. No more playing escort to one spirited and unruly woman whose lips tasted of sin. And no more snooping to find information on Millington or Stephen Duddlecott. The whole lot could go hang for all he cared. And yet that was the problem. He did care that Millington, in particular was getting away with what he was doing and under the roof of the Trium Impiorum. He could not stand for it. As for Cecily? She was no longer just anyone. Not any longer. She had become someone who mattered a great deal to him and he couldn't bear her thinking badly of him, even if he had been trailing after her purposefully to gain more information.

'Well?' she said, raising a brow. 'Nothing to say?'

Dominic leant forward and placed his elbows on the table, steepling his fingers together, and inhaled deeply, as though he was readying himself for battle. 'Fine. About two, perhaps three months ago the bald man whom you saw me conferring with in Hyde Park approached me and made me aware of certain facts about a few of the clients of the Trium Impiorum who were, shall we say, involved in things that they shouldn't be.'

'One of them being Samuel Millington?'

Dominic nodded. 'Yes.'

He watched her for a moment as she processed that information before lifting her head and met his gaze. 'And the other?' When he glanced away, she spoke again. 'Please, Dominic. Don't you think you owe me that?'

'I had not realised we were trading in anything that we might owe one another. But very well, if you insist. The other was your...brother.'

Her brows furrowed in the middle. 'Stephen? What would he have to do to with any of it?'

'Quite a lot, as it happens.' Dominic got up and made for the side cabinet again and held up the crystal decanter that used to belong to his father. 'Care for a top-up?'

'Yes, thank you.' She nodded. 'I think a restorative top-up might be needed for what I'm about to hear.'

Dominic took Cecy's glass, which she'd placed on his desk and poured a splash of brandy before handing it back to her, their fingers touching for a brief moment before she pulled her glass away, taking her hand with it. He itched to touch the woman again, not she'd ever let him now.

'I'm guessing that the man you met in the park has given you some sort of task regarding Mr Millington and Stephen?'

Clever girl...

He nodded. 'And made it quite impossible for me to refuse.' He took a sip.

'In what way?'

'Well, for one thing, I don't want whatever Millington is involved with associated with the Trium Impiorum. So, yes, I agreed to co-operate and work with the Intelligence Office to uncover the truth about whatever he is doing both at the club and elsewhere. It helps to remove any doubt that the club is not involved with the man's strange activities and whether they are in fact illegal or not.'

'I see. And what exactly have you been asked to do?'

'To watch their movements whenever they are here in the club, which is around three or four times a week.'

'What else?'

'How typical of you to know that there was more.' He flashed her a brief smile before continuing. 'I was also asked to note anyone else who joined their party while they played loo, whist, or at the hazard table and monitor their every movement. And observe anyone else who joined them in the dining room. Names, faces, every detail of their comings and goings at the club has been collated all of this time. I started to see a pattern in their behaviour.'

'Oh? And what was that?'

'Well, your brother would always arrive first, order a drink while reading one of Millington's papers—the *London Veritas* or the *Herald Reporter*. Millington would then arrive about an hour later and meet him. They'd have an early dinner together and chat. Sometimes a guest would also join them for dinner, sometimes not. Every other Friday night they asked my major-domo to arrange an exclusive invitation-only game of whist or loo in one of the private salons with a few of your brother's Parliamentary colleagues and a few of Millington's cronies. Your brother, of course, no longer ventures on the hazard tables—Millington's influence, I expect. They always leave before two in the morning and always separately, except on the alternate Friday nights, when they'd play their exclusive game, which goes on well into the early hours, sometimes finishing by the break off dawn.'

'None of this sound very damning.' She frowned. 'Is that it?'

'Not quite. You see, while both Millington and Stephen were engaged in seemingly mundane activities here at the club where they conducted many meetings with all sorts of characters, some of whom it's assumed they had business dealings with, they were also engaged in something else that looked seemingly innocuous.'

'What was that?'

'Their high-stakes game, of course. You see, they would recruit some of the same people they'd had meetings with into the game, which produced certain, shall we say, outcome for their own gain.'

'They threw the game?'

'How is it that you know about such things?' He smiled, impressed as always with the woman who shrugged, but didn't say anything else. 'But, yes, they manipulated the game in very subtle ways, so as to try to fool the people who work for me. Every time it would be slightly different. One time Millington would win, another time it would be your brother. I suppose it is why I never interfered.'

'I don't understand. To what end?'

He took another swig of the brandy, enjoying the warmth as it travelled down his throat. 'So that they could continue with their ruse and not to have anyone suspect what they were up to.'

'But did you find out why they were manipulating the outcome of the game?'

'Eventually. I realised that their efforts were a way to control the table, which seemed rather important to Millington, who didn't like not knowing the variables of the game or by taking any unnecessary risk. I believe it's all organised and devised by him, regardless who it was they had sat around the table. A senior politician or one new to the Houses of Parliament. Perhaps even a business magnate. He'd invite them all.'

'But why would he need to do it in such an exposed setting? Even if your bald friend had not asked you to keep watch on them, you, your brothers or any number of people who work for the club might have suspected what they were doing.'

'As I said it was subtly done, so it might have taken longer for us to realise that anything was going on, until my, er…bald friend's warning.'

'But I still cannot comprehend what they're trying to achieve with all these exclusive games of theirs?'

'That is what we're trying to find out.' He grimaced

after taking another long swig of the brandy. 'Perhaps the guise of an exclusive game provides the perfect opportunity to extract information or set in motion whatever scheme Millington has in mind.'

Her brows furrowed in that way it did when she was thinking. 'But does the club not also keep a record of its clients? Track and hold on to their markers, IOUs and leverage them with secrets if need be.'

'What a ruthless streak you have, Cecy.' Dominic's smile showed his surprise at her keen mind, as though there hadn't been enough examples of that. 'But, no. If we want to preserve our business, we hold on to everything that you mention without resorting to use them as leverage. After all, no gentleman wants their finances to be made public. And we take great pains to assure them our discretion. Unless…'

'Unless?'

'Unless they give us reason to divulge it.'

'Well, this is such a case, is it not? Why would you allow Mr Millington to continue with these stratagems and schemes if there is so much suspicion around him?'

'Because there is still not enough evidence of wrongdoing.'

'Oh I see. You're waiting to gather more.'

He nodded. 'Exactly.'

She sighed, shaking her head. 'And this is the man that Stephen would have me wed…'

'I'd imagine that your brother would do anything that is asked of him by Millington.'

Cecy paled. 'Do you mean that he's under Mr Millington's power?'

'That's one way of putting it. It must come as no shock that your brother has none of your strength of mind. And especially none of your principles.'

'How could you have guessed?' she said with a small rueful smile of her own.

'It comes down to the fact that Millington owns a lot of your brother's markers. As I said, Stephen was a fool and used to have a penchant for the hazard table, one that lasted quite a few years, which eventually got him barred from playing on the tables here. But he found many less salubrious gambling hells where he was welcomed with open arms, only to rack up even more debt. That was until he made a favourable marriage. When Millington befriended him, he took an interest in his political ambitions while buying up all his IOUs behind his back. He then proceeded to take him under his wing, whether he wanted it or not. So, as a way a way to pay this back, Stephen does Millington's bidding in Parliament and brings him news and leaks information that can be printed in any of his papers and used against Millington's adversaries.'

'He bribes Stephen?'

'Yes. But take heart, he bribes many men.'

Cecy covered her face with her hand as she shook her head in disbelief.

'I cannot believe this…'

'The common belief is that Millington trades in secrets and sells them to the highest bidder; sometimes keeping a few more important ones for himself to use when and how he chooses.'

'Good God. Why would he do such a thing?'

'Who knows?' Dominic shrugged. 'Perhaps it serves his business dealings, especially if it's tied up in administration and bureaucracy. But more than that, it's a way for Millington to acquire more and more power, which is something he is addicted to, it seems. Power he can yield to build or destroy anyone he wants, while creating stratagems where he can exaggerate or fabricate the truth to whatever or whomever he chooses within the pages of the *London Veritas* and the *Herald Reporter*.'

Cecy's eyes widened in shock. 'But he can't get away with any of it…can he?'

'He already has.' Dominic grimaced. 'Think about what happened yesterday—a peaceful march for the most part until it descended into absolute chaos.'

'Surely you're not suggesting that Mr Millington was in any way involved? He wasn't even in London.'

'Oh, I'm not suggesting it. And after a very informative conversation yesterday with the bald man in the park…'

'Whose name is...?'

'Something you need not know.'

'I see. Well, what did he say? Did he confirm that Mr Millington was involved with what happened yesterday at the march?'

'He did.' Dominic grimaced. 'Millington paid a few agitators and rabble rousers on his books to infiltrate the march and clash with some of the horse-backed bobbies on duty, creating the commotion, which resulted in the mayhem yesterday.'

'But why would he do that?' Cecy stood up and started to pace. 'For God's sake, someone could have got hurt.'

'Yes. They could.' Dominic rubbed his jaw. 'And as for why he did it? Well, it could be any number of reasons, but mainly because he could. Millington can then manipulate the news for his own gain and sway public opinion however he wants. I believe you shall find out soon enough tomorrow.'

'You mean to say that what happened at the march will be featured in the *London Veritas* or the *Herald Reporter*?'

'That's what I have been informed. Both papers will feature the march while his satirist paper, *The Witty Cavalier*, will depict what happened with their delightful caricature cartoons. You can only imagine how the women will be depicted.'

She sank back in the chair, her lady-like posture all

but giving way with her shoulders slumped and head tilted to the side. 'I assume not so favourably.'

'No,' he said, his lips flattening to thin line. 'Not so favourably.'

'Devil take him!'

'Quite.' He exhaled. 'And adding insult by having the articles on the same page as those declaration of love columns. You must have seen those before?'

'Yes, I have.' Her eyes momentarily filled with a wistfulness that he couldn't quite comprehend. 'I always thought those declarations to be utterly romantic. So exquisitely forthright and honest.'

Cecy blinked several times and frowned, the wistfulness quickly masked over as though she'd suddenly realised that she had confessed something far too intimate.

'Yes. I suppose they are,' he said carefully, not knowing what else to say.

Neither of them spoke for a moment as they quietly sipped their brandy and seemingly reflected on everything they'd discussed thus far.

'Millington cannot get away with this,' Cecy said quietly.

'No.'

'But may I ask, what is in this for you, Dominic? And don't tell me you were forced to comply with that nameless bald man you met because I shan't believe it. And I understand that you would not wish the

Trium Impiorum to be associated with Millington, but if you had not wanted to have anything to do with this then you, along with your brothers, would have handed Millington and Stephen over to the authorities and declined any further assistance while protecting your own interests and the club at the same time.'

She really was very clever...

'For the simple reason that I will not have everything that Sebastian, Tristan and I have worked for and built here at the Trium Impiorum tarnished by the machinations of one man using our club for his schemes and stratagems. So, yes, Cecy, I agreed to co-operate and assist the Intelligence Office, in lieu of a better understanding between us and the authorities.'

'Ah, your co-operation in lieu of favours?'

'Precisely. Of our choosing. But for now, evidence is needed as all that I have told you is supposition only, without a hint of sufficient proof.'

'I'm at a loss for words,' she muttered after another long stretch of silence. 'I had never expected any of this when I made my way here today. This is all beyond anything I...' She frowned. 'What I don't understand is where I fit into Mr Millington's schemes? What was his interest in *me*?'

Dominic's eyes softened as he gazed at her a moment. She really was so guileless and unaffected, something he'd never encountered in a woman before. But Cecy seemed oblivious to the effect she had on men—well, the ones who looked at her properly at any rate. The ones who bothered to see what a marvel she truly was.

'I believe that *you* are Samuel Millington's one weakness. Millington might be a corrupt unscrupulous bastard, but he has by all accounts excellent taste in everything: from his properties, his thoroughbreds, his many other assets and the artwork and collectables he owns. He can also see a rare diamond when others have failed to.'

'Surely you're not implying I'm this rare diamond.'

He gave her a slow smile. 'Oh, I am.'

'Well, it's just as well that he considers me a rare diamond, as you put it.' She laughed mirthlessly. 'God knows what he would do otherwise if I was anything less. As it is, he's only bribed my idiot brother into doing Lord knows what after buying up all his markers and IOUs. And as if that was not enough, he sabotaged the march yesterday just because he could, to then presumably have the whole thing depicted in a vile objectionable manner in all of his awful papers.'

'I doubt he knew you were there at the march, Cecy.'

'I don't care. Somebody needs to stop him.'

He smiled. 'That is what I'm trying to do. Find proof of wrongdoing. And then stop him.'

She rose and started to pace the small space in his office. 'Does anyone else know of this?'

'No. Neither of my brothers has been apprised of

any of it. Sebastian has a lot on his hands and Tristan is far too busy with his work at the British Museum. I can handle the situation myself. And outside a handful of people who work here, you are the only person who now knows about this. To be frank, until you came barging into my office, I had no plans of telling you either.'

'But you tried to warn me off Samuel Millington.'

'Yes.'

Cecy stopped pacing, her gaze hardening towards him. 'Well, I should be thankful of that, at least.'

'I am sorry, Cecy.' He sighed deeply. 'About all of it.'

'Why? You've provided me with so much clarity,' she muttered as she slumped back in the chair. 'I just need to think a moment about what do with this newly found clarity.'

Dominic could only admire her resolve as she quietly reflected on everything he'd said. Any other woman might be overcome with everything that he'd informed her about, but Cecily Duddlecott was tackling it in her usual inimitable way, despite the fact that it must be difficult having to listen about her own brother's involvement.

'I admit to finding this hard to take in,' she said at last. 'Especially Stephen's part in it. He and I have never seen eye to eye over many things. We are indeed very different people, but I never thought him capable of this...this betrayal of our family name and everything it stands for.'

'Money and power make people do the most desperate of things. In your brother's case there is also the addition of Millington's blackmailing him to do whatever he wants.'

'It's quite extraordinary.'

'Yes. It is.'

'And of all the weak, foolish things to do.'

'Quite. And by using the Trium Impiorum as the stage for their charade.' He nodded slowly. 'But I will end it.'

Dominic still did not know why the Trium Impiorum had been the club that had been singled out for Millington's nefarious dealings, but he would do as he vowed. He would end it.

'As will I. But how?' Cecy leant forward, her elbows on his desk, watching him intently. 'How do we stop them?'

There was something deeply gratifying that she'd used the word *'we'* even if it had been inadvertently done, as it implied an understanding and camaraderie between them which at this moment, Dominic was not quite certain existed, even after telling her the truth. He rather doubted that he'd been let off the hook, after his own behaviour in all of it. Cecy must have realised her mistake as she winced a little and sat back in the chair. Even so, there was no way that he would have her involved in *stopping them*.

'I did not tell you this so you could embroil yourself. Rather to remove yourself from the situation.'

'But I am already embroiled, Dominic. Surely you can understand that.'

She did have a point; he had to give her that. But even so, it could be dangerous with Millington, once he realised that they were on to him and that the woman he courted knew of all his misdemeanours.

'Cecy…'

'Besides, there is also your part in all this?' She raised a brow. 'I still haven't made up my mind whether to forgive you or not.'

As he thought, he was not off the hook. 'My part, as you put it, was not as bad as it seems.'

'You bent the truth. And all done under false pretences.'

'I was never quite as mercenary as that.'

Cecy rose again and stood her ground. 'I believe I shall be the judge of that, Dominic.'

'Very well.' He walked around the table to stand in front of her. 'But bear in mind that nothing was done under false pretences. Nothing.'

'Are you quite certain? Because I do recall things slightly differently. I do remember that you seemed to use the flimsiest of reasons to sit in on one of the TWERM meetings, where you feigned interest in our organisation. Then there were all the various things we spoke about, the many happy coincidences when you happened upon me at Hatchards or even that evening at Verrey's.'

'I don't think that is quite true,' he retorted. 'Despite appearances, I was actually looking out for you. That's why I followed you everywhere and, yes, I may have told you a few white lies about the reasons I was at those various places, but the intention was always sincere.'

'Sincere, was it?' she asked sardonically. 'Because you were looking out for me?'

'I hate the idea of you being in any way tangled with a man like Samuel Millington. God knows where his web of lies could take you.'

'And what of your lies and your deception?'

'Are you really comparing me to that...that miscreant?'

'Certainly not, but it does not excuse your own conduct, Dominic. Why, even the kiss we shared wasn't real. From where I'm standing you did a fair bit of manipulating yourself.'

What the devil...

'Never to hurt you, Cecy. And how the hell could you think that kiss was not real?' He locked eyes with her, studying those expressive eyes of hers, alight with longing. Yes, longing... Cecily might not like him at this moment, but she was certainly not immune to him. And if he closed the small gap between them, he could show her again how real his kisses were. 'I have hardly been able to think of anything but that kiss.'

'That may be so,' she said, taking a step back as he reached towards her. 'But I believe we should forget what happened between us down that alley.'

Dominic allowed his arms to fall to his side, knowing that she was still angry with him. He understood it, but didn't like it. Not one bit. He felt a sudden loss of something, something quite precious and rare; Cecy's trust and regard for him, which he'd now destroyed, possibly for good. And that chafed. He hated the idea of Cecily Duddlecott thinking badly of him and he would have to work hard to make her believe otherwise. 'Very well, if that's what you wish.'

'I think it for the best, Dominic,' she said. 'Especially if we are to work together.'

'What do you mean, work together?'

'I could be useful, now that I know everything. And don't forget that it's me Millington is courting.'

'Precisely,' he murmured, leaning forward. 'Which is the very reason you should be nowhere near the man.'

'All that would do is make him far more suspicious of me, my brother and possibly even you. And I know what you might say about Stephen…'

'That he's an idiot.'

'Yes, and I would agree. But he's not terrible. Unbelievable as it might sound, Stephen does have many redeemable qualities.'

That surprised him. 'Despite everything I have said? For your sake, Cecy, I do hope so, but the fact that your brother is in favour of an alliance between you and Millington does not speak well of him.'

She sighed. 'Yes, but it does show Stephen's desperation and possibly fear. That he'd want me to... Wait a moment.' She blinked. 'That's it, Dominic!'

He did not quite like the sudden change in her. 'Oh God, Cecy, tell me you haven't got some clever yet ridiculous idea?'

'Oh, hush.' She gazed into his eyes, willing him to agree with whatever she was about to say. 'What if I do not decline Mr Millington's suit?'

What the...

He blinked in disbelief. 'What the blazes would you do that for?'

'To give him the impression that all of his plans are going ahead smoothly. Think about it, Dominic. You said yourself that no proof has been found for any of this. What if it is inside his home? Or his office?'

'I already have one of the young boys from the club as well as another who works for the bald man, who have both infiltrated his home as well as the *London Veritas* offices. But nothing has been discovered yet.'

Cecy lifted her head, her blue-violet eyes fairly glittering with...oh, bloody hell, but the woman could hardly contain her excitement. 'Yes, exactly. It suggests that more needs to be done, do you not think?'

'No. This is nothing that you need to worry about.'

'How can I not? And think about it for a moment, Dominic,' she said. 'Think of all the various rooms and places I could have access to as his affianced bride, where neither your men nor your bald man could ever hope to go.'

'Stop,' he said, shaking his head. 'Stop thinking about putting yourself in harm's way again.'

'Are you being gallant again, Dominic? Because in this instance it is not needed.' She held up her hand to stop him from responding. 'This affects me as much as it does you. And I have to help catch Millington after he nearly caused a riot at the march with many who could have got badly hurt. As it is I have been informed that many women have been detained by the authorities and could face imprisonment, just so he might get a story in one of his blasted papers and for what? To sway public opinion and paint a poor opinion of the women's movement. No, he shall not get away with it.'

'And he won't. Not if I have anything to do with it.'

'Which is why I shall agree to his suit and come up with a plan.'

He shook his head. 'God knows what the man would do if he learnt of this.'

'I won't do anything that might jeopardise what

you've been doing so far, Dominic. Although admittedly, from what you've said, it hasn't been too fruitful.'

He couldn't help but smile at that. 'No, not too fruitful.'

She exhaled as she met his eyes. 'However, none of this means that I trust you, Dominic.'

'I know.'

'After everything I'm not sure I can.'

'I know that, too.'

'But I admit that I enjoyed kissing you, too.'

Well, there it was. The very problem if they were going to 'work together'. The fact that they were attracted to one another even if it meant nothing. Even if she wanted to forget it ever happened. His eyes dropped to her lips as he took a small shaky breath. God, but why did this woman affect him in such a way?

A knock at the door brought him back to where they happened to be. At the Trium Impiorum, and in his office.

Cecy picked up her reticule and gave him a bland smile. 'I should leave. Thank you for…finally letting me know everything about Millington, my brother and the real reason you followed me about London. Now that I know it all, I know how I should proceed. I'm glad we're of the same mind. Good day, Dominic.'

'Wait one moment, Cecily Duddlecott.' He stood,

towering over her. 'I never said we were of the same mind. What if something happened to you? Eliza will take a horsewhip to my hind.'

Her lips twitched at the corner. 'Is that what concerns you? Your sister-in-law?'

'Of course not. But I can't in good conscience allow you to get involved.'

'You can, Dominic.' Cecily lifted her hand to his jaw. 'After all you got involved because much of Millington and Stephen's dealings happened under this roof. And Stephen is my worthless brother and Millington is my miscreant of a suitor.'

Dominic tipped his head back and let out an exasperated sigh. 'I know I'm going to regret this.'

'You won't.'

The knocking at the door became more incessant before he heard the major-domo's voice on the other side of the door. 'Mr Marsden, you're needed on the floor.'

'I'm coming, Hendon,' he said, his gaze fixed on Cecy. 'The moment it becomes too dangerous, you'll remove yourself from the situation. Do we have an understanding?'

'We do.' She held out her hand, which he took. The warmth from her touch spread up his arm and he quickly dropped her hand as he clenched and unclenched his hand.

God, but he had a terrible feeling he would regret

agreeing to Cecily Duddlecott's involvement. The woman was getting under his skin, and in more ways than one.

Damn it!

Chapter Eleven

The next time Cecy saw Dominic again was a week later, in the most unexpected of places in Hyde Park and quite unlike the time she followed him to a secluded part where he had the meeting with the bald man whose name she still did not know. Of course, she could have guessed that he would come. After all, she had apprised him of where she'd be and with whom, their correspondence being furtive while she pretended that she was writing to Eliza.

Yet to watch him promenading with his younger brother, Tristan, near the Serpentine, looking so handsome and refined made her pulse hitch. Strangely he blended in so well with the fashionable set who were dressed in swathes of frothy pastels while the men were impeccably turned out in their dapper day suits. Far better than the man she was accompanying.

She could not fail to notice all the young women's eyes following the two Marsden brothers smiling and chatting as though they didn't have a care in the world.

They were that devastatingly handsome, in particular Dominic.

'I see the Marsden *boys* have made an appearance here,' Samuel Millington said as he covered her gloved hand, nestled in the crook of his arm, with his own.

'Ah, yes, so they have.' She tilted her head and smiled at the odious man, hoping that it seemed genuine.

God, but it been a strain having to lie when she'd finally agreed to Millington's suit on his return to London. She certainly made Stephen's day when she'd told him of her happy decision, although he had looked far more surprised than she would have believed.

'Oh, yes. Well, that's good news.' Her brother had uttered this so warily and she'd nearly told him that it wasn't true. Cecy had wanted to shake her brother until he explained why he'd made such a hash of everything and why he'd ruined their family name, but she didn't. There was no guessing what her brother would do and she no longer trusted that it would be the right thing. Still, Cecy was excessively uncomfortable with this charade that she'd devised and willingly got herself embroiled in.

Her plan was simple. Agree to Millington's suit and temporarily become engaged to the man, and wait until an opportune time for Cecy to infiltrate his house or offices in search of evidence to prove the wrongdoing that Dominic and his bald friend believed Millington had committed. And the only plausible way for her to do that, as she'd explained to Dominic, was to accept his suit. Not that she was comfortable deceiving anyone, but then Samuel Millington was not just anyone.

But as soon as she'd agreed to his suit, she found herself in the blasted man's company practically every day and for too many hours for her liking. And the engagement was racing ahead at an alarming rate, thanks to Millington's eagerness. Only her sensible pleas that she desired a long engagement and needed to allow the lawyers to trawl through the settlements, which thankfully her brother agreed with, finally mollified the man. Otherwise, he'd have opted for a special licence.

Yes, it was staggering how much the man wanted her for his wife. She could not quite understand any of it. But he'd told her of his attraction to her and how couldn't wait to beget heirs on her. Good God, they needed to find something soon, otherwise Cecy was going to find herself married to the reprehensible man.

And he *was* reprehensible. From controlling her brother, and having other politicians, industrialists and businessmen in his pocket dancing to whatever tune he played, to the terrible aftermath of the march where, as had Dominic predicted, his broadsheets the *London Veritas* and the *Herald Reporter* put the blame of what happened at the march solely on the shoulders of the women who'd participated, calling them hysterical and wholly unnatural with their violent disposition.

To her horror a few women had even been put in jail with some awaiting trial. And all because of the vile man who stood beside her. And *The Witty Cavalier*'s caricatures were the final blow of humiliation and condescension by the ruling class, taking their women's movement back by many decades. For all that he'd done, Cecy wanted vengeance against the man who might be self-made, but had drawn up that ladder for every group in society, including women. And the fact Millington knew nothing of her involvement at the march made it far easier for her to pretend that she shared the same principles as him, when in truth the opposite was true.

'They seem to be heading this way,' Millington said from beside her. 'I suppose we have to acknowledge them—after all, I do patronise their establishment.'

'So you do.'

The two Marsden brothers had made their way around the periphery of the Serpentine waters before stopping in front of Cecy and Samuel Millington, who was gripping her hand much too tightly.

Her heart skipped a beat since Dominic Marsden was near her again. God, but her stupid treacherous heart longed for something she could not have. After all, Dominic had admitted lying to her all along, so that he could look out for her, apparently. Of all the most ridiculous things. How could she trust him? This was yet another thing that kept her up all night apart from Millington's proprietorial manner.

Could Dominic not have trusted that she would have comprehended the position he'd been put in by the bald man, who no doubt worked for the intelligence office? Could he not have told her the truth, rather than have her believe that he was interested in her in a way that made her pulse hitch? So, no, she had not yet decided how to feel about Dominic Marsden despite wanting desperately to kiss him again. How pathetic did it make her that she longed to be in his arms again? But, no, enough of this nonsense. She could not become entangled with yet another inappropriate man. That she had done before and look where that had got her.

'Good day, Miss Duddlecott.' Dominic held her gaze for a moment longer than he should, as he tilted his top hat and inclined his head before flicking his gaze to the man beside her. 'Millington.'

Tristan Marsden also greeted them, as Cecy returned their salutations while her fiancé merely smiled.

'I'm surprised to see you out and about at this time, Marsden.'

Dominic raised a brow. 'I presume you are addressing me, Millington?'

'Just so.'

'True, I am usually asleep at this time, what with running the club all night, but it was such a glorious afternoon that I couldn't resist basking in some of the autumnal sunshine.' He gave a bland smile. 'And you? I would have thought that promenading would be far too frivolous for you.'

'Yes, well, I had a little time to spare between a few meetings and thought what better way to spend it than with my beautiful fiancée.'

Dominic's glare prompted Cecy to speak quickly in the hope that Millington failed to witness his animosity. 'We were just discussing the Trium Impiorum and how Mr Millington likes to give his patronage there,' she added pointedly.

'Were you indeed? Well, we are naturally honoured, sir.' Dominic's steely eyes were filled with unfettered loathing.

Millington, though, barely noticed the Marsden brothers as he smiled and lifted her gloved hand to his lips. 'Yes, and I have not forgotten, my dear, that you wished to visit the Trium Impiorum. Perhaps I shall be charitable and take you there myself.'

'Thank you, Samuel.' The muscles of her jaw ached for having to smile inanely at every asinine comment that he made. 'I would be intrigued to visit at some point.'

'Interestingly, my brothers and I have decided that we will host an inaugural night when the ladies would also be invited to the Trium Impiorum.'

'Oh?' Tristan Marsden frowned. 'I wasn't aware that we had come to that decision. But then again if my nose was stuck in one of my papers at the museum, I would probably not have noticed anything else around me.'

That self-deprecating comment earned the young man a smile from Cecy and Dominic and a snort from Samuel Millington.

'You do agree with the decision though, Tris?'

'Absolutely. I thoroughly approve.' He smiled at Cecy, who couldn't help beaming at the younger man, who looked a lot like his older brother, but was a few inches shorter and with lighter brown hair and blue-green eyes behind those round spectacles of his. Still, he was a devastatingly handsome man. 'And I hope you shall join us on that night, Miss Duddlecott?'

'I would love to, Mr Marsden.'

'Very good.'

'Perhaps after our little engagement ball, we can venture to the club together, my dear. Although I'm afraid I will have to forbid you from actually playing. That I could never allow.'

She smiled demurely. 'Of course, Samuel.'

'Apologies, but did you say your *little* engagement ball?' Dominic raised a brow, his eyes fixed on hers before flicking back Millington.

'Indeed. I can't think of a better way to announce to the world that I've caught my little dove.'

Cecy clenched her teeth as she smiled at the older man, but, dear God, Dominic looked as though he'd like nothing better than to throttle Millington. Still, he would do well to hide his feelings better. It was what Cecy was forced to do when every smile, every inadvertent touch made her skin crawl. With every outing that she'd gone on with the man, Cecy's resolve against Millington became stronger and more determined.

The more time she had had to digest everything Dominic had said about Millington's scheme that dragged her brother into it, the more disgusted she was. The man was ruthless and did not care about anyone whom he might destroy along the way. So, no, she did not feel any guilt about what she was doing. Samuel Millington was a power-hungry monster and he cared for no one other than himself.

'Ah, yes,' she murmured a little breathlessly. 'These past few days have truly been a whirlwind, but even so, Samuel rightly pointed out that we needed to host a gathering to formally announce our engagement. It had been intended to be a small party, but with so many important people in attendance from politicians to merchants and industrialists, it has now become so much bigger.' She laughed uncomfortably. 'Indeed, it has become an engagement ball.'

'How...wonderful?' Dominic said a low voice.

'Nothing but the best for my little dove.'

God, if the man called her his bloody little dove one more time...she'd hit him over the head with her parasol.

'Yes.' She smiled. 'And at such short notice. You think of everything, Samuel. Even hosting the evening at your elegant home, which I have yet to visit.'

'Ah, but you shall. It will become your home, my dear. Soon, very soon.'

'Yes.' She laughed nervously, avoiding Dominic's eyes, but hoped he'd understood her implication: that they could try to search for the evidence they needed against Millington at the ball. Which was why she quickly added, 'And you must both come, Mr Tristan Marsden, and you, too, Mr Marsden. Especially since, Eliza will still be in confinement. You must attend in her stead.'

'I'm afraid my obligations at the Trium Impiorum will prevent me from attending your *little* ball.' Dominic replied coolly, a muscle ticking in his jaw.

'Oh hark, Mr Marsden, I have not informed you when the ball will be held.'

And could you stop acting the jealous swain... 'I am happy to say that it will be held in a fortnight, on the evening of the eleventh.'

'How expediently you have arranged it.'

'Indeed. There is much to do, but I'm certain we can get it done in time if we put our minds to it,' she retorted, hoping the exasperating man had sensed what she was trying to tell him about the possibility on that night.

'May I ask why the rush?'

'That's rather impertinent of you, Marsden.' Millington's lips curled into a sneer. 'But it is true that I want our wedding arrangement settled as soon as possible. I'm impatient to have my dove ensconced in my home. Nay, in my bedroom.'

Cecy's jaw dropped. What a thing to say and in front of the Marsden brothers as well as in front of her. The man liked to affect being a gentleman, but he was far from it.

'I always like to strike when the iron is hot, as it were, and in all my business dealings. Not that I view you as such, my dear.' Millington lifted her gloved hand to his lips again, this time lingering, his gaze molten, making her feel uneasy and apprehensive.

She pulled her hand away and made a note to throw the gloves away when she had the chance. God, she hoped she hadn't overestimated their ability to find evidence of the man's wrongdoing because there was no earthly way she would attach herself to a man like Samuel Millington. No wonder Dominic had tried to dissuade her from getting involved. Still, she knew she could be of help here. She would do her bit, if not for herself, then the women from the march.

Even so, the more she spent time in Samuel Millington's company, the more uneasy he made her feel. There was something that disturbed and frightened her about the man. From the way he looked at her, or held on to her hand, to the way he told her blatantly about how he would oversee every aspect of her life once they were married. And there was more. Not that she could quite put her finger on it.

'You will attend, won't you, Mr Marsden?' How else could Cecy convey that she needed Dominic to be there? Perhaps later she might have to send Mary to Marsden House, with a message to spell out exactly what she was trying to say to the cloth ear.

'I'm afraid I would still not be able to attend, Miss Duddlecott. But I wish you both my felicitations. Good day to you both.' He touched his top hat and inclined his head at her, holding her eyes for a moment before looking away. 'Tristan, shall we?'

Tristan Marsden's eyes darted from her to his brother and back again before his eyebrows shot up. But thankfully he kept whatever he was thinking to himself and turned to bid them farewell as he strode to catch up with Dominic.

'I do believe that Dominic Marsden has a tendre for you, my dear,' Samuel Millington said as they watched the retreating forms of the brothers. 'But I believe the better man has won your affections.'

God, how she wished she could have left with Dominic and Tristan Marsden.

'Yes. Of course.' And just then Cecy felt weary and knew that she couldn't keep up the pretence of her attachment to Millington much longer. She exhaled a shaky breath as Millington took her hand. She had to find something that could be used against the man at their sham engagement ball. And then all of this would be over.

She would end her fake engagement with Millington. Her brother would hopefully be free of him and the corruption that the man had wielded at the heart of government would also come to an end. More importantly, the women from the march who Millington had wronged would also get their day. But all this would mean that her association with Dominic Marsden would also come to an end and her life would go back to what it was before she'd come to know him.

Cecy lifted her head and smiled at Millington. 'If you don't mind though, Samuel, I would like to return back home. I feel a headache brewing.'

For a moment the man seemed annoyed and a little angry at her request, but his expression suddenly softened a little as he nodded. 'Very well, Cecily. Perhaps I shall allow our plans to change. Although I will say that as an extremely busy man I am not used to having my schedule suddenly altered. But I will have to reflect on to how to placate a wife.'

Was that supposed to be a compliment to her? Either way, it was obvious he had no real interest in her or her feelings. Cecy also knew from some of their earlier discussions that he wanted her to express opinions, but only as long as they aligned with his. In fact, he would not stand for any kind of insubordination, as he'd told her. He had lived longer in the world and much of that time as a bachelor and, while he welcomed intelligent conversation, he would not tolerate any form of disobedience or fundamental disagreement, which Cecy took to mean the kind of disagreement they had had at Verrey's restaurant.

She could also remember the afternoon when he'd expressed his wishes to her and in front of Stephen who remained silent as he listed off all his requirements for a wife as though he was purchasing his new brood mare. Even so, the man couldn't have been more wrong as she possessed none of the virtues that he sought. But then he didn't really know her or even took the trouble to do so. And that was what puzzled her. Why would such a man want her as his wife? Not that it mattered because it would never come to pass. She would never actually marry Samuel Millington.

'Thank you,' she said as he ushered her back.

'Very well, Cecily, but I expect your company tomorrow afternoon.' He drew his finger around her jaw, making her shudder from revulsion. He naturally took her reaction for something akin to desire.

He leaned forward, his head close to her hear. 'I share your feelings, my dear. I cannot wait to take you to be my wife in every way.' He actually wet his lips, making her want to cast up her accounts.

For the first time since she had undertaken the task of trying to discover proof of wrongdoing with this pretence of being the man's fiancée, she felt uncertain about her abilities to see it through. 'May we go now, Samuel?' They made their way back to the house and thankfully he took his leave.

The following days, she was relieved not to have to suffer Millington's company as the man was far too busy with an ongoing situation at his newspapers… thank God. It meant that she could send missives via her maid Mary to Dominic Marsden as she went for fittings for her evening dress for the engagement ball at the Maison Fleur, the haute dressmakers. She needed him to be there, so that they could look for evidence at Millington's home. But the message she received back stated;

'Do not concern yourself with it, Cecily. It will be taken care of...' Which was unhelpfully cryptic. And then the man ended the note with, *'But your part with Millington must end before it becomes dangerous. And he is dangerous. It has gone too far.'*

This Cecy could hardly dispute, but then she had never relied on someone else to do her bidding. Still, she hoped he would come.

As the days and nights had slipped by until it was the evening of the ball, Cecy's unease continued to mount. She was poised, standing there with Samuel Millington, whose hand loitered at the small of her back as they welcomed the guests to his home. She had to admit his servants had done a fine job in readying for the engagement ball. The Venetian cut glass decorated the ballroom and the overhead chandeliers burned with beeswax candles, while the walls were fitted with the same Venetian glass lights using oil lamps to create a soft glow throughout the room. Arrangements of hothouse flowers in creams and blues were also dotted around adding further extravagance to the decor. Yes, she'd give Millington that. His house was stylishly refined as Dominic had said and there had been no expense spared for this evening. Nevertheless, it filled her with unease and guilt that the man did not deserve. She had to constantly remind herself of the power Millington held over so many people, including her hapless brother.

Cecy found the evening repressive, and increasingly difficult to breathe as she stood there welcoming guests and watching the ballroom fill with people. Her eyes settled on Tristan Marsden as he was announced, but she was disappointed to find that the young man had come alone after all. Her heart sank.

'My brother sends his apologies, Miss Duddlecott, however, I am delighted to be attending this splendid evening. Thank you for your invitation and my felicitations again to you both.'

She forced herself to smile as she curtsied. 'You are most welcome, sir.'

She opened the ball with Millington as expected, who held her far too closely as they danced the initial waltz. The evening wore on in a haze of endless chit-chat and well-wishers wanting to meet her as well as more dancing. God, it was awful and the only way she got through the night was the many flutes of champagne that she picked up from the passing trays—mainly from a tall blond-haired servant who seemed to be there whenever she needed another drink and, strangely, looked vaguely familiar.

After the light supper, Cecy found herself for the first time alone by the side of the ballroom, finding it a good place to watch and observe while finally being able to breathe properly. It was then that she caught Tristan Marsden's eye. He stood at the furthest corner of the room beside a huge potted plant and an arched alcove. He beckoned her over to his side with a flick of his head. And although it a strange request, Cecy found herself weaving around the throngs of people, her eyes flicking to find that both her brother and her 'betrothed' were chatting to a group of stuffy Tories.

She approached Tristan who inclined his head and took a couple of flutes of champagne from a passing servant—the same efficient blond-haired servant who served them before moving away.

'Thank you, Mr Marsden. I hope you're enjoying this evening.'

He smiled at her, pushing his spectacles back along his patrician's nose so like his brothers'. 'Very much, Miss Duddlecott, but please call me Tristan.'

She returned his smile. 'Very well… Tristan.'

'You've certainly got a good turnout for this evening.'

'Indeed, I believe your cousin, the Earl of Harbury, has also honoured us with his presence. We even have a foreign princess in attendance.'

'Quite.' A spark of emotion crossed the younger man's eyes before being masked over. He took a sip of champagne before changing the subject. 'Allow me to say how captivating you look, Miss Duddlecott.'

'Thank you, that's very kind. And please call me Cecy,' she murmured. 'It is a shame that your brother could not attend as well. I have much to discuss with him.'

'Do you indeed?' a low voice said from behind her, coming from the direction of the alcove. A voice that could only belong to Dominic Marsden. 'No, no, don't look behind. Look ahead and carry on as through you're continuing your conversation with my brother. Give him all your attention, Cecy, while we have this discussion you're so desperate to have with me.'

'I did not say I was desperate to do anything with you,' she muttered under her breath, while she trained her eyes towards Tristan Marsden, as though she was talking solely to him.

'Are you sure about that?' Cecy could not see the man, but felt him grinning at her from wherever he was hiding behind in the alcove. 'Oh, and, Tris?'

'Yes, dear Brother?'

'Stop flirting with Cecily Duddlecott.'

Chapter Twelve

In truth, Dominic was the one who had been desperate to get inside Millington's palatial home, not just to put in motion the plan that he'd carefully orchestrated, but also to see Cecy again. He'd been fretting about the woman ever since she'd had got the hare-brained idea of becoming betrothed to the very man who was involved in corruption, blackmail and nefarious wrongdoing. The man they were trying to bring down.

As well as this, the last time he'd seen Cecy was at the Serpentine, when Dominic thought he might actually strike Millington. The misbegotten bastard had his hands on Cecy, touching her as though she belonged to him—although in his mind as her affianced betrothed he probably felt as though he had such a claim, the knave. Still, it had been a coup to have access to Millington's home, which was usually closely guarded and it would never have been possible had Cecy not agreed to this Goddamn fake betrothal, resulting in this ridiculous sham of an engagement ball.

'How did you come here, Dominic? I don't recall welcoming you.'

'That's because you didn't. I didn't come in the usual manner.' Cecy began to turn her head to look around behind her. 'No, keep your head looking ahead at the ballroom itself and only, and I mean only, address Tristan while you're talking to me.'

'Very well,' she said, smiling at Tristan Marsden who pushed up his round spectacles and returned her smile. 'It appears you and I are to be engaged in conversation, Tristan.'

'Indeed, Cecy. May I say again how happy I am to be here on this auspicious night?'

'Quite. I am so glad that you're here, but it seems you smuggled in a stray.'

He chuckled. 'I was just doing my bit. And had it not been for the stray I would have asked you for a turn about the room. Or perhaps even a dance.'

'And I should have been happy to accept, but sadly it seems we will have to wait for another auspicious moment.'

'I look forward to it.'

'Have you both quite finished?' Dominic muttered through gritted teeth.

'I am just addressing your very charming brother as you wished,' Cecy said taking a small sip of champagne from the flute he'd just served her. 'And hopefully that would suffice?'

'Yes,' he said, rubbing his forehead. Really, he had no reason getting irritable with Cecy, or Tristan for that matter, when his brother had done him a huge favour by agreeing to assist him here tonight. But this whole situation was delicate and dangerous and needed to go off as seamlessly as possible. 'I trust you are well, Cecy? And that Millington has been behaving as he ought to. I should, perhaps have asked you this to begin with?'

'It's fine and, yes, he has been tolerable, I suppose. But I can't wait for an end to this charade.'

'I quite agree.'

'Tell me, Dominic, how did you manage it, though? I don't quite understand how you could have got inside without gaining anyone's notice. Most of these men know you well.'

'True,' he muttered from behind as he pushed down the leaves of the plant for a better look at her. 'But not if I came inside from the back, through the servants' entrance. And in case you're wondering, I was serving you just a moment ago.'

'Ah, so I was right. You were the servant with blond hair and little round glasses?'

'Which he borrowed from me,' Tristan said, raising a brow. 'I can't account for the terrible wig and whiskers or the strange cosmetic make-up he's had plastered on his face to make him look a little older, but the spectacles are mine.'

'Very ingenious. I wondered why you looked familiar.' She took a shaky breath. 'Although I doubt most of the guests will look too closely at a servant. Or at least I hope so.'

Dominic smiled, marvelling at how perceptive his Cecy was. He gave his head a mental shake at that. Cecy was not *his*, but at that moment he wanted to reach for her and take her far away from this place and these people. He allowed himself just a moment to admire this beautiful woman from the back as he gazed at her elegant poise, her body wrapped in that stunning dress that allowed all that exposed smooth flesh and her dark hair piled up high with a few curls falling down the curve of her neck. God, how he wanted to put his mouth there on the pulse beating at her neck. It was startling how much he wanted Cecily Duddlecott.

Exhaling a shaky breath, Dominic brought his mind back to the reasons he was there. 'Yes. I was one of many servants who had been hired along with a couple of my men from an outside agency for this engagement ball, where I managed to gain access inside Millington's home.'

'To do what? What exactly have you planned? What are you about to do?'

'Hush, Cecy, it's all in hand. I want you to take a deep breath and act as though Tristan is saying all sorts of interesting and amusing things to you. But nothing that might cause any of your guests, and in particular your esteemed brother and fiancée, to look in this direction.'

'Fine. Very well. Tell me, Tristan, how do you cope with having such a heavy-handed older brother telling you what to do?'

The younger man chuckled. 'With great difficulty.'

'Very funny, you two,' Dominic said quietly.

'Is this all you require me to do? Chatting aimlessly while you get up to God knows what and possibly getting caught by Millington?'

'No, I want you to listen carefully. All I need you to do is to keep Millington and your brother occupied, while I search his house. That would be the most helpful thing you can do at this moment.'

'I'll come with you,' Cecy whispered.

'No, absolutely not. You're supposed to be the man's betrothed or have you forgotten? Besides, you'll be missed if you come snooping around the place with me.'

'You know something, don't you, Dominic?'

'Possibly. But I will explain later.'

She turned her head to the side. 'Can't you tell me now?'

'There's no time. But I do need you to do something for me. I want you to make certain that Millington does not leave the ballroom and, if he does, he doesn't go anywhere near his office.'

'His office? But that room is heavily guarded.'

'Not tonight it won't be.' He took a deep breath before continuing. 'And if I am successful in finding ledgers and the files that contain the evidence we need, then I want you to take particular care. Millington is not a stupid man and might think it very coincidental that all this happened on your supposed engagement night. He might start to have suspicions about you. If he does then you need to leave your brother's house immediately and come to the Roseberry Hotel and meet me there. Use the code name Rowan.'

She gasped. 'You cannot be serious.'

'Deadly so.'

Dominic sensed Cecy's embarrassment as her back stiffened and, even from the back, he could see that she'd flushed. But he didn't have time for her reluctance about meeting him somewhere that could cause her ruin. He'd take that risk if her life was in danger. He would do everything in his power to avoid that in any case. All he wanted was for her to be as far away from Millington and even her brother if she needed to. No one but his two loyal men, who were also pretending to be hired servants, as well as Tristan knew Dominic was there.

He'd made sure that he was seen at the Trium Impiorum several times that evening in the gaming hell salon and had hired someone who looked like him to then retire to his office, so as far as all his clients and workers at the club were concerned, he was there and had never left the premises. He'd then used the Roseberry, a small discreet hotel, to get changed and alter his appearance before venturing here. Indeed, the fewer people knew of his movements, the better.

'Promise me that you'll leave and come to the Roseberry, if you have to?'

He realised then that he must have frightened her, as she took a sharp breath in. But Cecy needed to be cautious around Millington as the man was capable of anything. 'Very well, but only if absolutely necessary.'

'Good. And, by the by, Tristan was right. You look ravishing this evening.'

'I believe I said the lady looked captivating.' His brother smiled, trying as he always did in moments like this to lighten the mood.

'That, too. Until later. Cecy, Tristan. Be on your guard.'

'Dominic?' she murmured.

'Yes?'

'Take care.'

Yes, he needed to. Dominic slipped away from the side of the alcove he'd chosen especially for this tête-à-tête, since it had two entrances. And one that opened to the servants' hallway running parallel to the main one. He moved stealthily down the dark hallway before turning right into another corridor and continuing until he got to the furthest door on the left-hand side, which he opened and checked to see if there was anyone there before stepping outside to another hallway. He took a few steps down the hallway and very quietly let himself inside Millington's office. He met one his men, Jakes, who handed him a round metallic disc that Sir Algernon Pendle had been able to get one of his men to filch for a few hours so that they could copy it before returning it.

'Stay outside and give me the usual sign if you see anyone coming this way.'

'Yes, boss.'

The disc was apparently some sort of key that unlocked a hidden contraption somewhere in the office. It was here that the damning proof of Millington's corruption, extortion and blackmail was believed to be held. But he needed to find this first. And to find it as expediently as possible. Dominic switched on a few of the wall oil lamps that flooded the room with a hazy light before starting to search for anything that might fit the round metallic key. He first went through his solid oak desk, which was so large it took up most of the space in the office. Perhaps there was some hidden drawer or cupboard built inside somewhere, which would explain the need to have a desk so huge. He felt his way around the solid wood and found nothing, even on the large hollowed side, where Millington's legs would be tucked underneath presumably, when he sat at his desk. He crouched low beneath the hollowed side of the desk and felt his way around the edges with his fingertips. He came across a protruding button and when he pushed it down, released a revolver onto the floor from the hidden box beneath the desk.

'Well, well, well. What could the bastard want with this, I wonder?' he whispered to himself. 'And I wonder whether he's ever used it.'

Dominic carefully placed the revolver back where he found it and closed the box before continuing his search around the desk before he heard three knocks and heard Jakes on the other side of the door.

'Boss, your brother and the lady are here.'

Dominic expelled an exasperated breath. He also heard a few whispered voices outside as he strode to the door and pulling it open.

'What the hell is going on here?' Naturally he found Cecily Duddlecott with Tristan standing with Jakes.

'I tried to stop her, Dom, but she was adamant that she'd be useful to you here.'

Adamant, was she...?

'This isn't a game, Cecy,' he hissed. 'I thought I told you to stay in the ballroom with your damn intended?'

'My damn intended and my damn brother have gone on the terrace along with a few of their damned Parliamentarian chums for cigars and brandy.'

'Then go back and wait for them in the ballroom.'

'I've just purposefully snagged the hem of my dress, creating a tear, giving me the perfect reason to be excused for a while to mend it in the lady's retiring room.'

'Cecy...'

'Please, Dominic. I'll be much better use helping you with the search, even for the fifteen or so minutes I've bought for myself, than staying in that stifling ballroom pretending to be the happiest of women. And if I have to suffer another person telling me how extremely fortunate I am as an old spinster of nine and twenty to be attaching myself to such a powerful and wealthy man, I shall scream.'

'You? Old? How dare they.' He threw her a brief smile before addressing the men. 'Very well, Miss Duddlecott will help me search here, if only for a short time. Jakes, as you were; make sure you're doing the whole servant routine and walk up and down the hallway carrying the tray if anyone comes by and, Tristan, wait at the edge of the entrance of the ballroom and signal to Jakes if Millington and Stephen Duddlecott venture this way.'

'Very well.' Tristan nodded before moving away.

Jakes nodded. 'Yes, boss.'

Dominic ushered Cecy inside the room, before closing the door behind her. 'Will you ever do as you're told?' he whispered, shaking his head at her, but privately relieved that Cecy was safe with him, even for a few minutes.

'No, sadly not. My nurse as well as my governesses

always complained about my wilfulness, not to mention my headstrong manner.'

'Never say. I simply can't believe it,' he teased. 'Come on then, we haven't got long. We need to find the bloody incriminating evidence and get the hell out of here.'

'What exactly are we looking for?'

Dominic dragged a hand through his hair, knowing that if he wanted to earn Cecy's trust and prove himself to her, he needed to tell her everything. Well, mostly everything. 'One of the men planted to work here has found this metal disc, which we think might be some sort of key. My bald friend had it copied, so that Millington wouldn't miss it before returning the original.'

'So that's the way of it?'

'Yes, and we think it might open a secret cupboard or box somewhere.'

'I see. We're looking for something that the disc might fit inside? Here in his office?'

'Exactly. That's the theory anyway.'

'What about the desk? It's a bit odd that's so large. Could have some hidden compartments?'

'That's what I was searching before you bounded in here. But since you're smaller than I, you're welcome to continue searching under the desk, while I check the drawers above it. Watch out for the revolver hidden underneath there, though.'

'God above, but why would Millington need a revolver?'

'Who knows? As I said before, anything is possible with an unscrupulous man like him, but unless we find proof to back it up, the man will naturally evade justice. He seems to be exceptionally good at covering his tracks.'

They continued to search the room, but found nothing in the bookshelf behind the desk, the small drinks cabinet to the side, the cupboards inside or the small bureau that held a lot of his business ledgers and other files.

'There's nothing here, Dominic.'

'There must be. We're missing something. Keep looking.'

It had to be there somewhere in the room unless they were all wrong and Millington kept his secret folders somewhere else entirely.

Suddenly he heard two knocks, a pause and then another two knocks. He caught Cecy's stricken eyes. 'Millington's coming. Get under the desk, Cecy. Now!' he hissed before crossing the room and switching off all of the oil lamps. He then hurtled under the desk as well, adjusting his large body so that he ended up lying on top of Cecy, folding his bloody great long legs around her with his upper body in between her bent knees. Thank God she was wearing one of those new collapsible bustles but he had to gather all the folds of the silky material of her dress and fit it underneath the desk.

His elbows were on either side of her, carrying his weight as he looked down at her. His body pressed against this desirable woman, from shoulder to groin, predictably hardened against her softness, while his face was inches away from hers. In fact, this would be exact position they'd be in if they were in his bed, rather than hiding in perilous situation underneath Millington's desk.

Damn it, his treacherous body didn't care about that, but registered Cecy's luscious body pressed against his, her scent wrapping around him. Good God, he did not need his body to betray him at such an inopportune time as this…

She shifted a little beneath him, making it even more painful for him. 'For God's sake, woman, don't move.'

'What is it?' she whispered.

'I said stop moving.'

'I'm trying not to, but what is that pressed against my…' she hissed. 'Oh…oh, heavens above, is that your rampant male…?'

He closed his eyes and groaned. 'Please do not finish what you're about to say.'

'But, oh my goodness. That's your…your…'

'My rampant male part?' he muttered on a shaky breath. 'A thousand pardons, I'm only a stupid idiotic male. And if you'd stop writhing and rubbing against me, I would be eternally grateful.'

'I am doing no such thing!'

'I beg to differ, darling. And to own the truth, I am flattered that you are moving in that way against me, but this is hardly the place now.'

'You're insufferable,' she hissed.

'I know, but you like me against your better judgement anyway.'

At least she was no longer nervous, her body no longer shaking uncontrollably beneath him as it had been when he first suggested she hide there. And that was what he had aimed for with his provocative words beyond his own painful predicament, even though they were true. He wanted Cecy to feel safe and have the fear he'd sensed in her, earlier in the ballroom and just now when they'd retreated beneath the desk, to dissipate. Perhaps that was why she'd come looking for him here, rather than spend another moment in that ballroom.

And just then someone, presumably Millington, entered the room with another man, speaking as he turned on the same oil lamps Dominic had turned off only moments ago.

'I'll need to put everything in motion, Duddlecott.' It was indeed Millington and he was evidently speaking to Cecily's brother. 'I need those votes, damn it. I need to get the bill through Parliament.'

'But even if it does go through, you'll need it to go through the Lords as well,' Stephen Duddlecott muttered.

'Never mind about that,' Millington said, his voice confident and assured, making Dominic wonder whether there were perhaps a few lords in his back pocket as well. 'I want to talk to you about Cecily.'

Dominic felt Cecy stiffen beneath him, panicked by the mention of her name. He trailed his fingers up and down her side in attempt to soothe her. *'I'm here, it's all right...'* He hoped his hands were conveying that message.

'What about my sister?' Duddlecott said after taking a sip of a drink that Dominic had heard being poured into glasses. 'She's accepted your suit as you wanted. What more do you want, Millington?'

Was it his imagination or had Stephen Duddlecott sounded a little defensive of his sister?

'Surely you know me well enough to know that I always want *more*.' The man laughed. 'I want the wedding to brought forward, Duddlecott. Cecily may have ideas of the banns being read and long engagements, but I want to be wed to her by next week at the latest. And I already have the special licence at the ready. All I need you to do is to convince her of this. And if not, well then, I shall convince her.'

'No...no need. I'll do all I can.'

'And by the by, where is she? I didn't see her in the ballroom when we returned from our little meeting.'

'I'm not Cecily's minder, Millington.' Just then, Dominic saw Cecy's fan—the fan that she must have left somewhere on the desk—land on the floor and a foot quickly slide it under the desk. Was Stephen Duddlecott...could it be that he was *helping* them? Did he now know that his sister was somewhere in this room? 'But in any case, my wife as well as Lady Honoria explained that Cecily snagged her dress or some such mishap and went to fetch her maid to mend it in the ladies' retiring room.'

Cecily's lips parted beneath him as she screwed her eyes shut for a moment. Dominic dragged his hand to cup her face, his fingers stroking and caressing, trying to calm and reassure her.

'Keep a close eye on her. I don't like how that Marsden Bastard is sniffing around her the whole time.'

Stephen Duddlecott laughed. 'Put your mind at rest, my sister detests Dominic Marsden.'

Cecily shook her head at him, contradicting Stephen Duddlecott, which made him smile. That was the thing about Cecy. She might want to present a buttoned-up demeanour, but beneath it all, she was kind and caring. Why else would she even be doing any of this when she could easily leave it to others? Because it mattered to her. The women of her organisation, the women on that march, the fact that Millington jeopardised their safety and made up lies about them in his damn papers—it all mattered to her. And she never failed to surprise him, so much so that it made Dominic's chest ache. God, but this woman, this woman… what was she doing to him? He needed his wits about him, especially in this precarious situation they found themselves.

Just then, they heard Millington speak again. 'Whatever you say, Duddlecott, but I still don't like it.'

'Don't worry about Cecy, she will be compliant, I'm certain of it.'

'Anyway, what I wanted to discuss is that we need to organise the next high-stakes game at the Trium Impiorum, so for now I'll let the matter lie.'

'Very good, Millington. And in the meantime I'll try to pass on your reservations regarding Marsden to Cecily.'

'Make sure you do.' The man's voice dripped with an unspoken warning. 'Now about the Tories. I want the Hubert Railroad Bill to go through. None of them have enough backbone, however, to challenge Gladstone. Not even Disraeli.'

'You know that you can count on me.'

'Yes…yes, but that is something I take for granted.' He laughed. 'No, I need the numbers, Duddlecott, pay attention. For it to go through we need to be strategic. From my sources, there's Bushey and Jarvis-Bailey whose secrets I own, less he fails to cooperate. And then there's Thompson, whose affair with Lady Maccleby, if it becomes public, would mean the end of his Parliamentary career. I have a few others written down. And aside from them there's the game at the Impiorum we need to organise for Lord St John Derryn, his cousin the Earl of Glynford, Anthony Fairview and Monty Caarth-Bevis. I own many of their vowels already, a bit like yours, Duddlecott, but with this game, I shall have the upper hand all together. Each one weaker than the last.'

'Making it easy to bribe, blackmail and extort.'

'Must you use such ugly language? It's beneath you, Duddlecott.' The man huffed as he made clanging noises, like two metal pieces grinding together. 'But, yes, as it happens, they will bend to my will.'

'I still marvel at the ingenuity of your contraption, Millington. To think all you need to do is to slot the key into the base of that vase on the bookcase, pull down the lever and it then opens to that.'

There was no denying it this time. Stephen Duddlecott was, without doubt, helping them out. For what reason, Dominic could not tell, but he was relieved for Cecy's sake. No one would want their brother to be working with a man like Samuel Millington, not even a man as pompous as Duddlecott. But here he was explicitly telling them, while being aware that they were somewhere inside this room, how to open the secret room using the copied metal disc which, as Dominic suspected, was a key.

'Yes, ingenious. And one of my own designs,' Millington muttered. And once again Dominic heard that sound again as though furniture had been moved around and a clanging of metal before Millington spoke again. 'Come, let us get back to the party.'

'Yes. And don't worry, Millington. I'm sure my sister will have returned by the time we get back to the ballroom.'

Millington grunted as he walked out of the room with Stephen Duddlecott.

Dominic and Cecy lay absolutely still for a little while longer; the only sound the rapid thumping of his heart or was it hers? He then expelled a long breath and rolled off Cecy, getting to his feet before helping her out of the tight spot they'd been hiding in. He missed the warmth of her body, her touch, her closeness.

'My brother…he's not working with Millington.'

'It does seem so,' he said as he stretched out his limbs, shaking off the longing he felt for her. 'I'm glad for your sake, but you best get back, Cecy, before you're missed.' He wanted to reach out to her, he wanted to hold her again, but that would be a mistake. 'I will see to finding this secret compartment.'

Cecy didn't say anything other than nod before turning and walking towards the door, holding herself straight as though she was about to go into battle.

But just as she closed her fingers around the doorknob, she turned and marched back to him, reaching up and winding her hand around his neck, pressing a quick kiss to his mouth. He pulled her close, revelling in this heat, this closeness before she pulled away and looked into his eyes for a long moment.

'Find it, but don't get caught.'

He smiled. 'I'll do my best, sweetheart. Now go, and, Cecy?'

'Yes?'

There was so much to say, so much to convey and yet so little time. So, he said the words that mattered at that moment. 'Remember, the Roseberry. I'll be there for one night more.'

Chapter Thirteen

Cecy paced back and forth along the Aubusson rug in the blue-and-gold parlour, wringing her hands as she waited nervously for news. After everything she had heard in Millington's office the evening before her head was reeling. She'd tossed and turned all night, wondering if Dominic had found the compartment and the proof against Samuel Millington that they desperately sought.

God, but the relief she'd felt when he approached her in the ballroom. She hadn't realised how much she had needed him there at the God-awful fake engagement ball until Dominic spoke to her from behind that alcove.

Every time Millington touched her or even smiled in her direction, it made the hairs on the back of her arms rise. He repulsed her in every way, yet the man wanted to bring their supposed nuptials forward. And everything that he'd said in his office confirmed what that Dominic had said about the man... He truly was a terrible person.

And, oh God, Dominic... Was he safe? Had he got out of that office and Millington's house without getting caught? The way he had calmed her, the way he had protected her, laying his rather impressive body over hers, while distributing his weight on his elbows so that he didn't crush her. He did everything he could to ease her as they lay there beneath that desk. Now it was his own safety that worried Cecy more than she could say.

She had wondered all night whether Dominic was well or if something had happened to him. Cecy realised that Dominic Marsden had been trying to shield and protect her from the first moment he'd attended one of her women's meetings. He was also the first man in her life, since her father, who listened to her, valued her opinion and treated her like an equal. In truth, her feelings towards him had gone through such a huge transformation that there was no longer any doubt about how she truly felt. She could not deny that she was not only attracted to the man, but cared about the great lummox. And a great deal, too.

Then there was her brother. Stephen had shown her again and again that he cared nothing about anyone other than himself, his career and the things that mattered to him. Cecy had always assumed that even his young wife came at the end of that list. But had she been mistaken in Stephen, all this time? He had gone out of his way to come to their rescue in the office last night when he'd made certain that Millington had not seen her fan that she had accidently left behind on the desk, by dropping it and kicking it under the desk. He'd known she was there, of this she was certain, and perhaps even Dominic, too, since Stephen then subtly informed them of how they would be able to gain access to Millington's compartment. What did it all mean? None of it made any sense.

She'd asked Clayton to enquire whether her brother could see her for a moment and when the door opened, she turned around to see Stephen enter the room.

'Good morning, Cecily,' her brother said.

'Stephen.' She inclined her head and took a seat, making him do the same beside her. 'A good morning to you, too.'

'Clayton informed me that you wished to see me? Is it about last night? Well, I must say that it was a splendid evening, my dear. So many felicitations from many esteemed politicians, so many important guests. An earl and even a princess, too. It seems that you have made a brilliant match with Millington, Cecily. You're a lucky woman.'

What on earth...?

Cecy blinked in surprise at her brother's words, so different from his actions last night. She opened and closed her mouth several times, wanting to ask what he meant before she noticed the smallest shake of his head. Did this mean that his words were not real? She didn't quite understand, but decided to play along… for now. 'Yes, it was a grand affair, one that will live in my memory for a very long time.'

'I'm so glad to hear it.' Stephen got up and moved to close the door before returning to sit beside her. He sat in a casual, relaxed manner, his smile and demeanour the same, but when Stephen spoke again, his words were uttered quietly and with a trace of concern. 'Look at me, Cecily, and listen carefully. But please act as though we're having a light conversation, about say the weather or any other banality.'

'The weather?'

'Yes.' He smiled at her. 'The inclement weather at present has been terrible, would you not say?'

'Indeed, it prevents us from venturing out to take long leisurely walks where perhaps we could converse more privately.'

'Yes, but we'll make do here, in this room.'

She lowered her voice. 'What is it, Stephen? And why the pretence here in our own home?'

'Because these walls have very adept ears listening in, at present, and there's very few people I can trust. Even within this house.'

She felt her jaw drop open as she watched her brother in a completely new light. 'You cannot be serious, Stephen. Who? The servants?'

'Yes, perhaps. But in the main, I have it on good authority that Lady Honoria Saxby spies for Millington, constantly watching our every move.'

Cecy took in a shaky breath as she stood and began to pace nervously again, before stopping to stand in front of the French door. 'Oh look, Stephen, it seems the rain has stopped.'

'Has it?' Stephen said as he moved to stand beside her. 'Then you may be able to leave the house for your leisurely stroll after all.'

'Good God, Lady Honoria? How do you know this?' she whispered.

'I did not know any of this until my marriage to Victoria, who has nothing to do with any of it, by the by. But Lady Honoria's husband was in Millington's pocket before his death and she has been ever since. Why do you think that I've given Lady Honoria the responsibility of the running of this house, Cecily? Because I was all but forced to, while giving the impression that it had all been my idea all along. So, yes, she reports back to that bastard.'

'Good lord. Why didn't you say something, Stephen? Why in heaven's name did you encourage Millington's suit?'

He laughed mirthlessly. 'Because I believed that you would do the very opposite of what I advised, as you have always done ever since we were young. Not once have you ever taken account of what I have said in the past. In fact, you have always done whatever you wanted within the bounds of propriety, except this one time when I was actually counting on your resistance to the match. It completely backfired on me. Believe me that I never actually wanted you to be part of any of this, my dear. Never.'

'But I am involved, am I not?' she said softly. 'And you used my engagement to find the information you sought regarding Millington.'

'But only so that I could extract myself, Victoria and you from his clutches, Cecily. And before you ask, I was never able to tell you any of this, since I stupidly believed that I could contrive this situation by myself. And then I also made an oath to keep my dealings with him entirely confidential. However, it is becoming more and more clear to me that you cannot stay here as it's no longer safe for you.' That was exactly what Dominic had informed her, last night. 'You are being watched, my dear, constantly from the moment you wake up until you put your head down on your pillow. And Millington is getting wind of your… er, partiality for Dominic Marsden, which means he will come after you if you betray him…he will come after both of you.'

Which meant they had to act now.

'Come now, Stephen, don't you think you're being a bit melodramatic. And Mr Marsden and I are only on friendly terms because he is the brother by marriage to my good friend.' She lied as smoothly as possible. The truth was at this moment, Cecy didn't want to contemplate what Dominic actually meant to her. But either way, it was no one's business but hers how she felt about the man and as a woman of nearly thirty years she had earned that right, within the bounds of propriety, of course. God knew what would happen if she ever stepped outside those confined boundaries. 'In any case, I doubt Millington will do anything until after this high-stakes game that he mentioned last night.'

'Ah, so you heard that, did you? Yes, however, while that may be true, you still need to take care, Cecy. You need to pretend that you are the happiest woman, impatient to wed your betrothed, especially while you are living under this roof. And until all this unpleasantness is dealt with.'

'I hope to give just as convincing a performance as you have.' She exchanged a brief smile with her brother.

'Good, because as I said you need to be vigilant. Lady Honoria even knew when you had gone to Marsden House while your friend was not in residence and passed the information on to Millington. What were you thinking?'

'I was thinking that she was not a problem, Stephen. But you… I cannot believe that all this time you have made me believe the worst of you.'

Her brother grimaced. 'I thought it would be for the best if you believed that.'

She shook her head. 'Oh God, what a mess.'

'Yes, it is. Perhaps it might be best if you go and stay with Eliza Marsden in Cornwall.'

'No, I don't believe in running away from such problems, Stephen. I did it once before, but I shan't do it again. And don't worry, I shall think of something. But it would probably be best if you do not know my movements.'

'You know that he means to marry you at the earliest opportunity, my dear, especially now that he believes that Marsden has stolen a march on him.'

She felt herself blush at the mention of Dominic's name again. 'Yes, but I can safely say that I will not be going to go ahead with it. I never was, Stephen.'

'Even so, you don't know him like I do. You don't know what the man is capable of. And you don't know how determined he is once he sets his mind on something.'

'Me?'

'Yes, you.' He sighed. 'He made me understand that if I was ever to go against him, if I ever told the authorities of all his dealings, his backhanders, the corruptions, lies and blackmail and everything he's involved with, as well as those blasted high-stakes games at the Trium Impiorum, then he would destroy me, completely and utterly. And he could do it, quite easily.

Professionally and certainly, financially, since he has bought every single one of my IOUs when I gambled and lost far too much.'

'I had no idea about any of it.'

'And why would you? It's not something one discusses with one's sister.' He shook his head and sighed. 'I feel thoroughly ashamed of myself.'

'You mustn't think like that, Stephen. We all make mistakes and I more than anyone understand that truth.'

'Thank you. You're far more forgiving than I ever was with you.'

Even so, Cecy did not want to constantly be held back because of everything that happened in the past. She wanted to move forward with her life. But that was only possible if she could let go of all these feelings she had carried all these years. 'Stephen, despite our obvious differences, you were there for me when I needed you.'

He shook his head. 'I should never have judged you just because what happened in Oxford was a convenient way for me to reaffirm my beliefs about further education for women. I should have done better by you.'

'Perhaps.' She smiled up at him. 'And perhaps if you and Victoria are ever blessed with daughters, you might encourage them to follow their dreams as our parents did.'

Stephen nodded, sharing a quick smile before returning back to the subject of Samuel Millington. 'Anyway, since my marriage I have had to endure Millington's company, while trying to find evidence of wrongdoing. I had no real proof, as he is very good at covering his tracks. That was until recently when I found that compartment in his office and told the necessary people.'

'Necessary people? Or do you mean necessary person? I wonder whether this might be a tall bald man, Stephen?'

'How do you know such things?' He glared at her incredulously and muttered under his breath, 'Damn Marsden.'

'It's not his fault. I followed him, you see, and saw him conferring with the man who I assume works for the Intelligence Office?'

'Yes.' Her brother dragged his hand through his hair. 'But let's hope no one then followed you.'

Neither of them spoke for a moment before Cecily asked something she wanted to know 'So, you no longer gamble, then?'

'No, I no longer have the desire to. But Millington… he forces me. He makes me do all manner of unpleasant things, Cecily,' he whispered. 'And I have done everything he asks, to protect myself, to protect my wife and to protect you. God knows how long I have tried to protect everyone as best as I can. Not that I have succeeded. All I want is to be free of him.'

'Dear Lord, Stephen.' She shut her eyes for a moment, as she tried to understand everything her brother had said. That it had all been unwillingly done. 'But why me? Why does Millington want me so much? I have never understood his pursuit of me. For one, we have nothing in common.'

'That has nothing to do with it. The truth of it is that it has actually little to do with you, but rather the fact you look like Mama.'

'*What?* I don't understand…' She frowned. 'Mama?'

'Yes.' He nodded at the painting of their parents' portrait above the mantelpiece. 'Millington knew Mama in his younger years and worked for her father in his law firm as a clerk. He fell in love with her, but I doubt his feelings were ever reciprocated as he was below her notice. So, he left and vowed to make something of himself to prove his worth, but it was too late when Papa came and I quote, "stole his dove from him", as if that bastard ever owned her, least of all any part of her heart.'

Her brother looked suddenly so weary, so deflated as he shook his head. 'From the very first time he set eyes on you, he felt as though he was looking at Mama, his one and only sweetheart… I suspect he decided then and there that he would have you as his wife. And went about making that happen, in the only way the man knows, by blackmail and coercion. I played my part as he expected, but as I said, I never counted on you to actually accept him.'

Cecily stared at Stephen in horror, unable to take in what he was saying, even though she knew it must be true. God, but Samuel Millington was truly mad. The power and money he'd amassed had obviously addled his brain in such a way that he believed anything could be his, if he so desired it—including her. She shivered at the thought.

'I haven't actually accepted the man, Stephen. I only pretended to.'

'Then as I thought you have put yourself in a dangerous position. Marsden, too,' he whispered.

She slid her hands into his and squeezed it. 'Do not worry about me. Just carry on behaving as his loyal partner, in the manner you have been to him and to Lady Honoria. Pretend that everything is fine and make certain that you are above reproach so that you're not suspected of anything. You are excellent at doing that, by the way, Stephen. And if Millington comes calling on me today, say that I'm indisposed, or unwell. Tell him that he will see me as soon as may be. But above all, make sure that the high-stakes game at the Trium Impiorum goes ahead as planned. Organise it for as soon as may be.'

'I had hoped that the game might not actually be necessary. Especially if proof of wrongdoing that would implicate Millington was finally found in his secret compartment and put an end to all of this. Was it found?'

'I don't know. I haven't had any word from Dominic.' Cecy would not tell her brother where he might be at that very moment. Not that she didn't trust Stephen now, but the fewer people knew the better.

'Even so, it cannot be taken for granted that if anything was found, that it would actually incriminate Millington. Think, Stephen, a man like him who has so many enemies is hardly going to make it so easy as to leave incriminating evidence lying about, even in a secret compartment. There's no choice in the matter. That's why if we want the full force of the law to come down on him then the game must go ahead at the Trium Impiorum. And you must continue to help him cheat at the game and leave the rest to us.'

'Us? You and Marsden?' He made a face. 'I do not like the sound of this, Cecily.'

'I know.' She smiled, an idea formulating in her mind. 'However, leave this to me. But make all the arrangements, Stephen. Make certain that the game is organised and he attends just as planned.'

'Are you certain of this?' he whispered as she strode towards the door.

'Yes. It's the only way to make certain he pays for everything he has done.'

'Fine,' he said in a resignation. 'But, Cecily? Take care.'

She nodded before she left the room.

A few hours later, after packing a small portmanteau, Cecy left the house and hailed a hansom cab from the road adjacent and changed to a different vehicle many times, going to different destinations, from Hatchards in Piccadilly to Fortnum and Mason, while the original cab delivered her portmanteau to the Roseberry Hotel, the place that Dominic had told her about. Eventually she made her way there, too, after making sure that she had not been followed.

She entered the hall and smiled at the concierge clerk, giving him the name that Dominic had told her to use: *'Rowan'*.

'Right-o, Mrs Rowan. Please follow me to the Lilac Suite. Your husband has already arrived and is waiting for you.'

Husband?

'Er, yes, I...thank you, sir.'

She was shown inside a beautifully appointed but modern suite on the second floor with a bedchamber, indoor plumbing with running water and a commode, and a small, tasteful but simply decorated parlour with a dining table and chairs. Dominic Marsden stood and smiled at her, the relief on his face, palpable as he watched her enter the suite. Cecy could not hide her elation at seeing him again either.

'Hello, Cecy.' He smiled that half-smile that made her stomach flip over itself.

'Hello, Dominic, it's so good to see you.'

'And you.' He strode towards her, catching her hand in his.

'I can't stay long. But I just needed to come and see if you had got away. I had been so worried, Dominic. So worried.'

'Hush now.' He kissed her forehead. 'You don't need to worry about me.'

'Somebody has to. How did you get away?'

'In exactly the way I got into Millington's house. Come, I'll tell you over supper, I've ordered a repast. I hope you're hungry.'

'I'm famished.'

Yet she didn't move. For a moment Cecy wanted just to be close to him. She laid her palms and her face on his chest, realising belatedly however that she had surprised him. Sighing deeply, Cecy recognised that she could be a bit presumptuous at times, forgetting herself. Yet after everything that had happened and everything that she had learnt she was throwing caution to the wind, grateful that the man had got out of Millington's mansion in one piece. That was all she needed and yet, as she tried to pull away, his big strong arms came around her, holding her to him.

'I've missed you, Cecy.'

She frowned in confusion. 'You have?'

'Yes. I have become rather used to that sharp tongue of yours in the last few weeks. And it seems that even an absence of only a day, has me pining for more.'

She tilted her head back and looked up at him. 'You tease.'

'Yes. And, no. Perhaps I'm a glutton for punishment.' He grinned before bending down and pressing a quick kiss to her lips, which made her a little breathless.

'Very funny,' she said on an exhale.

'I try.' He winked. 'Come now, let's eat before the food gets cold.'

He uncovered the silver platters to reveal a round flaky crimped pastry of steak and kidney pie, suet dumplings, carrots and greens, with baked cinnamon apples and cream for afters. She did the honours and served the food on their plates before tucking into in the simple but delicious fare in contented silence, while Dominic filled both their glasses with a rich dark red wine.

'So, Dominic…'

'So, Cecily?'

'Will you not tell me whether you were successful in gaining entrance inside Millington's compartment?'

He took a swig of wine and nodded. 'It was just as your brother described. There was a small vase on the bookshelf, only it wasn't actually a vase at all, and once the metal disc was slotted inside fitting the base, it became a lever.'

'A lever? That you pull?'

'Yes. And when I pulled it down, it made the bookcase slide across a little to reveal a secret room behind it. As your brother said, it's very ingenious.'

'Did you find anything?'

'As expected there were ledgers and files inside.'

She beamed up at him excitedly. 'Then…then you've done it then, Dominic. You've found the evidence to get him with?'

'Not quite. I had a scant few minutes to look for what we needed before I might have been discovered, so I could not linger. And frustratingly most of the ledgers pertained to his papers, the *London Veritas* and the *Herald Post*, and I didn't have time to go through all of them.'

'Oh, I see.' Cecy tried not to show her disappointment.

'However, I did find this.' He pushed a black notebook towards her that he'd left by the side of the table. 'It was hidden behind a stack of ledgers neatly piled upon a shelf. And, Cecy, there were more than half a dozen of these little black notebooks.'

Her brows furrowed in the middle. 'Did you find anything of interest inside?'

He leant back and sighed. 'That is the peculiar thing.

If you look through all the pages, they have dates and names, but the rest is in some sort of codex.'

'Codex?' She reached out for the notebook. 'May I see it?'

'Be my guest.' He rubbed his jaw and sat back taking a swig of wine before speaking again. 'I haven't had time to study it properly, but it suggests to me that once we break whatever codes he's used, we'll then be able to understand the contents inside the book a little better.'

'The very fact that he's needed to use a code in the first place suggests that there might be highly sensitive and important information in here.'

'Any ideas how he's done it, because everything he's otherwise used in the book looks like a load of undecipherable nonsense.'

'I may not be good at reading people, but I am rather good at mathematical puzzles and deciphering codes. I might be able to do it, or at least have a bash at it,' she said flicking through the notebook. 'But I shall need time.'

'Time, we don't have.' He sighed, shaking his head.

'Then as I expected the high-stakes game is where we need to focus our attention,' she said absently wondering how they were going to pull this off.

'And as soon as possible before Millington realises that one of his black notebooks has gone missing and becomes suspicious.'

'Yes, I asked Stephen to organise the game for Millington as soon as possible and approach the Trium Impiorum in the usual way he does. Hopefully he'll make it seem as though it was his idea all along.'

'So, you managed to speak to your brother then?' Dominic said, leaning forward as he steepled his fingers together and watched her.

'Yes, and the long and short of it is that, like you, he works for your bald friend.'

Dominic shook his head and muttered a few oaths under his breath. 'Yes, thank you for that. It seems that my "friend" did not trust either of us enough to tell us the truth about one another. If he had, then much of the past few weeks could have been avoided.'

Avoided...? Such as befriending her?

Cecy stopped herself from asking the question, knowing that she might not like the answer. The truth was that the only reason she was even tangled with Dominic Marsden in the first instance was because of this intelligence officer who obviously didn't trust either man and had enlisted Dominic to spy on both Stephen and her. If not for this reason, then she would still feel exactly as she used to about Dominic Marsden. And he would have been able to avoid her and this predicament he found himself in these past few weeks.

'Never mind about that now,' she said stiffly, dabbing her lips on the crisp napkin before leaning back and meeting his eyes. 'We have other more important things to discuss.'

'Such as?' he said, raising a brow, his smile wry and knowing.

He really was handsome and Cecy was glad that Dominic was far from the vain, self-absorbed man she'd believed him to be, now that she knew him better. Really, though, the man was too much of a distraction, especially when he smiled at her like that. 'Come now, Dominic, we don't have long and you need to teach me whatever game it is that Millington usually plays.'

'Wait…' he said. 'Wait one moment, Cecily Duddlecott. Do you mean for me to teach you a card game?'

She nodded. 'Yes.'

'The one that Millington usually plays?'

'Indeed.'

'Samuel Millington who is rather an experienced card shark and attends the Trium Impiorum often to arranges high-stakes games. That Samuel Millington?'

'Of course.'

'Have you lost your mind?' He stared at her in disbelief. 'The man thinks you're engaged to him.'

'I do realise that, Dominic. However, Millington will need to find out that we are not.'

'Oh, and you think the best place to tell him would be at a high-stakes game at the Trium Impiorum?'

'Where better?'

He stood and threw his napkin on his plate, and

moved away from the table. 'For God's sake, Cecily, I'm trying to keep you safe from the man by keeping you as far away from his clutches as possible, and here you are suggesting something so outrageous, I can hardly believe it.'

'Don't you see that Millington has made a mistake here and we need to use it against him, just as he has always used people's worst weaknesses against them. We'll turn the table and use his weakness against him.'

'And what pray is his weakness?'

'Me.' She said on an exhale, 'It seems I am his weakness. Don't look at me like that, I am repulsed just thinking about it, but it's the only way.'

'I was correct with my initial observation. It seems that you have lost your mind.'

She slipped her hand in his. 'Don't you see that this will bring the element of surprise that we need for the high-stakes game. It would certainly catch him off guard.'

'Oh, I'm sure it would, but that's not the point, my gorgeous, beautiful accomplice.' He shook his head. 'He won't like it and God knows how he might react. What if he then refuses to play if he sees you there and makes a scene because his betrothed has arrived unannounced. It will all be for nought.'

No, Cecy did not know what she would do if Millington refused to allow her to join the table and would need to come with an alternative plan.

She smiled and hoped it conveyed a confidence she did not yet feel. 'I'll make him an offer I doubt he'll refuse.'

'It's madness what you're suggesting. Absolute madness.'

'Yes, it probably is, but I must do this. Please.' She pulled him around gently so that he faced her now. 'The man wants me to be his wife and yet knows nothing about me, nor any of the causes that are close to my heart or even what I stand for. He knows none of it and doesn't care to know either. Yet he wants to own me. He wants to extinguish everything that matters and all because I resemble my mother.'

His brows shot up. 'Your late mother?'

'Yes. Apparently, she has everything to do with his interest in me.'

Dominic frowned. 'How so?'

'I don't quite understand all of it, nor to own the truth do I wish to. But it seems that Millington was in love with Mama as a young man and, since she is no longer alive, then the daughter will do. After all, we're interchangeable as women, aren't we?' She shook her head. 'This is why I want to be the one who also plays at the table, Dominic. To bring him and his whole house of cards down.'

'But you don't know how to play, sweetheart.'

'That's where you come in because you can teach me.' She caught his gaze and waited while he seemingly mulled it over. 'Please, Dominic. I will be doing it for you because he used your club for blackmail, extortion and criminal activity—under your very nose, may I add. I will also be doing it for my brother who he's had under his control for a very long time, and I'll be doing it for the women's groups, including TWERM who he's smeared lies about in his newspapers, and finally for me, because he assumed that he could own me and change who I am.'

'Cecy...' He squeezed her hands gently. 'Allow me to handle this.'

'Why? Because you believe that I can't manage it?'

'That's not what I said. We don't have the time needed for me to teach you. You said yourself that you couldn't stay long.'

'I can stay for as long as needed. Please, Dominic. Please let me be of some use.'

He exhaled through his teeth for a long moment, muttering under his breath before he lifted his head. 'Oh, God, I know I'm going to regret this. But very well. I will show you, Cecy—however, if it becomes evident that it will be too...er, challenging, then we will abandon the whole scheme.'

'Challenging?' She raised a brow. 'Surely you believe I can do it?'

'To grasp the basics of the game in one evening, yes. To beat hardened gamblers at said game, no. But I do like to be proven wrong,' he added with a wink, his humour at once again restored. It was something she liked very much about Dominic Marsden. That optimism against the odds, which was not only attractive but highly addictive as well.

'Do you…enjoy being proven wrong?'

'With you, sweetheart, undoubtedly.' He lowered his head and touched his forehead against hers. 'And I have been proven wrong again and again with you, to my eternal surprise.'

She was for a moment captivated, wanting to melt into him and learn something quite different to a card game and instead discover everything about him that would make her pulse race, her blood soar, leaving them both breathless.

'You almost sound as though you actually like me.' She glanced up and caught his eyes filled with so much longing. The same longing that she felt. God, but Cecy had tried to forget this simmering attraction between them ever since that day in the alley when he'd kissed her soundly in the aftermath of the march. And then there was the night of the engagement ball when Dominic had covered her body with his, beneath Millington's desk. He looked as he did now, as though he wanted more. Just as much as she did.

'Heavens above, do I? Then there's really no help for me, if I succumb to *liking*.' He bent his head and touched his lips to hers, gliding them across hers, then slowly, excruciatingly slowly, coaxing her mouth to open, deepening the kiss. Her arms came up and around his neck as she kissed him back, anchoring herself to him, wanting that rich decadent taste of him. Oh God, this was what she had wanted every time she saw him. Yet, Cecy had to remind herself that while she enjoyed Dominic's company and all his incredible kisses more, there could never be anything more between them.

They had come together because of Dominic's assignment and once all of this was over, they'd have to go back to how things were before; and she'd go back to being his sister-in-law's friend and nothing more. No promises had been made. If only she could get her body to be of the same mind.

'You know, Dominic, I might share the same affliction as well,' she whispered against his lips.

'Then there's no hope…' His voice was low and portentous. 'For either of us…'

But Cecy had to stop her foolish heart from imagining there would be more. As Dominic reminded her, they'd never have needed to spend all this time together and could have *avoided* all of this unpleasantness had they not been thrown together by that unscrupulous intelligence officer, who'd obviously asked him to keep an eye on Cecy, or words to that affect. And just because they'd found a spark of attraction that lit a fuse whenever they happened to be in the same room as one another, it did not mean anything more, did it?

Her professor and lover at Oxford all those years ago had taught her that. He'd qualified their attraction, claiming it had been nothing more than carnal connection between them and none of it had actually meant anything. The bastard. But Cecy had been young and she'd been a romantic. She had been led to believe that marriage would follow after she'd allowed such intimacies with the professor. After all it had been her first time and she had believed herself to be in love. But all she was left with was a broken heart.

'We shouldn't be doing this now. Not when there is so much we need to do before the game.'

'On the contrary,' he said, kissing her down her jawline, his fingers digging at the back of her neck, her hairpins falling out of her hair. 'I can't think of anything better than this right now.'

And while Cecy knew that not all men were alike, she was no longer naive. She knew that she was not the type of woman that most men would want more than a friendship of sorts or even a dalliance with. She was far too opinionated and far too set in her ways and far too difficult. A challenge, yes, but once she'd succumbed to their attraction, then all interest was lost. It had happened before with a few of Stephen's Parliamentary friends who she always managed to scare away. For who could live with a woman like her? An intellectual, a woman who championed social justice and equality for all in society. Not many and anyway, this whole hullaballoo with Samuel Millington made her realise that perhaps her destiny was to remain a spinster. After all, a man like Dominic Marsden probably had many such attractions, many such affaires. These kisses, this closeness, this attraction did not necessarily mean anything and she was not prepared to risk her heart as she once had before.

Cecy pulled away slowly as Dominic continued to kiss his way down her neck. 'You are trying to distract me.'

'Is it working?'

'Yes.' She gasped as he sucked on that rampant pulse at her neck. 'But we can't, Dominic. I need to learn the...oh, my.' He nipped her at the corner of her lips before kissing her open-mouthed, tasting her and deepening the kiss.

'Mmm, that feels wonderful.' She tilted her head back, giving him better access to her neck as she moaned. 'But surely one of us must be sensible?'

'Must we and dear God, Cecy, how many layers are you wearing?'

'The correct amount.' She chuckled lightly. 'And, yes. At such time as this, when we have so much to do, we must.'

'Spoilsport.' He smiled slowly as he untangled her arms from around his neck and pressed a kiss on the inside of both her hands. 'I must say, you look thoroughly ravished.'

'I feel thoroughly ravished,' she murmured and stepped back, just in case she acted more foolishly than she already had and threw herself in his arms again.

He touched a tendril of her hair that had fallen down, brushing it between his thumb and fingers. 'It suits you, being ravished.'

'As it does you.' She dragged her finger along his jawline, making his green eyes smoulder, darken and fill with unfettered heat. 'But perhaps later.'

'Later?' He turned his head and caught her finger with his teeth, licking the tip, making her intake a gasp. 'I'll hold you to that.'

Cecy moved around him as she tried to rearrange her hair, her fingers trembling a little. It amazed her how much Dominic's touch affected her. 'In the meantime, will you make me into a card player?'

'A promise is a promise, I suppose. Yes, I'm at your service.' Dominic held her eyes, lingering for a long moment before nodding. 'Let's get to it.'

Cecy watched him as he moved stealthily around the room, her heart thumping wildly and, oh, how much she ached for him. Dear God…she couldn't…she just couldn't be falling in love with Dominic Marsden. It would be the biggest disaster if she did. And worse, when the time came for him to let her down as he'd surely do.

Dragging her eyes away, she pulled her mind back to what needed to be done. She got out a deck of cards and a small leather-bound notebook and pencil from her portmanteau as she sat opposite Dominic. 'Shall we begin?'

Chapter Fourteen

Dominic watched Cecy's face as he went through the rules of playing a few of Millington's favourite card games and smiled to himself at how perceptive she was, grasping concepts so quickly.

'Millington sometimes insists on a fast and loose game of Macau, the long and strategic game of whist or the unpredictability of a few hands of vingt et un, but he usually likes to play a five-card loo in high-stakes games because it needs strategy, yes, but is also a much faster-paced game than whist.'

It had surprised him that it was Cecy who had correctly reminded him of the reasons she was there in the first place, even if it was a little humbling. Because it was not for his charm or his company per se, but his knowledge about card games. And now quite adeptly she had not only manoeuvred him to agree to her attending the game itself, but was mastering it beforehand. It was madness, but he knew why he'd done it. Why he'd succumbed to Cecy's insistence to be there.

Because all her life she had been denied admittance to every institution solely because she was a woman—this he understood very well now and how important it was for Cecy to gain that validation. From the extreme scrutiny and suspicion she'd aroused when finally being allowed inside the hallowed walls of Oxford University to her passionate belief in the emancipation of women, which was constantly side-lined and ridiculed by the political establishment as well as society at large compounded by the vicious lies in Millington's newspapers.

It meant that the downfall of a man like Samuel Millington had now become far more personal to Cecy because he represented everything that had always sought to muzzle and control her. Which was wrong... so wrong for a woman like Cecy, who was by far the cleverest person he'd ever known. And for someone like her to have to prove herself constantly and have her worth constantly challenged was nothing short of an outrage. No, she had every right to be there and he would do everything he could to help her. And if this decision would later be criticised by his brothers, especially Sebastian, then so be it. He would not let her down.

'Right. So you understand everything I have said so far?'

'I think so.' She referred to her notebook. 'Players are dealt five cards each and ranked just as in whist, except that the knave of clubs, which is called the "Pam", is the highest trump card. The aim is to win at least one trick, under penalty of increasing the pool.'

'And you remember how the pool is determined?' He raised a brow, but quickly added, 'Without referring to your notes.'

'Let me see,' she said, tapping the side of her face. 'The pool is formed by dealer's contribution of five chips or counters.'

'Yes.' He smiled. 'The players, having seen their hands, can either abandon them free of charge or elect to play. Any player failing to take a trick is "looed", with a penalty of adding five more chips to the pool. Does that make sense?'

'I believe so.' Cecy's brows furrowed in the middle as they often did whenever she was thinking. 'Before play, each in turn announces whether he will play or throw his hand in. If one player exchanges and the others all pass, the exchanger then wins the pool.'

'And what you're aiming for is for someone to hold a Pam-flush-four cards, whether dealt initially or obtained by drawing cards, he or in our case, she…can sweep the pool before playing. The next best hand to the above is a trump-flush-five cards of a trump suit and this sweeps the pool. The next best hand is that of a flush of other suits, which sweeps the pool.'

'I understand.' She nodded. 'What I want to know is how I need to win and win everything.'

'Devise a strategy and push for the game to become an unlimited loo, if no one at the table suggests it first. It's risky to do that with seasoned gamers like Millington, especially if he takes it in his head to push you out or even isolate you from the beginning.'

'That is something I am quite used to, Dominic.'

'Quite.' He flashed her a wry smile. 'But we're not going to let that happen, love, and you never know, you might surprise him.'

'Oh, I aim to.'

'I know you can.'

'Thank you.' She lifted her head and smiled. 'Now, shall we play? It will be good practice for me to formulate the strategies as you said.'

The one aspect in all this that struck Dominic was how quickly she'd forgotten that they'd been in the midst of their er…ravishment only moments ago. It had ignited so quickly, with a heat so potent that Dominic had wanted to lift her skirts and bury himself inside her, until she had the foresight to put a stop to it. How incredible that she could so easily put aside their attraction and, while it was a bit of a kick in the teeth, she was certainly far better at controlling herself then he was. Damn, but the surge of desire coursed through his veins, whenever she was near. Her face, those eyes, her lips plump and reddened after their kiss.

She had said, *'Perhaps later…'*

What the hell did that mean? To continue where

they'd left off? And was it later tonight, tomorrow night, mayhap never? It was enough to drive a man mad. *She* was enough to drive him mad.

Dominic lowered his gaze down to the deck of cards and swallowed uncomfortably. 'Fine, let's play. The first game will be for practice and to run through everything I've said, ironing out anything you're still a little unclear about.'

'And the second?'

He met her eyes. 'Will be for real with real stakes.'

'Indeed?' she said, raising a brow. 'And what stakes do you propose?'

'I think I shall allow you to decide.' He winked.

'Very gallant.'

'I'd like to think so.' His gaze dropped to her lips again before rising back to meet her eyes again. He gave himself a mental shake. 'Choose wisely and think very carefully about it, Cecy. But above all remember to be single-minded and determined and more than anything be ruthless if you want to succeed. Use everything and anything in your power to achieve your aims.'

'I understand.' She nodded. 'Shall we begin?'

He shuffled the deck of cards in a swift extravagant manner that the dealers at the Trium Impiorum would do, making Cecy's jaw drop a little. 'Indeed. Ready?'

'Yes. And that was very impressive by the by.'

He grinned. 'Glad you think so.'

* * *

They spent the next hour or so on that first game, the practice game, the one that he'd purposely allowed to be loose and easy for Cecy to get a grip with. She asked questions, many questions. Asking whether alternatives were possible and making more notes in her little book, her eyes glowing, her teeth dropping down on that plump bottom lip. He realised then that she was in her element, that this was what she enjoyed: problem solving.

'What are you writing down?' he asked, trying to look over at the page that she was scribbling lots of symbols and shapes. 'Wait one moment. Are you applying mathematic theorems to a game of loo?'

'Yes, if I can. I'm trying out a few theories to see if they could work and then how I could implement them in the game. After all, most card games, including loo, are a matter of probability. I want to see whether I can somehow use factorials to be used here.'

'And what, may I ask, is a factorial?'

'Factorial is a mathematical concept that exists and serves as a fundamental operation for counting arrangements and combinations of objects.'

'And you can see a way of using it here?'

'Possibly.' She nodded. 'The thing I'm wondering is whether it could provide a way to calculate the total number of possible outcomes in various different situations.'

'One being a card game such a loo?'

'Precisely.'

'Very well,' he muttered, crossing his arms over his chest. 'But promise you'll never mention it again if you find that this could be one such situation.'

Cecy giggled, a sound so throaty, unexpected and seductive that it went straight to his groin. Good God, did he...did he find this talk of mathematics and theorems arousing?

'Very well. We'll keep this a secret between us, shall we?'

He crossed his chest with a swipe of his hand. 'Whatever is said in this parlour shall remain in this parlour. And only between us. Cross my heart.'

She copied him and made a single solemn nod. 'Mine, too.'

'Well, are you going to expound your theory? This, I must hear.'

'Well, the idea I have is that since there are fifty-two cards in a deck, then it's reasonable to assume that I should be able to apply a theorem of James Stirling's. He was a Scottish mathematician who came up with his theory based on the fifty-two factorial decks of card. It can be useful in a game of loo for instance, as factorials are particularly useful when dealing with permutations and combinations of different set of objects and patterns.'

It seemed that he did find her explanations exceedingly arousing. God, he could listen to her to talk like this for hours. 'Without this descending into the realms of a scientific hypothesis, tell me what would determine permutations and combinations in the case of a card game such loo?'

'Permutations of different hands refer to the arrangement of the cards in a specific order, while the combination refer to the random selection of cards in the game without a particular order.'

'And you can determine either the permutations or combinations using this fifty-two factorial theory, then?'

'That is the idea.' She smiled mischievously before catching her bottom lip between her teeth as though she was trying to contain her excitement. 'You see, the concept of factorials can be applied in practical terms here in this very game either by counting the possible number of permutations and combinations of any given hand, by then arranging the hand in a specific order or selecting the cards without considering their order.'

'And you can predict this?'

'Or make a very mathematical stab at it.'

'How, precisely?'

'I would say by using probability to calculate the number of favourable outcomes against your opponents in a game of cards, by using a fifty-two factorials deck of cards, especially when there are more than two people playing,' she said, leaning forward. 'That way you can determine the probability of a specific hand coming up or at least the likelihood of certain outcomes.'

'I'm impressed.' He looked at her agog for a moment before a slow smile curled around his lips. 'And I presume you can do all of that.'

Cecy shrugged, looking a little self-conscious. 'I can give it a go.'

'Yes, I can see that you will.' He gripped the edge of the table from stopping himself from reaching out for the delectable woman sitting across from him. 'However, while you apply whatever mathematical theorems you wish, I have a proposal to make.'

'A proposal?' she said, her brows shooting up.

'Yes, by making the game a little more interesting.'

She frowned. 'How so?'

Yes. He wondered what had suddenly made him blurt out the need for a proposition. Things were rather interesting as they were.

'By introducing another element into the game, one that might allow another strategy that you could use—one of diversion.'

'And what, pray, could that be?'

'Anything you wish. Something that you can use in your favour.' He caught her eyes and smiled. 'Or perhaps one that I could use. State the terms of the stakes, sweetheart.'

'Ah, so you're allowing me to choose what the stakes might be?'

He inclined his head and took sip of brandy. 'Just so.'

'All right, but allow me a moment to think about it.'

'Hasn't there already been a lot of thinking for one night? God, but numbers, factorials, probability, permutations, combination and mathematics can frazzle a man's brains.'

'Not yours, though.' She flashed him a cheeky look before leaning across the table. 'You enjoyed all that talk about numbers, factorials, probability, permutation, combination and especially mathematics. I can tell.'

'Oh, and how could you do that?' Dominic murmured, leaning forward in his chair as well so that he was only a few inches away from her.

'Because of what I can see in your eyes and that is all I'm prepared to say at present.' She grinned and sat back. 'For now, I'd be much obliged if you could pour me a glass of brandy and then shuffle the deck.'

Dominic chuckled before reaching for the decanter and filling a tumbler and pressing it into her hand. 'Go easy, though, sweetheart. You don't want to be foxed and unable to hold your drink. That is also something to keep in mind when trying to outplay Millington and the others at loo, no matter how well you try with your mathematical strategy.'

'I can hold my drink as you discovered that first time I drank brandy. But thank you for your caution. Now, deal the cards if you please, Dominic.'

'And the stakes?' he said, shuffling the deck again.

'Yes, about that,' she said, picking up her cards. 'I've been thinking about what you said and wondering how I could make it as interesting as you said I should.'

'And?'

'I'm still pondering on it.'

'We could play for half a crown.' He shrugged. 'That should keep things interesting.'

'But hardly interesting enough.' She laughed softly, her mouth hitching at the corner, clearly enjoying herself. 'I can hardly describe playing for half a crown as either interesting or original. Even if it will pauper you.'

He whistled. 'Fighting talk, Miss Duddlecott.'

'Indeed, Mr Marsden. I would also wager the need to add a new requirement for the stakes of this game.'

'Oh and pray what is that?' Dear God, the woman was making his head spin.

'Perhaps it should also be original…and challenging.'

'So interesting, original and challenging?'

'Yes.' She studied her cards and arranged them in order of the suits, just as Dominic had explained earlier before flicking her eyes over the top of them and giving him a challenging look of her own. 'Do you accept?'

'Well, if you're going to the trouble of thinking of a stake that could be all those things, then it may as well be outrageous as well.'

Cecy raised a brow. 'Outrageous, eh? The only stake that encompasses all that is if we played for items of each other's clothing.'

He froze momentarily before his eyes snapped to hers. Cecy obviously meant something far more innocent than what his depraved mind was thinking. 'What did you say? Items of clothing?' he ground out, his voice hoarse even to his own ears.

'Well…yes.' She blinked, perhaps realising what she had inadvertently alluded to. 'But don't worry, I am only half-jesting.'

'And the other half?'

She smiled slowly. 'Would meet the…the terms of my exacting specification.'

'How daring of you. Allow me to get this right. You're saying that after we conclude this practice game, the stakes will be for one another's clothing?' He returned her smile. 'Have I got this right?'

She shrugged. 'I can always propose another wager for the game if you'd prefer.'

'No…no, wait one moment.' He threw her a cheeky grin before scratching his jaw. 'It's certainly an outrageous proposition.'

'Perhaps it's too outrageous...for you.'

The minx. Two can play at that game....

'No, I think it perfect. I'm game if you are.' He raised a challenging brow. He could hardly believe that she would actually walk blindly into this outrageous proposal of hers. 'It's your choice, Cecy.'

Dominic watched her as she battled with herself, perhaps wanting to be daring but then knowing that what she had proposed had been far too indecent for her to actually consider. After all, Cecy was nothing if not a proper gently bred woman no matter what she had experienced. Even if this suggestion was to peel away their clothing for a game was not actually as sinful as proposing that they succumbed to their carnal desire. Perhaps it was for the best because God knew that Dominic would find it very difficult to sit there with a half-dressed Cecily Duddlecott.

'Don't worry about it, love. Perhaps it is as you said—*too* outrageous.'

'Absolutely not. You were right the first time. What I proposed would be the most challenging stake as neither of us would want to lose. And it would be interesting, original and most outrageous. I doubt even you have ever played for such a stake.'

Oh, love, if only you knew... 'So what are you saying?'

She shrugged. 'You did say that you wanted me to play into my strengths.'

Cheeky minx. 'Is that what you'll be doing, sweetheart?'

'Yes.' She nodded before smiling wryly at him. 'And I am game, Dominic. Are you?'

Shock rippled through him at this audacious and, yes, outrageously scandalous proposition. *Her* outrageously scandalous proposition.

Perhaps she was teasing him. Perhaps if Dominic went along with this madness Cecy might come to realise that she would also be out of her depth at the game at the Trium Impiorum, and decide to sit it out altogether, despite all her mathematical theorems.

'If I said yes, what would you think?'

He noticed Cecy worry her bottom lip and perhaps wonder what she had got herself into, but then she seemed to make some kind of decision. 'I would think that this wager would be a good way for me to then deploy bolder tactics that are not only outrageous but necessary. After all, you told me to be determined and single minded about what I am doing and remember to use anything and everything at my disposal. If it works this evening then I might even use some of these tactics at the high-stakes game at the Trium Impiorum.'

'You are not taking your clothes off during the game, Cecily Duddlecott.' But only for me...he wanted to say, *only for me...*

'Who said that I would be the one doing that?'

'Oh, yes, very bold.' He chuckled darkly as a wave of uneasiness settled over him.

The last thing he needed was her distracting the game, but more importantly he'd be damned if he was going to expose Cecy to possible danger. Yet as he sat there staring at his cards, he couldn't help think that the danger was not just contained to the game tonight or even the one being arranged at the Trium Impiorum, but something far more dangerous to him personally. His chest ached terribly when he thought of Cecily Duddlecott, her kindness, her intelligence, her causes, her mathematical theorems, her enticing mouth and everything else he loved about the damn woman.

What the devil?

It could not be true, could it? That he loved Cecily Duddlecott? Oh hell, perhaps he was the mad one after all.

Chapter Fifteen

Cecy didn't know what had possessed her to be as bold or even as outrageous as she'd been when Dominic had teased her to name her wager. It had been a jest at first, but she had maintained her reasons anyway. She didn't know where she'd found her daring and rather ridiculous indecent suggestion of the stakes this evening but it might have been something to do with the casual way that Dominic had presented himself this evening or rather his *dishabille*.

His stiff collar had been removed and his shirt was unbuttoned to reveal the long column of his throat going down to a wide expanse of chest with a smattering of crisp dark hair which was just about visible beneath, if one looked hard enough. And she had; she had looked at him from top to bottom. This naturally roused her curiosity to such an extent that she had been unable to tear her eyes away from him. It had made her want to see more, resulting in that poorly judged wager for one another's clothes.

It was ridiculous as she'd blurted it out, forgetting all the implication of what she was saying. For one thing, while Dominic Marsden would have to peel off this clothing when he lost a hand, so would she. It had given her pause—*he* had given her pause. Yet, even then, she had not heeded the warning of such a wager. After all, she could not lose face, or take it back now and have Dominic believe she was not only a prude, but someone who backed off a wager.

Besides, Cecy trusted Dominic, she cared for him and knew implicitly that he would never do anything that would make her feel uncomfortable. No, it wasn't Dominic she feared but herself. In truth at that moment, she trusted him far more than she trusted herself. And, dear God, she wasn't certain what she would do if she had to reveal herself, all of herself, to him or if Dominic had to strip off for her.

It made her giddy just thinking about it. Perhaps she'd gone too far. Perhaps the stakes were too high. Perhaps it was too much of a risk to be playing such a game with a man like Dominic Marsden whom she longed for and couldn't stop thinking about, despite the predicament they were embroiled in. Yet it was too late for her to back down as they were playing. They were playing now and for real.

'Remember that I can no longer give you any more pointers or handy tips, sweetheart.'

And did he also have to do that? Did Dominic have

any idea that each time he called her *sweetheart, darling* or *love* and looked at her as though he wanted to take her to the bedroom and have his wicked way with her, her heart tripped over itself?

'I am aware, Dominic. I'll rely on my own instincts now. Besides, they've never let me down before.' Not unless it was to do with matters of the heart. In that, she could not trust herself at all. 'But then again that is not a bad thing as I will have to do so when I play with Millington as well.'

Cecy laughed, trying to mask her nervousness, even though she felt it in in her clammy hands, her body which held tremors of anticipation that rippled down her spine and spread throughout, as well as those pesky metaphorical butterflies that fluttered incessantly in her stomach.

'So, shall we name the pieces of clothing we want to divest or shall it remain a surprise?'

Cecy had just enough surprises to contend with, without inviting any more. Oh, blast it. Why had she set this nonsense in motion in the first place? Her gaze slid to Dominic, who looked far too amused by this whole situation.

'What do you mean?'

'You know exactly what I mean.'

'Well, naturally, I'd rather not invite any further surprises.'

'Very well,' he muttered as he dealt the cards. 'How many items of clothing, then?'

'Really? Must we name and number them?'

He shrugged. 'If you wish for no further surprises.'

'Fine, then let's say four.'

'Three.'

'Done.' She made a single nod.

'And the items are clothing are…?'

'Do you seriously wish for me to state them?'

He smirked. 'Shout them, if you wish. But tell me the three items of clothing that you will have off my back in the unlikely event that you win this hand.'

'Fighting talk.'

'I like to think so.' Dominic flashed her a grin, making him look much younger, with his hair tousled, his dishevelled appearance and that one dimple that popped out at in his cheek when he was overly amused. 'Well, are you going to tell me what items you'd have me divest?'

She looked him up and down and licked her lip before answering, 'Your shirt.'

He raised a brow. 'My shirt? May I ask why?'

'No reason,' she said, her voice a little hoarse. 'Other than the fact that it's already practically undone.'

'Noticed, did you?' He winked.

'Hard not to.' She smiled and started to enjoy herself. 'And I'll have your trousers along with your shoes and stockings.'

'Very enterprising to go for more than your quota,' he said on an exhale. 'My turn.'

And just like that her smiled slipped from her lips. 'What?'

'Well, you stated your items, now I shall return the favour and tell you mine. That is how this works. Really, Cecy, do you need me explain?'

'No...no, of course not,' she said, feeling a little faint. 'I forgot that you would also need to make your... selection. Very well, what will it be, Dominic?'

'Let me see... I shall want your skirt with that terrible bustle contraption, along with your bodice.'

Cecy blinked as she felt her jaw drop. Dear God, this was highly improper. 'You're a scoundrel to suggest such things.'

'Come now, it's not as though your er...undergarments won't be covering your naked form.'

Cecy felt herself flush and become warmer by the minute. 'This is the most indecent, shocking conversation I believe I have ever had.'

'Well, then, let us stop.' Dominic sighed deeply, as though he had meant to bring her to this point, hoping for her to change her mind. 'Let's forget the wager and think of something else.'

Yes that would possibly be the best solution rather than the unwelcome awkwardness that this whole game had roused at her own insistence, foolish as it was. But it would not do. She had never been someone to give up just like that. If she did that now, then there was no point in participating in the game with Millington.

'No,' she said forcibly, as though she needed to convince herself as well. 'No, we have both agreed to this, so we shall see it through. I need to be prepared for the game with Millington and remember what is at stake.'

'And this…game…this wager will remind you of that?' His eyes fairly smouldered as he spoke.

'Yes. I believe so.' The wager also reminded Cecy that she could not afford to lose, because if she did then she'd have to sit in front of Dominic Marsden in this blasted room divested of the garments he'd specifically chosen for her to remove. How bloody mortifying would that be? And yet…and yet…there was a part of her that wanted them both to do just that— be half-naked in the same room as one another with their unbanked desire and attraction fully on display as well. Cecy could only imagine what might then happen between them.

And, yes, if she was honest with herself, the secret wanton part of Cecy's heart would secretly want all that mutual desire to reach a natural conclusion and for her to end up in bed with Dominic Marsden. It was a shocking thing to admit to, even to herself, but, dear God, she had imagined it often enough as she tossed and turned in her own bed these past few weeks.

'Very well.' She nodded. 'My skirt and bodice. What is your third item?'

'It's not quite an item of clothing, but something else. I will have your hat as well as all your hairpins removed.' His voice was low and hoarse. 'I will have your hair undone and unadorned.'

She took a sharp intake of breath, feeling that this was somehow worse than the request for her skirt and bodice and because Dominic's eyes flashed with barely disguised desire. Good God, there was no way in which Cecy could allow him to win. 'I accept. All of your choices.'

'You do?' He frowned slightly, almost surprised that this was actually about to happen.

'Yes.'

'Fine… Good. Then in that case let's begin, shall we?'

Dominic dealt the hand for the real game now that the practice one had been played and with questions Cecy had asked and received answers for. He had allowed her to try different variations and possible hands and showed her how she could put everything he had taught her about the game into practice.

But now that was over. Now the game had become real and she needed to muster everything she knew, everything she'd understood in the short time she had learnt the game into beating Dominic who knew the game inside and out. But the area she outmatched him and his experience was how she could apply her mathematical knowledge and use it to her advantage. This was how she could best Dominic and then perhaps use the same tactic in the game with Millington.

But the longer the game went on the less and less Cecy thought about the game with Samuel Millington and the more she focused all her attention on the man who presently sat opposite her.

'Remember that it's not just what's in front of you with the cards you have, but also make a study of your opponents. Be observant of their ways and be as sly and surreptitious as you can by learning their movements, their little idiosyncrasies, their mannerism. And as quickly and as efficiently as you can.'

'Such as?'

'One example is whether they fidget or not during the game and compare whether a man like Millington usually does or not. Being observant during the game can tell you a lot about what kind of hand your opponent might have.'

'Really? In what way?'

'It might reveal secrets that a player might want to keep hidden: a spark of emotion in their eyes, the hint of a blush in your cheeks…' His eyes fixed on hers, making her think for a moment that they were speaking of something other than the game. He shrugged and looked down at his cards. 'Or even the sheen of perspiration on the brow. It can all be signs and if you're able to decipher these signs, then you might also be able to read your opponent.'

But this was the one area that she was not at all good at—reading people. Time and time again she hadn't seen all these signs even when they had been staring at her in the face. Far too many times she had been fanciful and hoping for something that never existed, trusting when she shouldn't have.

Even now she longed for a man whose touch she wanted, a man she cared about and a man she was starting to fall in love with, even though she knew it was a mistake to venture down such an unknown and dangerous path…again. She didn't want to risk getting hurt again, but despite all her best efforts, she knew that it all been for naught.

The heart had a canny way to seek and find the one it truly desired and wanted anyway. And for Cecy, it was Dominic. It had been Dominic for quite some time. But she could not act on it. Could she? Lord knew that had not been the reason she had come here tonight, nor the reason why she'd wanted him to teach her how to play cards.

She pushed these unbridled thoughts away. 'And can the opposite be true?'

Dominic frowned. 'In what way?'

'What if you do everything that you have mentioned and observed and understood the signs that you speak of—from the gleam in an eye, a smile that conveys so much, to that loquacious tongue, with smooth honeyed words that promise so much—but realised it was all a lie.'

Cecy realised the moment that she'd spoken she had not necessarily referred to this or any game and her meaning was not entirely to do with any tactics, but something else entirely. Something that always made her doubt herself, as it spoke of those swindlers and tricksters who she could never quite recognise, never could quite see, however hard she tried because she always wanted to believe in their lie. She wanted to believe that she could be accepted and could be loved.

Cecy studied her hand, swallowing down the lump in her throat, and wondered what had brought on this tumult of emotion at a time when she needed a clear head. After all, this was supposed to be a prelude to the real game.

'Perhaps,' he muttered softly. 'Perhaps what you are describing is the art of bluffing…at least in a game of cards it is.'

'Bluffing?' Cecy knew that she'd erred when she'd unintentionally spoken of something so personal—well, personal to her. She had to keep her mind on this dratted card game. Just this game. And nothing else.

'Indeed. Bluffing is exactly what you described earlier. Giving the impression or pretending to have a certain hand and even revealing certain mannerisms to mislead and deceive the opponent.'

'So, lying, then?'

'In a manner of speaking. You're making your opponent believe one thing when in fact the opposite is true.'

'So, play acting comes in handy?'

'When playing a high-stakes game? Yes.'

Strange but that could also relate to life itself. Cecy knew first-hand about liars and schemers.

She sighed as she processed this. 'I am grateful to you, Dominic, for passing all your valuable knowledge to me. I shall endeavour to put it into practice. Now, in fact.'

'Good.' He smiled. 'You can certainly try.'

They continued with the game, the only noise in the room the ticking of the small clock on the mantelpiece. Suddenly and with much aplomb Dominic threw down a queen of hearts which meant that the probability that he might have a higher card with a better suit value was quite high. She needed for him to think her hand was weaker than hers for him to believe that he was about to win. A bluff—that was how he'd described it and along with Cecy using the factorial model she quickly calculated whether it was even possible for his hand to be as good as hers. There was obviously the chance that perhaps he was doing the same as Cecy and bluffing as well. But in this case, she thought not. His features were set in neutral, but only a small twitch above his brow.

She flicked her eyes to meet his and worried her lips with her teeth, not overly much but enough for him to believe that she had poor odds. She wanted to ask him whether this play acting would do? Had she taken him in?

'Well?' he said, in such a cocky manner that Cecy looked forward to wiping it off his face. 'What are you going to do now?'

'If you'll allow me a moment.' She glanced down at the cards that were available to pick up. She reminded herself that Dominic was not overly concerned about any of the cards on the table which gave her an insight into what he had to have in his hand.

'If you like, we can forget that we agreed to play this game for real and I can then guide you the best way to proceed.'

'No, I don't think that will be necessary.' Her hand hovered over the queen that he'd thrown down. 'You're constantly eager to renege on the wager, Dominic. Not worried, are you?'

He chuckled and shook his head. 'Not in the least. Well, are you going to pick up a card from the table or one from the dealer?'

'The table would suffice,' she said as she finally picked up the queen, discarded her king and laid out her cards on the table. 'There, I believe this is a queen flush.'

He inhaled sharply. 'You need to call it beforehand, sweetheart. But I'll allow it this time.'

'So that is it?' She lifted her head. 'I won, then? I won this hand?'

'You did, yes, congratulations. Well done,' he said as he stood up. 'Now what was it again? My shirt, my trousers and my shoes and stockings?'

All the euphoria she felt for besting a man who knew this game better than most dissipated at the thought of what Dominic was about to do, his eyes gleaming wickedly at her as she swallowed uncomfortably.

'Yes.' Her voice was barely audible, so she just nodded, her heart hammering in her chest. 'I believe it was.'

Dominic grinned as he tugged the shirt over his head, pulling it off and throwing it on the chaise longue set against the wall. His shoulders were broad and powerful, his arms sinewy, and the wide expanse of his muscular chest had a smattering of hair running down the length. He then sat and unlaced his boots, tugged them off and started on the buttons on his trousers, his eyes never once leaving hers, pinning them to his, keeping her totally captive. And, worse, she couldn't look away even if she'd wanted to.

In truth, Cecy didn't want to. The man was far too fascinating, drat him. Her breath caught when his trousers finally slipped down his narrow hips, revealing his bare legs, his powerful thighs, taut and lean, his body a perfect specimen of masculine beauty. Dominic kicked the garment away before bending down to retrieve it and adding his stockings to the pile on the chaise longue.

He prowled back towards her and lifted a brow. 'Well? Shall we resume the game?'

Cecy's mouth became dry, unable in that moment to trust herself to speak, so she nodded instead. God, she wished she could stop herself from reacting in this unbecoming manner, but she couldn't. In truth, Dominic was gorgeous and with that knowing smile that he flashed at her, he knew exactly the effect he was having on her, the scoundrel. Reaching for the tumbler, her hand shaking a little, Cecy tossed down the remainder of the brandy, welcoming the burning bite of the amber liquid as it slid down her throat.

'May I have a little more?' she asked, holding out her empty glass.

Dominic obliged her by pouring another measure from the decanter. 'Shall we see if I can even this out a bit? Are you ready for another game?'

'Perhaps.' She took another sip from her glass and tilted her head. 'You're very sure of yourself. What happens if I win again?'

His lips twitched at the corner. 'I think I'll leave that to your discretion.'

She knew she was poking the devil in him, but she couldn't stop from herself from saying words that no properly behaved woman would say. 'And if I asked you to remove every stitch you're wearing, you'd oblige?'

God, how Cecy hated the breathlessness in her voice which hardly disguised the longing she felt for him.

'I suppose I would have to,' he said softly. 'I'm not a man who'd go back on a wager. But perhaps you're getting a little carried away here, Cecy. Perhaps it will be I who shall have the pleasure of winning the next game.'

'We shall have to see, then.'

'Indeed we shall.' He started to shuffle the cards in that extravagant manner of his, making the cards curl and flow through his fingers effortlessly before he stacked them on the table and dealt them.

Once again they descended into silence as they became engaged in the game, but this time she found it hard to focus with Dominic's nearness so very exposed to her, while he acted as though nothing was amiss. Perhaps he was comfortable with his nakedness but she could hardly keep her eyes from his person, watching the dip and angles of his body move when he stretched and flexed.

'Concentrate, Cecy. I can just imagine that I am distracting you, but you must keep your mind on the game if you want to be triumphant again,' he said sardonically.

'You find this amusing.'

'Perhaps a little.' He grinned. 'What man doesn't enjoy being at the centre of a woman's perusal from time to time?'

'I wasn't...'

'Weren't you?' He raised a brow. 'My mistake.'

'I hardly comprehended that your physique would be so...?'

His lips curved upwards on one side. 'So?'

She felt herself getting even warmer, if that was possible. 'Oh dear, I shouldn't be speaking in such an unseemly manner. It's highly improper. I apologise.'

'As we have established, this whole encounter is highly improper. But never, ever apologise for it, even if does put me to the blush. My, er...manly physique was forged on the streets of London when my brothers and I were forced to fend for ourselves.'

'What did you have to do?'

'Many things. There's one time when Sebastian and I found work on the docks carrying cargo from dawn to dusk. It was hard, dirty, difficult work for little reward, but it taught us pampered boys, as we were back then, to graft for our keep.' He shrugged, as though he was tossing away that memory. 'But lately, it's the pugilist clubs that Tristan and I frequent that keeps us on our toes. It helps shape a man.'

Cecy sensed that none of that was ever supposed to shape Dominic or his brothers. As sons of a powerful and wealthy earl they were never meant to have had the lives they had. They were never meant to get their hands dirty and do a labourer's work carting cargo on the docks. And they were certainly never meant to open up a lucrative and successful gaming hell. Yet they did. That was their story made of threads of chance, opportunity, as well as terrible circumstance. God, but they more than earned their keep. She flicked her gaze up and down his body before meeting his eyes.

'That's admirable,' she murmured, knowing the truth of it. Dominic Marsden was quite simply the most impressive man she'd ever met.

'Thank you.' Without taking his eyes off her, Dominic laid his cards down in a fluid motion and leant back against his chair. 'And I have high king flush, which gets the win.'

Cecy's head snapped down, taking in the cards he'd placed on the table before lifting her head back up again. It seemed that Dominic Marsden was not only an admirable, impressive and tempting man he was also exceedingly annoying. A blasted card shark.

'How did you do that?'

'The usual way.' He was watching her as he leant back and threaded his hands behind his head. 'I win, Cecy.'

'So it seems.' Her heart was racing, knowing that it was now her turn to undress and take off the particular garments that he'd requested along with his interest in her unbound hair. And of course, she would do it, though. She would honour what she'd wagered.

Cecy stood before him and took a deep breath, feeling so ridiculously nervous. As she started to unbutton her bodice, which were thankfully at the front, Dominic's hand shot out and wrapped around her wrist.

'Wait.' He shook his head. 'You don't need to do this. I won't hold you to it. Not if you don't want to, sweetheart.'

He'd naturally misunderstood, believing that she regretted the wager that they'd made. That it was obligation alone that propelled her to honour the wager when in fact the opposite was true. When in fact, the desire she felt for Dominic threatened to consume her.

'But… I want to.'

Chapter Sixteen

For a moment Dominic just stared at Cecy, wondering whether perhaps he had misheard her. How was it possible that this woman was saying she would actually go through with their wager, when he'd given her ample opportunities to get out of it. He had tried again and again to make her see that there was no obligation for her to do it.

For God's sake, this was getting out of hand and the last thing he wanted was for Cecy to do anything she would be uncomfortable with. Or, worse, that she would come to regret later. He wouldn't allow that. If she wanted to take off her clothes, he would be the last man to stop her, but it couldn't be because of a wager.

However, like the simpleton he was when it came to Cecily Duddlecott, he realised that he'd got it all wrong. She wasn't nervous because she didn't want to go through with her end of the wager. No, she was nervous because she did. She did…

The woman surprised him, just as she had done so

many times before. The knowledge that she actually wanted to peel off the garments he asked for made him realise something else. It made him understand with alacrity that Cecy was holding back on all that unbanked passion that she'd held within herself, just as he was. All of that tension simmering to the surface, with neither of them wanting to give in to it. Not wanting to take that step and give in to that desire.

Dominic might have it wrong, but he would wait and see what Cecy would do next. He would allow her to lead, for him to follow. And God knew he would follow her anywhere.

His eyes fell to his hand that was still wrapped around her wrist and quickly removed it, placing both hands on his knees.

'Very well,' he said hoarsely, tamping down the unbridled excitement coursing through him. Damn, but he needed to remind himself again and again to proceed with caution.

Cecy took a step towards him and continued to unbutton her bodice. One small pearl button popped open and then another, and another until she'd reached the last one. She then took off the garment and dropped it on to her chair. His breath caught as he studied the smoothness of her skin, the dips and the curves that he wanted to explore, to touch, along the long lines of her neck, her arms and tops of her breast that dipped under her cream-cotton combination.

Over the top of this was her turquoise-coloured corset, embroidered with silver thread—the one flash of extravagance in an otherwise modest undergarment. He felt himself smile at this new revelation about her, this contrast between the prudent and the small bit of luxury she'd allowed herself.

As with everything to do with Cecily Duddlecott, it was all contained, all her feelings meticulously controlled. Not allowing more than she was prepared to give. But lately it seemed that the lady was becoming more and more daring, as though she was testing the boundaries of what she would allow. How much she would accept. And what she was engaged in doing, at that moment, was yet another such test.

She undid the ties of her green-and-black herringbone-checked skirt that matched the bodice. It came loose on both sides of her waist and she allowed the ruched skirt to collapse and fall down to the floor. Cecy stepped outside her skirt and then proceeded to untie her petticoats, which followed the same path as her skirt, as well as the collapsible bustle which she untied and piled all the clothing on the chair along with her bodice.

He swallowed uncomfortably as his eyes skimmed over her form, clothed in a light cream-cotton combination edged in cream embroidery anglaise trimming, and all the way down to her calves. She sat and took off her half-boots and rolled down her stockings before standing up. Moving in front of the looking glass, she removed the small hat perched on the side of her head and then started to take out the pins holding up her thick jet-black hair which had been artfully arranged in a high chignon at the top of her head.

Dominic realised that he was breathing heavily now, watching totally spellbound as Cecy's hair slowly started to tumble down around her face. That long, luscious, dark, almost black hair that he wanted to wrap around his hand fell heavy, cascading around her. He almost groaned out loud.

'Do you mind giving me a hand here?' she said, glancing back at him. 'I can't seem to get these last pins out from the back of my head.'

He ambled towards her and paused for a moment, his hands shaking, as he searched for the pin that Cecy couldn't reach and gently pulled it out, making another length of her glorious hair fall down. He dropped the pin on to the mantelpiece and then went in search of another pin and another until he found the last one, releasing her hair, which now fell in waves around her.

He inhaled through his teeth as she turned around to face him. 'God, Cecy, you're beautiful. You're so damn beautiful.'

He'd never seen Cecily Duddlecott looking as she did just then. Achingly young and achingly vulnerable. She made him want to wrap his arms around her and hold her for just a moment. His spirited, fierce little suffragist. Dominic reached out and dragged her hair around his wrists, his fingers running through the silken strands.

'Come here,' he said in a low voice, pulling her gently into his arms. 'You're trembling. Are you cold?'

'No.' She tilted her head up and their gazes caught. 'It's just…'

He bent his head and dragged her hair over one shoulder before placing a kiss at the base of her neck. 'It's just…?'

She snapped her eyes up to meet his. 'I want you, Dominic. I want you like I have never wanted anyone in my life.'

How like Cecy to just blurt out her wants and needs without pretence or artifice. 'That's a good thing as I want you, too, sweetheart. Quite desperately.'

'You do?'

'Yes,' he whispered as he stroked her lower lip with his thumb. 'How could you doubt it?'

Before she could answer, Dominic swooped down and carried her in his arms, bending his head down and catching her mouth with his. He moved across the parlour and opened the door of the bedroom before shutting it closed with his foot, without breaking the kiss. Laying her down in the centre of the bed, he strode across to turn on the oil lamp.

'Behold, lights.' He smiled at her.

'Really, Dominic? Lights at a time like this?'

'No better at a time like this. I want to see you, Cecily Duddlecott.' He moved back towards her, dipping the bed as he sat down, swinging his legs across to lie beside her. 'All of you.'

He watched her as her blue eyes darkened, filling with a mixture of tenderness and lust. For him…all for him. His fingers skimmed the smooth skin above the tops of her breast flushed pink down the length of her body and up and down her bare arms, watching her shudder. Dominic started to unhook her corset from the front and watched her as her chest rose and fell rapidly, her eyes clinging to his. He pulled the corset away and dropped it to the floor, and took a shaky breath, taking in her pert breasts beneath the gossamer cotton combination, so light he could see her hardened nipples through it.

With a groan he covered her mouth with his, tasting her, his tongue tarrying with hers. Cecy's arms came around him, her hands touching, exploring his chest, his shoulders, settling at the back of his neck, holding him close as he hungrily plundered her mouth. She tasted of brandy, of sin and a particular sweetness that was all hers. And God, how he craved more of her.

He dragged his mouth to the side of her jaw, along her throat, sucking on her pulse at the base of her neck while gently tugging the top of her shift to expose more of her smooth skin. He nipped at her collarbone, circled his tongue in the hollow of her throat and heard her gasp as he cupped her breast, his thumb circling around that her nipple.

'Oh my…you're so…this is all…too much,' she murmured breathlessly.

'Oh sweetheart, I've only just begun.' He smiled before pausing for a moment. 'But I can stop if you prefer?'

'No.' She grabbed his wrist as he started to pull away. 'Don't you dare, Dominic. That is, unless…unless you want to stop this madness between us.'

'This madness, as you put it, has been brewing between us since we first met.' He gave her a wolfish smile before continuing to kiss, touch, nip and lick along her body, his nimble fingers busy undoing the small buttons of her combination shift. 'And I have spent a long time thinking about this, wanting desperately to give you this surfeit of pleasure,' he murmured against her skin, his hand tracing her body, as he continued to peel away the last few remnants of clothing, revealing more and more of her flesh, wanting to learn every part of her. 'All the things I'd like to do to you.'

'You're a scoundrel, Dominic Marsden.'

'That I am,' he said, winking at her. 'But I never pretended to be anything else.'

Dominic ran his fingers down her body, tugging down Cecy's shift and throwing it on the floor before sitting back on his knees and taking in her glorious form head to toe, now without a stitch of clothing to cover her. She groped about for the coverlet to cover her body.

'No, Cecy.' He cradled her cheek. 'Don't hide yourself from me. You're exquisite, sweetheart. Quite exquisite.' He smiled down at her.

The tenderness he felt for this woman who made him feel things he had vowed never to feel again surprised him more then he could say. He wanted Cecily Duddlecott with a fierceness that shocked him to his core. And not just for tonight, but for many, many nights. Endless days and nights and yet, he couldn't quite find the words to tell her. He was shocked to realise the truth of that, but wouldn't dwell on it now. Instead, he would show her how much he wanted her, how he needed her and had fallen…yes, fallen deeply and madly in love with her.

He kissed her, devouring her mouth as his fingers explored, learning the shape of her, wanting to know every inch of her luscious body. He tore his mouth away and followed the trail set by his hands along her body, using his teeth and tongue. She moaned as his mouth closed over her breast, his fingers skimming down the length of her body and finding the heat between her legs.

'Oh God, Dominic, this is all too much,' she said breathlessly. 'Far too much.'

'I can stop, love.' He brushed his lips to the side of

her breast and then moved down, circling his tongue inside her belly button. 'Whenever you want me to.'

'No.' She arched her back, almost coming off the bed. 'No, don't stop. Never stop.'

He grinned at her before making his way down her body and placing an open-mouthed kiss on the inside of her thigh, which made Cecy moan and grab the coverlet with her fingers on either side and twist it tightly.

'Dominic?' she whispered as he showered her legs with kisses. 'Oh Lord, what are you…? Oh, my God.'

And then he put his mouth to her core, that sweet junction between her legs, and made her scream out his name.

What on earth was happening to her? Cecy felt as though she was melting into a big heap of nothingness. Good lord, what was Dominic doing? It was so wrong, so indecent, so sinful, yet so utterly decadent at the same time. What did that make her, then? That she would take everything he was giving. And want more. It made her nothing other than wanton…oh, so wanton. God, but when he kissed her on her mouth, on her face, her neck, her skin, her breasts, when he touched her and kissed her *there*, in her most private of places, she had lost all intelligible thought. It was astonishing. Cecy had never known pleasure quite like this heat…this scorching potent heat.

This want.

This man.

She turned her head and threaded her fingers through his hair as he moved back up her body, kissing and nipping his way up. Feeling emboldened, Cecy began her exploration of him as well. She allowed her hands to feel, to touch, to caress his skin, the corded sinew on his powerful arms, his shoulders, the rippled bands of muscle across his chest and that rock-hard stomach with a smattering of hair that disappeared under his smallclothes. His skin was hot to the touch, smooth and yet so different to her own.

'You are far more overdressed than I am, Dominic,' she murmured.

'What do you suggest we do about it, then?' His lips curved on one side of his mouth in that usual teasing manner of his. How incredible that this would have once annoyed her, when now she'd shifted her view and welcomed his humour, his levity and calmness in moments of difficulty. It was a balm for her very soul. He made her laugh; he made her see the ridiculousness of their world and yet still find a place within it.

'I could tear it off with my teeth?' she said, raising a brow matching his playfulness.

He laughed and shook his head. 'I must say that I like you this way, Cecy. Undone and so very bold. But I think on this occasion I shall decline your tempting invitation, in case I expire from sheer excitement.'

He undressed quickly and prowled towards her on

his hands and knees, rising above her. The intensity with which he gazed at her, his eyes soft and filled with longing, nearly undid her. How was it that Dominic Marsden wanted her as much as she wanted him? She could hardly believe that this beautiful, wonderful man wanted her, was enthralled by her and most importantly accepted her as she was. It was all so astonishing. But she felt cherished, needed, wanted…*loved*.

She reached out and cupped his jaw as he turned his head and kissed the inside of her palm. And in that moment Cecy wordlessly asked him something from her heart. Something she dare not say out loud. Something she could hardly believe and yet it was true. Everything she felt for Dominic was in her gaze, in her touch, in her kiss and everything that had transpired between them at this moment.

But perhaps he understood. Perhaps he sensed the same longing in her. A longing for that someone of her heart. The one whom she had always been searching for all her life. Dominic covered her body with his and in one long thrust entered her body, making her gasp, filling her so completely. He angled his body and shifted his weight, burying himself deeper inside her, taking her breath completely away. She arched her back, wanting to meet his thrusts, building and building to an exquisite sweet point.

She wrapped her legs around his hips, drawing him deeper, urging him on. Threading his fingers with hers, Dominic moved her hands above her head, his movement becoming erratic, fevered, as though something he'd been holding on to had burst free. He moved faster and faster. The pleasure now becoming almost too much, almost unbearable. She wanted to close her eyes and be lost to this sensation, but she couldn't tear her eyes away from his smouldering gaze locked on to hers.

Sensations rocked her to her core and again as she heard herself scream his name once more, feeling as though she had come apart, as she reached that point of complete bliss. Dominic suddenly groaned loudly, pulling out of her in time as he reached his release. Both seemingly shattering into tiny little pieces before being put back together again, replete but never quite the same again.

Neither spoke for a while as they both tried to catch their breaths. As they both tried to steady themselves back to some semblance of normality. Cecy curled herself against to his body, resting her hand on his chest which rose and fell rapidly, anchoring herself to him. He wrapped his arm around her, simply holding her close. And apart from feeling the rightness of being with Dominic, at this moment she did not know what any of it meant. So many emotions were bubbling inside, but perhaps it might be best to keep them all contained. She felt exposed as it was.

'That was…'

'I know.' He bent his head and kissed her forehead.

'I was going to say unexpected.'

'Oh, really? You thought we would divest our clothing during our daring little game of loo and then take tea?' She felt him smile beside her. 'I saw that glint in your eyes, Cecily Duddlecott. You wanted me with a burning passion and I was never going to be able to deny you that.'

She felt herself blush. 'Oh dear, I was that obvious?'

'It was obvious to me. But then I wanted you just as badly and to continue the ravishment from where I left off.'

'Oh, Dominic. You really are ridiculous.' She giggled.

'Ah, but that's just my appeal.'

'Is that so?'

'Yes,' he said, softly trailing his finger down across her jawline, making her shudder.

'But there's more to this than passion and ravishment.'

'There is,' he said with so much tenderness that it made her heart ache. 'And more than anything, I *see* you, Cecy. I see every part of you.'

In that moment Cecy felt his words open a part of her that she'd hidden for so long. It made her feel a certain vulnerability. A certain uncertainty. 'That's a lovely sentiment, Dominic, but none of us can truly see one another as we really are. Without artifice, without hiding who we really are. Even Millington only liked me because I reminded him of my mother.'

'You know, love, it's really not the done thing to mention a man's name when in bed with another.'

'Dear God, you're right, it's unpardonably rude. I'm so sorry.' She sighed deeply as she sat up, drawing the coverlet around her. 'You can comprehend my meaning, though. I often blurt things out without thinking about what I am about to say.'

'It's one of the many adorable things about you.' He brushed his hand down the length of her arm.

'Do be serious, Dominic. I know what I am and I know what people think when they see me—a far too opinionated spinster who is nine and twenty years old. God above, but who'd want that?'

'*Me*. I want that. Because when I look at you, I see a beautiful, intelligent woman who is opinionated and intelligent which is far more attractive than someone who isn't passionate about anything and doesn't know their own mind. I like that about you.'

'You do?'

'Very much. I always have. Besides you shouldn't care what others think of you. And I'm not all that different from you anyway. People have always misunderstood and judged my brothers and me. Initially when we were heirs to an old and glittering earldom, it was to gain our good opinions and desire our friendship and even our affection,' he said. 'But then when we were shunned, when we became destitute once we were declared to be illegitimate, no one then wanted our good opinion. No one wanted to know us and every single one of those sycophants flitted away.'

'You didn't need any of those people.'

'No, we didn't and neither do you,' he said, drawing her down towards him. 'We turned our backs on the society we once knew and made something of our lives, reinventing ourselves as the notorious Marsden Bastards, owners of the Trium Impiorum. No one knew what to make of us, but that didn't stop society with their usual judgemental ways.'

'Oh, Dominic, I believe I was one such person. I judged you before I got to know you. It was very wrong of me.'

'To be fair, sweetheart, I believe I did the same about you. I think we were both at fault.'

She smiled. 'Yes, I'm sure you are right.'

'After all, I did mercilessly tease you.'

'You still do, although perhaps with a little more affection?'

He brought her hand to his lips. 'With far more affection than you could ever imagine.'

His words made her pulse hitch, but Cecy needed to be careful not to get carried away with her feelings as she once did. 'Could it be that you did it as a way to keep anyone from getting to know you?'

'Yes, I always hid my feelings behind my humour.

When my father died, I tried to keep up everyone's spirits, especially my mother who was inconsolable at that time. Sebastian couldn't help since he'd retreated behind a wall of silence. In any case he effectively became the head of the family, always worrying and taking the world on his shoulders. Tristan was too young and too stunned by the sudden loss of our father, our home, our standing in the world and then later the devastation of losing our mother. So, all in all, it was all left to me to play the part of nonchalant jester. To keep everyone from descending into some wretched Gothic melancholy.'

'Even though you were hurting, too?'

'Even then.'

'Oh, Dominic.' She smoothed her hand across his chest.

'So you see, it might have pricked our pride at first, but for a very long time now, none of us cared for the opinions of those who didn't matter to us. I certainly didn't.'

'You once alluded to the same heartache that I once spoke of?'

'Good God, you want me to talk of another woman at such a time as this, when we are in bed together? It is the same as I mentioned before in regards to being bad form.'

She cradled his jaw, her fingers caressing his skin. 'Tell me, Dominic.'

'There's nothing to tell other than what I already expressed, sweetheart. The *ton* in my experience is shallow, sanctimonious and filled with condescension and hypocrisy. Her name no longer matters to me, Cecy, but, yes, there was a young woman who also caused me to experience the same emotion that you described.'

'Heartache?'

'Come now, Cecy,' he said. 'It is rather humiliating talking about all of this.'

'And you needn't do it, if it's too difficult. But know that I have already experienced it, too. I know all about the humiliation, Dominic.' She reached across and covered his hands with hers. 'What happened, if you don't mind me asking?'

He sighed deeply. 'It was exactly as I mentioned before. People's behaviour which drastically changed the moment we Marsden brothers were declared illegitimate and no longer heirs to the Earl of Harbury. For me, it was a young lady whose family was close to mine. We had made promises to one another that one day we'd marry, despite my being the second son and all that. And not only was she was my friend, but I even imagined myself to be in love with her—well, calf love that it was.

'Nevertheless, her assertion that we could no longer be associated with one another, after my father's death, cut me deep. I understood it and wasn't naive to have any expectations of her and yet... I had known her for as long as I could remember. Our mothers were close friends and had always wanted an alliance between their children. Yet everything changed when our circumstances did, Cecy. And I could never forgive her betrayal of that memory, of that friendship. I remember seeing her years later at some function or another, with her husband, where she gave me the cut direct as though she didn't know who I was. So, yes, it was all very humiliating.'

'I'm so sorry. You deserved better than that.'

'I suppose I did.' And just like that his mood changed again, his gaze soft and tender. 'We both deserved better.'

'Yes.' She smiled down at him before pressing her lips to his. 'We did. We do.'

He threaded his fingers with hers and studied them for a moment before bringing them to his lips. 'The truth is that I learnt a very important lesson back then. I learnt that I could never rely on anyone other than my brothers.'

'But you can,' she said, mirroring him by bringing his fingers to her lips. 'You can always rely on me. Always.'

Dominic looked stunned for a moment before a slow smile curled around his lips; a smile so true and unfettered that it made her heart trip over itself. He pulled her towards him, catching her lips with his, kissing her with abandon. Wrapping his arms around her, he tugged her to the side before rolling them both over so that he now had her beneath him. His kiss tender, soft but unbelievably passionate. As though he was trying to express something without words.

Cecy knew that after everything that happened she should contain the surfeit of emotion that was bubbling inside, but she knew she shouldn't give her heart so quickly. And it was all because of Dominic Marsden. A man she felt a powerful connection to. One who consumed not just her body, but her heart and soul as well. She realised then that she might not survive this…connection. It blazed far too hot for her to try to temper it. But it was too late anyway. She loved him.

'I love you.' Cecy could see that she had shocked him, as he then opened and closed his mouth several times as though he was searching for the appropriate words. Her heart sank, with the realisation that, once again, she'd spoken too soon and without thinking. 'No, don't…please don't say anything,' she added quickly.

Cecy couldn't bear that he might respond just because he suddenly felt obligated to. Whatever Dominic would say now would come across as though he'd forced himself to say it. And the last thing she needed was that. A terrible thought plagued her. Had she once again been mistaken in a man's feelings for her?

Chapter Seventeen

Dominic knew the moment that Cecy had stepped into the private room, far removed from the main gaming rooms at the Trium Impiorum, that he had blundered. Badly.

He had sent word to her the morning after teaching her how to play loo, when they had ended up in bed together, that Millington had brought the private game forward to that night. And, damn it, this whole situation worried Dominic. After all, Cecy had only just learnt the card game and no matter how many mathematical strategies she had up her sleeve, it would be too much to expect her to triumph over seasoned gamblers. Not that he didn't have any faith in her, but the unpredictability of it made him feel on edge.

This game had now become an important one, as a way to stop Millington from cheating and bribing the men sat around the table in this room. He would have shown Cecy a few methods of cheating if only the game had been scheduled for a few nights later.

Besides her time would've been better served trying to decipher the little notebooks they'd found in Millington's office. But now everything had to be brought forward, increasing the risk of failure. And, more importantly, a risk to Cecy, which he would not allow.

But dear God, Cecy looked like a queen standing at the entrance of the room with Hendon, the club's major-domo, ushering her in. All the men sat around the table looked stunned at her presence, but manners dictated that they stand as she moved to sit at one of the chairs and before they could also take their seats.

'What are you doing here, my dear?' Millington said in what he hoped was a pleasant voice, as a muscle leapt in the corner of his eye.

'Good evening, gentlemen.' She smiled, her spine straight, her demeanour graceful. 'I thought it was quite obvious, Samuel. I have come to play.'

'You jest, of course, since women are not permitted in the Trium Impiorum.' Millington smirked, gaining a few echoes of laughter from the men sat around the table. 'Is that not so, Marsden?'

'On this occasion, we have dispensed with our normal rules and have allowed women to attend the club and to play, naturally. But perhaps you missed the ladies in the main gaming salon, Millington?'

'I thought they were a different kind of…but no matter.' He turned his head. 'I would, however, prefer you not to play tonight, my dear.'

'And yet I prefer to do so.' She smiled sweetly. 'Dear Mr Hendon, the major-domo, has been so obliging as to show me around and I admit I never thought the Trium Impiorum to be so elegantly appointed. It's a credit to you and your brothers, Mr Marsden.'

It was the first time since the night before that she'd acknowledged him. 'Thank you, Miss Duddlecott. Very kind of you to say so.'

'Look at me. Look at me, damn it!' he wanted to shout, but of course they both had their part to play this evening.

'I do not approve of this, Cecily,' Millington sneered as Dominic clenched his fists so tightly he felt his nails digging into his skin.

'Oh, for the love God, Millington, let the lady stay,' Lord St John Derryn, one of the men invited for this game along with his cousin the Earl of Glynford, muttered. 'You don't need to be such a stickler.'

'Indeed.' The Earl smiled across at Cecy. 'You are very welcome to play, m'dear, if that's all right by you, Marsden?'

'Of course.' He noted the flush of anger on Millington's face. *Good, you bastard...*

'Well then, it seems I'm outnumbered, but I am surprised you sanctioned this rebellious outing, Duddlecott?' Millington said in a clipped tone.

'I saw no issue with Cecy's presence here. It might liven things up.'

'It will certainly make us behave with more decorum in your presence, Miss Duddlecott,' Mr Jarvis-Bailey, another of the men who was present at the behest of Samuel Millington, said while the rest of the table chuckled.

'I should hope so,' Cecy said with a small smile.

She had said she loved him. And his response had been terrible. It had been nothing short of a metaphorical slap in the face when he just gaped at her in disbelief. Because he couldn't believe that the woman had the same feelings as he did. Damn it, of course he loved her. But he hadn't had the chance to rectify the situation as Cecy erected those protective walls around herself so swiftly before needing privacy to get dressed and leaving to get back home.

He couldn't have gone with her, in case they were seen together by Millington or any of his damn spies, but Dominic followed to see her return back safely. Yes, he'd blundered very badly. And the thought that he might have inadvertently hurt her was torturous. He wished he could have a private moment with her to explain that she'd caught him off guard. That he'd fallen for her and wanted her in his bed, in his life...

Dear God, how glorious she had been in his arms. He'd never known anything like it; never felt anything remotely close to the feelings that had coursed through his veins when she'd come undone. He wanted Cecily Duddlecott. All of her. And it shocked him how much he did. He loved the woman—that much he did know. That much he should tell her. That much he needed to. And he would, in good time.

'Well, shall we begin the game?' Duddlecott said, looking around the table.

Still, Dominic wished she had not come tonight. How could he protect her from Millington if she was here in the same room, about to attempt to bring his whole of house of cards down, as she eloquently put it? The bastard was a slimy, slippery snake and extremely unpredictable.

Cecy looked across at her brother. 'I assume we're playing loo? May I ask what the stakes are?'

To prove Dominic's point, Millington glared at Cecy before answering, 'No. Not loo. Not tonight.'

'What do you mean?' Jarvis-Bailey lifted his head and scowled. 'What do you propose, Millington?'

'Poker...stud poker.' The man directed this not at Jarvis-Bailey, but at Cecy. 'I assume we all know how to play the popular American card game?'

'If the lady has no objection to the change of card game?' the Earl of Glynford muttered, showing the others that at least he knew how to behave in front of a woman.

Damn Millington to hell, for Dominic knew perfectly that this was part of his intimidation tactics against Cecy, whom he was no doubt furious with for going against his wishes. And in public, too. God, he wanted to wipe that smug look from his face.

But Cecy did not cower, nor look away. She looked at the man straight in the eyes and smiled serenely. 'Of course, my lord. I have no objection, as long as one of you gentlemen can apprise me of the rules of the game.'

'Gladly, Miss Duddlecott.'

Dominic could not help but admire his Cecy. She was a lioness in the face of adversity and he realised in that moment that while he would've preferred for her not to take part tonight, she naturally felt that she had to. She felt she had to go toe-to-toe with Millington, and face her fears head-on.

For Cecy, it wasn't just the corruption and blackmail that the man was involved in, but a far more personal reason why she wanted to bring him down—that much Dominic did understand. She was also doing this for all the women whom Millington had wrongly arrested after the march. The women who were languishing in jail. She knew she had to fight, otherwise what good were her words and beliefs if she didn't stand up to the likes of Samuel Millington?

Dominic knew then that she was woman who would always have to fight for her beliefs and he would always support her. Always… After all, men like Millington and even Dominic and his brothers could always rise from adversity by starting over and making something of themselves. Whereas society judged women far harsher and placed obstacles only to trip them up within the rigid confines of what was expected of them.

In truth, Dominic didn't know if he'd ever known anyone as brave as Cecy. She was extraordinary. So, no, he could never stand in her way. He could not deny her this moment, to face Millington whether or not she succeeded. But he had every faith that she would. She was by far the cleverest person in the room. Of that he had no doubt. Still, he crossed his fingers behind his back after the game of poker was explained to her by the men around the table, just as he had done with other card games the night before.

'I think I understand it all now, gentlemen.'

'Then let the play commence.'

The game started in earnest with everyone around the table allowing Cecy a practice game. All except from Millington, whose complaints regarding having Cecy there—in truth, all women admitted to the club—becoming tedious. Just like the bastard himself.

'What are the stakes?'

'A guinea,' Millington said. 'But this is a fast-paced game and the stakes reflect that, my dear. So they will continue to rise up and up and up. Perhaps you might still wish to reconsider playing, after all?'

'Oh, for goodness sake, Millington,' Dominic

snapped. 'Cease putting Cecy off. She's already stated she'd like to play.'

The minute Dominic had uttered the words, he knew he'd made a mistake as he'd inadvertently drawn attention to both of them. But the man's attitude was grating.

'"Cecy," eh?' Millington picked up the cards that the croupier had dealt and arranged them in his hand. 'How familiar you are with my betrothed, Marsden. Some might say too familiar.'

'I meant no disrespect by it,' Dominic said quickly, knowing he must bite his tongue if he wanted their plan to work. 'Accept my apologies, Miss Duddlecott.'

'Of course, sir. No harm done,' she added smoothly.

The first game was played with the Earl, Lord St. John Derryn and Duddlecott folding, and Cecy and Millington eventually losing to Jarvis-Bailey. The second game was played with stakes reaching ten pounds as all around the table played the game, but this time it was St John Derryn who was triumphant, against Duddlecott who was the last man standing in the game. And so it went on, the same pattern with either Cecy or her brother consistently blocking Millington to win and frustrating the man at every turn. And the more this went on, the angrier Samuel Millington became, especially at his partner, not knowing of course that Duddlecott was now doing everything in his power to prevent Millington from winning even if he had a good hand, and thus stopping him from being able to use the high stakes to dominate his opponents and bend them to his will.

Millington wanted to control the game using his and Duddlecott's wins to exert influence over the other men around the table and bribe them into doing his bidding in Parliament. He needed the men to back the controversial Hubert Railroad Bill, that would plough through many green areas of southern England, without the usual careful legal assessment of the land beforehand. Millington had much to lose if the Bill did not go through Parliament as he had sunk so much of his own capital into the scheme. And as it was so close to call, he needed the vote of the other three men sat around the table, making the assumption that he already had Duddlecott in his back pocket.

But nothing was going to plan for Millington this evening, First was the addition of Cecy to the proceedings and then there was Duddlecott, who was not playing to Millington's usual script. Not in the least.

Dominic could see the mounting frustration building in the bastard. The clammy brow, the scowling face, the clenched jaw. And those glares he threw at Duddlecott who pretended not to see them. All of which was part of the plan. To frustrate Millington at every turn, squeezing him so much that he'd eventually resort to cheating to win, thus exposing himself. Even now, Sir Algernon Pendle, the head of the intelligence services, was waiting outside with a handful of his men ready to reprimand Millington once he'd fallen into their trap. And within thirty minutes if they were successful, once the go-ahead was given, Pendle would send more of his men inside Millington's office to open the secret room and retrieve more of the notebooks they'd found as evidence against the man. But timing was crucial to their success. One wrong move could spell disaster and so they needed to tread with caution.

'For God's sake, Marsden, why are you still here hovering around the room like a bad smell?' Millington snapped after losing yet another hand, this time to the Earl of Glynford.

'Since this is my club, mine and my brothers, I assumed I could go anywhere I pleased, Millington,' he said sardonically. 'And that bad odour, I assure you, does not belong to me.'

'I don't care. Just stop moving about the place, as you're distracting me.'

Dominic didn't respond, but exchanged a look with Cecy, who read what he was trying to convey. They were close now, very close. As it stood, the Earl, was coin high, then his cousin, Jarvis-Bailey, Duddlecott with Cecy and Millington having the least amount of coin left. But this was going to be the last game of the night so anything could happen.

The croupier dealt the final cards and almost immediately the stakes rose, again and again and again. But it didn't put any of them off as the participants declared that were all in; the whole table was playing. Dominic silently prayed that Cecy would remember everything that he'd taught her. To study her opponents by trying to read them and use tactics such bluffing and application of mathematical processes where necessary.

'I must say that I am enjoying playing immensely,' Cecy murmured, smiling sweetly at St John Derryn to her right, as the stakes rose again to a staggering fifty pounds. 'I think I shall come again.'

Millington frowned. 'I will not permit it.'

'Oh, do not be a bore, Samuel.'

He sneered, 'I would ask you to cease this nonsense, Cecily. You have made enough of a fool of yourself.' Dominic had to catch himself before he did something stupid and pounced on Millington, but thankfully St John Derryn and the Earl both stood demanding an apology from Millington, who stood his ground. 'You forget that the lady is my betrothed.'

'And you forget that she is my sister,' Duddlecott retorted, growing a backbone. Good for him that he was finally prepared to stand up to Millington.

'I shall deal with you later,' Millington hissed at Duddlecott, almost giving himself away. He was now so furiously angry that he was holding on to his temper by a thread. 'And how disappointing, Cecily, as you are nothing like your dear docile mother.'

'Is that so?' She smiled, not rising to his bait.

'Yes.' Millington, though, was getting more and more vexed. 'I'm raising it. I'm raising the stakes to one thousand pounds.'

There was audible gasp around the table as all the players, including Cecy, froze momentarily, shocked by the outrageous amount that Millington had raised the stakes by.

'Come now, Marsden, will you allow such brazen behaviour?' The Earl of Glynford scowled.

'I'm afraid so,' Dominic lied. 'This is, after all, a high-stakes game, my lord.'

One by one the Earl, St John Derryn and Jarvis-Bailey and Duddlecott folded, leaving just Cecy and Millington in the game.

'Well, Cecily, what shall it be?' Millington sipped brandy from the tumbler. 'Are you in or out?'

Cecy held the man's gaze, her face impassive, not betraying any emotion save the slight tremor of her hand. 'I think… I think that I will play. I'm in.'

'No, Cecily, I will not allow it.' Duddlecott stood, playing along as he was instructed. 'Where are we going to get such a sum together?'

'Sit down, Duddlecott.' Millington smiled menacingly. 'I should very much like to teach your sister a lesson here. Never to cross me again and in public, too.'

It was working, judging by the worried glances the

other men exchanged with one another. Millington had unravelled fast with all his energy now focused on Cecy. With the tension high in the room, his heart pounding in his chest, Dominic watched as Cecy asked and received a guarantor for that exorbitant amount. Everything was now in place. The only thing needed now was a win for Cecy.

'Lay down your cards, Cecily.'

'After you, Samuel. After all, I asked to see you. That is the correct expression, is it not?'

'As you wish.' He laid down his five cards, slowly revealing that he had three aces and two kings in his hand. 'Very little beats this, my dear. But no matter, I shan't call in the debt especially since we are soon to wed.' The man was practically preening, far more engaged with imparting whatever lesson to Cecy as opposed what he'd come to this room for.

'Not so hasty.' Cecy held up her palm just as Millington was about to gather all his winnings from the croupier. 'You are, of course, quite right. Very little beats your hand, except perhaps this…'

Cecy laid out her cards revealing four aces and thus winning the entire game. For a moment no one moved. Millington had a dangerous glint in his eyes, glaring at her before he stared at the cards in disbelief.

'You cheated!'

'I did not.' Cecy looked down her nose at him. 'Perhaps the words you might be looking for are "well done"? Oh, and by the by, I wouldn't marry you if you were the last man on earth. And you're quite right, I'm nothing like my lovely mama. Not that she'd have anything to do with a snivelling toad like you.'

'You bitch!' It all happened so quickly; Millington lunged for Cecy as he bellowed at her, Dominic getting his hands on the bastard before he did and punching him so hard the man flew across the room and landed on the floor. It was then that lots of counterfeit cards fell out of his many secret pockets.

'It seems that, it is you who cheated, Mr Millington. Not that you managed to win. Not this time.'

Within seconds, Sir Algernon Pendle and his men piled into the room and dragged Millington away. Dominic knew that with all the evidence that they'd also uncover in the man's home, they would be able to bring the charges of extortion, bribery, blackmail, coercion and corruption against him. But all Dominic cared about was the woman standing in front of him.

'Are you all right?' he asked Cecy, glad that the room had emptied, leaving the two of them alone.

'I am now.' She gave him a strained smile.

'I am glad. As I am that this is all over.' He crossed the room towards her.

'You are?'

'Yes, and surely you must be, too?' He held out his hand to reach for her, but she sidestepped around him.

'I suppose I must be.'

He tried to ignore the way she seemed to move away from him now that just the two of them were left in the room. 'And by the by, you were magnificent, Cecy.'

'Thank you.' She shrugged as she wrapped her arms around herself. 'And by the by, I'm indebted to you. In truth, I should thank you for arranging this evening at your club.'

What the blazes was she talking about?

'Indebted to me? I think not. We did this together, sweetheart.'

'So we did.' Her smile did not quite reach her eyes. 'And now as you say, it's…it's over.'

Panic swelled in his chest. What the hell was going on? There was something at play here that he could not quite understand.

He caught her hand and laced his fingers with hers. 'Yes. And once all this settles there will be time. Time for things that need to considered. Time for words that need to be said. Time for us to realise what we truly want.'

She screwed her face and shook her head. 'If this is about what I said last night, I think perhaps we should forget it.'

Not a chance…

'I'm afraid I cannot do that.'

Her eyes flicked up and met his, wary and uncertain with that mask that he so detested firmly back in place. And to think he'd not seen that look since that day in Marsden House.

'Cecy...'

'Please, Dominic,' she said quietly, taking a step back. 'You do not owe me anything. I hope you know that.'

Why was Cecy putting those damn protective walls around herself again? Did she doubt herself? Did she doubt him?

'No. I don't owe you anything. Just as you are not indebted to me. But that is not what I meant.'

'Then what?'

How could she not understand? How could she not see? If he could trust again, if he could love again, could she not give them a chance? For God's sake, he was in love with her. He loved Cecily Duddlecott, every wonderful, beautiful irascible part of her. And yet the words were stuck at the back of his throat.

Bloody, bloody hell!

He was mucking this up.

He wanted her; he wanted her badly. But perhaps this was the wrong time to declare himself. After all, they'd just dispatched Millington and were now weary from everything that had come to pass.

And it must be done properly, not at a time like this.

He dragged his fingers through his hair and released a long slow breath. 'It's late. Perhaps we should discuss everything on the morrow.'

'Yes, very well.' Cecy closed her eyes momentarily before opening them again and then quickly moving towards the door without sparing a glance at him.

'Wait,' Dominic said, following her and gently tugging her around by the elbow so that she faced him. 'What is it, sweetheart? What are you so scared of?'

'Everything,' she whispered, rubbing her forehead. 'But perhaps you're right. Perhaps we shall talk about everything tomorrow.'

'I shall come to you in the morning if that is amenable to you.' He skimmed his fingers down her jaw, making her expel a soft gasp. 'You'll wait for me?'

She nodded. 'I will. Goodnight, Dominic.'

He gave her a quick kiss on the lips. 'Until then.'

Cecy waited for two long days in the parlour for Dominic to come to her but by the third day, she gave up. He wasn't coming. She had to wrap her head around the fact that she had once again misunderstood a man's intention. How foolish had she been, thinking that Dominic Marsden felt the same way as she did about him and yet…yet there had been times where he had expressed his feelings to her, pledging his intent and his love for her not by words, but by showing her his feelings.

Perhaps Cecy had misread it all and seen only what she wanted to see. Perhaps that night at the Trium Impiorum, that was he was doing: letting her down gently. But why not do it in person, as he'd said he'd do. The whole blasted thing was mortifying.

And it was this realisation that brought all her insecurities crashing over her. She couldn't stay in this room, in this house, in this city any longer and needed time away to be able to come to terms with everything that had happened. And quite a lot had happened. From Millington to her brother and most importantly, finding herself in love with Dominic Marsden. Perhaps on her return she might have a better control on this mess that she'd found herself in.

After leaving behind a letter to Stephen to inform him of where she was going, she made her way to Paddington Station, where she boarded the train to Exeter with her maid in tow. She grabbed a copy of the *London Veritas*, which surprisingly had continued to run even after the debacle with Samuel Millington's arrest at the Trium Impiorum a few nights ago, needing something to read to while away the hours and stop her mind from drifting back to Dominic Marsden.

After placing their trunks away, Cecy found their carriage, settled in her seat while her maid promptly fell asleep. She opened the *London Veritas*, curious to find out if there had been any further news regarding Millington's demise in his own paper, when her eyes caught a column in the corner regarding the fact that the many women who'd been imprisoned after the march and even those awaiting trial, were all pardoned...thanks to her uncovering the truth about Samuel Millington.

Cecy read the article twice before taking it in, her mind racing. What did this all mean and how had the journalist known about her involvement? She turned the page and again another story, but this time regarding a fire at the Trium Impiorum. Good God, a fire? With her heart racing, she read that the fire was put out swiftly and no one had been hurt. Inhaling sharply, Cecy realised that perhaps this might be the reason why Dominic had not been able to come to her. Oh God, and she had thought the worst of him. And then in the corner, a square column caught her eyes with words that made her heart trip over itself.

"To Miss C.D., the one I love more than life itself. Be mine for ever...?"
Dominic Marsden of The Trium Impiorum.

Cecy's eyes filled with tears as she raised her trembling hand to cover her mouth. This declaration was for her. Cecy remembered revealing to him how she adored those columns in newspapers. And he remembered. He had committed every little thing she'd said to memory.

He loved her...

Dominic loved her after all. And yet she was here. On this train. About to depart. And he did not know. Dominic had had to deal with the aftermath of a fire at his club, while he was unaware that she'd abandoned him. Oh Lord, what a mess.

Could he not have sent word to her about it? It mattered not. What did was that she needed to see him. She needed to tell him of her feelings. She needed to make certain that he was safe. She rose abruptly and threw the door of the car open before crashing into a wall. Except the wall was not a wall at all, but a man. And not just any man, but a beloved man.

'Going somewhere, Miss Duddlecott?'

'Dominic!' His name came out on a gasp. 'I was about to get off the train and come looking for you.'

'And instead, I came looking for you.' He raised a brow as he ushered her inside the carriage. 'What on earth were you thinking, running off like that, sweetheart?'

'I had no idea. None whatsoever. Not until I read the *London Veritas*.' She stared into those unfathomable green eyes.

'Ah, so you read it?'

'Yes.' She smiled at him, catching her bottom lip between her teeth. 'And you had those…words printed. Why?'

'Well, a wise, brave and may I add beautiful suffragist who fights for others but never actually for herself, once revealed quite by accident how she always thought those declarations in newspapers to be utterly romantic. She believed them to be exquisitely forthright and honest.' He wrapped his arms around her waist and tugged her a little closer. 'So I thought that I'd like to indulge her with words from the deepest, most secret part of me and hoped...yes, I hoped that she'd find them equally romantic and honest.'

'She does.' She lifted her hand to his jaw. 'I do.'

He covered her hand with his. 'I'm glad.'

'Do you mean it?'

'Every word.' He smiled softly at her. 'But if you don't want me, then tell me now and I'll never trouble you again.'

She caressed his jaw and wrapped her other arm around his neck. 'I doubt I'll ever stop wanting you.'

'Well, that is a relief.'

She lifted her head and looked into those gorgeous eyes of his. 'You love me, Dominic?'

'I do.' He grinned, clearly bemused.

'And...you want me? For ever?'

'That I do.' He chuckled as he removed his top hat and threw it on the chair. 'If you'll have me? So, tell me, Cecily Duddlecott, will you be mine?'

'I'm already yours, Dominic Marsden. I'm already yours,' she murmured before closing her eyes and pressing her lips to his in a long, lingering kiss.

Epilogue

Four weeks later...

'You're here, both of you! Come and meet the newest Marsden.' Eliza beamed at Cecily and Dominic, who had arrived at Trebarr Castle only a short while ago and were duly ushered in to Eliza's confinement room. They found Eliza sat on the day bed swaddling a baby in her arms, as well as the elder and younger Marsden brothers, both of whom rose as they entered the room.

'Here is our little man. Come and meet Christopher Simon Edgar Hugh Marsden.' Eliza beamed. 'Isn't he a peach?'

'He's beautiful,' Cecy said, kissing her friend's cheek, while Dominic shook both of his brothers by the hand and light-heartedly slapped Sebastian's back before coming to greet his sister-in-law and nephew.

'Indeed, he is.' Dominic dropped a kiss on Eliza's head. 'He's another handsome Marsden male. Felicitations to you both.'

'Thank you, Dom,' Sebastian said, taking the tray of champagne flutes from a footman before handing them out. 'And you would have met our newest addition had you arrived earlier. Indeed, we expected you to arrive with Tristan.'

'Apologies, but I'm afraid I got waylaid.'

Sebastian frowned. 'Not anything to do with the Trium Impiorum, I hope?'

Dominic flashed a quick smile at Cecy and shook his head. 'No, not that.'

It amazed Cecy that her heart still tripped over itself as it always did whenever Dominic gazed at her in that smouldering way of his, the exasperating man. Yet, it always did. Always.

'Well, you're here now and a good job, too, as you bumped into Cecy, so that you could travel down from the train station together.' Eliza smiled.

Dominic winked at Cecy and grinned. 'Yes, it was a pleasure.'

'I think it's a time for a toast, don't you?' Sebastian raised his glass and smiled. 'To my beautiful wife, Eliza, who safely delivered our precious son, Christopher Simon.'

'To your health. Eliza and Christopher Simon.' They all took a sip of champagne.

'And yours, too, Sebastian.' Eliza chuckled, pressing a kiss on the baby's forehead.

'Thank you, my love.' Sebastian bent down and kissed his wife and son before turning his attention back to Dominic. 'So come now, what was it that caused you to be waylaid, Dom? Anything I can help you with?'

'No.' Dominic smiled. 'I very much doubt it.'

'What happened? Until you walked into this room right now, we had no idea where you had been.'

'Ah, about that...' Dominic glanced at each one of them, before his eyes landed on her.

Cecy intervened, 'I'm afraid it's my fault.'

Sebastian Marsden turned towards her and frowned. 'Yours, Miss Duddlecott?'

Cecy worried her lip before laughing nervously. 'That is just it, Mr Marsden. You see, I am no longer Miss Duddlecott.' She took a deep breath before speaking again. 'I am, in fact, Mrs Marsden... Mrs Dominic Marsden.'

There was a collective stunned silence—well, except for Tristan, who raised his glass at her before they all descended into a rapturous cheer. Dominic's younger brother had become an ally and good friend these past few weeks. But little did any of them know that when Tristan left for London the following day in preparation for the new Persian exhibition at the British Museum, which would open the following year, his life would change in the most unexpected of ways.

'Oh my goodness, I had no idea,' Eliza cried excitedly. 'But in truth I had wondered whether Dominic was...'

'*Taken with Cecy?* Yes, you were right there, dear Sister.' Dominic looked across at her, his eyes filled with so much tenderness.

'Well, I must say, this is wonderful news.' Sebastian Marsden slapped his brother on the back.

'It is, yes.'

'I think felicitations are in order!'

'I think another toast is in order!'

The Marsden family continued to celebrate a birth and a clandestine marriage well into the small hours. It was a remarkable if not unconventional gathering that would soon welcome Cecy's brother and his wife.

'Happy?' Dominic said much later as he wrapped a shawl around his wife's arms when they were alone in the gardens staring up at the nights' sky.

'Very.' Cecy smiled up at him. 'I was thinking how fortunate I am to have found you, how life has infinite possibilities with you by my side. And how I love you, Dominic Marsden. I could never have imagined any of it.'

'Nor I. And I love you, too, Cecily Marsden. More than you will ever know.' Dominic lifted her hand to his lips. 'I am beyond proud and honoured to be the lucky man to stand with you, from now to wherever life takes us.'

He sealed this oath with a lingering passionate kiss under the stars, and showed Cecy in every way that he did *'see'* her.

Together they continued his mother's legacy with

the Alice Marsden Education Fund and expanded it to become the Alice Marsden School for Girls, one of the first in the east end of London. The Trium Impiorum continued to thrive especially the nights where women were admitted, with Cecy and Eliza leading the way. Dominic showed Cecy that he shared the same causes as her and attended marches, rallies and meetings with Cecy. But the tour de force was when Dominic encouraged Cecy to finally finish her degree in mathematical sciences, at University College London, later becoming one of the first female professors in the field of mathematics. It might not have been the same as those dreaming spires she had once longed for, but for Cecy it was so much more. And all because of the love of her very own scoundrel.

* * * * *

If you enjoyed this story, why not check out one of Melissa Oliver's other great reads

Stranded with Her Forbidden Knight
The Lady's Bargain with the Rogue

And you'll be sure to love Melissa Oliver and Ella Matthews' Brothers and Rivals duet

Her Warrior's Surprise Return *by Ella Matthews*
The Knight's Substitute Bride *by Melissa Oliver*

MILLS & BOON®

Coming next month

DARING TO DREAM OF THE DUKE
Lauri Robinson

Book 1 in Brides for Sworn Bachelors

There was something in Michael's eyes, the way he was looking at her, that was stealing the air from her lungs. Making it hard to breathe and impossible to look away. It felt as if time stopped. As if the world forgot to keep turning.

She had the strangest sensation that he wanted to kiss her. Or maybe those were her thoughts. For that was exactly what she wanted. With every part of her body.

His finger was still beneath her chin, and his thumb was caressing her cheek and sending a thrilling heat through her face, down her neck. Her lips were tingling, her heart was pounding, and the rest of her had the greatest desire to rise on her toes so her face was closer to his.

She'd never wanted something so badly. So completely. An unusual excitement was growing stronger and stronger at the mere idea of kissing him. Of his lips touching hers. She could imagine that it would be better than dancing with him. Better than anything she'd ever known.

Just as she was giving in, about to rise onto her toes, a piercing sense of reality struck. This was Michael. The one man she'd always dreamed of kissing and the one man she couldn't kiss. Couldn't ever let him know about the dreams she'd had for years. He'd merely been being kind to her this weekend, watching out for her, because as Nora had mentioned that first day, he thought of her as another sister. Someone he had to protect. Nora had said that would never change, and he certainly hadn't done anything to make Rosemary believe otherwise.

She'd been the one wishing it would change, and she shouldn't have. It wouldn't matter what she wore—he would never see her as a woman he could be interested in for something more than friendship.

Coming to her senses, she jerked her head backwards, and knowing that wasn't enough, she took a step backwards, too, all the while struggling to catch her breath.

The hand that had been touching her face fell to Michael's side, and it suddenly felt like she'd lost something precious.

He stared at her for yet another stilled moment, and she wished with all her might that she could read his mind. She couldn't, so all she could do was hope that he hadn't realized how badly she'd wanted him to kiss her.

Continue reading

DARING TO DREAM OF THE DUKE
Lauri Robinson

Available next month
millsandboon.co.uk

Copyright © 2026 Lauri Robinson

COMING SOON!

We really hope you enjoyed reading this book.
If you're looking for more romance
be sure to head to the shops when
new books are available on

Thursday 26th March

To see which titles are coming soon, please visit
millsandboon.co.uk/nextmonth

MILLS & BOON

FOUR BRAND NEW BOOKS FROM
MILLS & BOON MODERN

Indulge in desire, drama, and breathtaking romance – where passion knows no bounds!

OUT NOW

Eight Modern stories published every month, find them all at:

millsandboon.co.uk

LET'S TALK
Romance

For exclusive extracts, competitions and special offers, find us online:

- **f** MillsandBoon
- **X** @MillsandBoon
- **◉** @MillsandBoonUK
- **♪** @MillsandBoonUK

Get in touch on 01413 063 232

For all the latest titles coming soon, visit
millsandboon.co.uk/nextmonth